W9-AQY-305

RECEIVED
APR 26 2016
By

THE INCIDENT ON THE BRIDGE

Also by Laura McNeal

Dark Water

You Can't Leave Me Now: Three Stories of True Crime

Also by Laura McNeal, writing with her husband, Tom McNeal

Crooked

Zipped

Crushed

The Decoding of Lana Morris

By Tom McNeal

Far Far Away

THE INCIDENT ON THE *BRIDGE*

LAURA McNEAL

Alfred A. Knopf
New York

THIS IS A BORZOI BOOK PUBLISHED BY ALFRED A. KNOPF

Visit us on the Web! randomhouseteens.com

Educators and librarians, for a variety of teaching tools, visit us at
RHTeachersLibrarians.com

Library of Congress Cataloging-in-Publication Data
Names: McNeal, Laura, author.
Title: The incident on the bridge / Laura McNeal.
Description: First Edition. | New York : Alfred A. Knopf, 2016. | Summary: When Thisbe Locke is last seen standing on the edge of the Coronado Bridge, it looks like there is only one thing to call it. As the town prepares to mourn the loss, her sister Ted, and Fen, the new kid in town, are not convinced and they set out to figure out what happened on that bridge and find Thisbe.
Identifiers: LCCN 2015024304 | ISBN 978-0-375-87079-8 (hardback) |
ISBN 978-0-375-97079-5 (lib. bdg.) | ISBN 978-0-307-97461-7 (ebook)
Subjects: | CYAC: Mystery and detective stories. | Sisters—Fiction. |
Bridges—Fiction. | BISAC: JUVENILE FICTION / Social Issues / Self-Esteem & Self-Reliance. | JUVENILE FICTION / Social Issues / Emotions & Feelings. |
JUVENILE FICTION / Family / Siblings.
Classification: LCC PZ7.M47879365 Inc 2016 | DDC [Fic]—dc23
LC record available at http://lccn.loc.gov/2015024304

The text of this book is set in 12-point Bembo Book MT.

Printed in the United States of America
April 2016
10 9 8 7 6 5 4 3 2 1

First Edition

FOR TOM

1

IMPULSE

Thisbe had to stop. She had to quit obsessing about Clay and Jerome and college and ride her bike down to Glorietta Bay, where she always felt better, where she had researched and written "The Effect of Pleasure Boating on the Mid-Intertidal Zone," the best paper Ms. Berron had ever seen from a high school student. She should stare into the murky water until she saw the rippling edges of a stingray as it fluttered its way along the rocks. That was a reliable thrill: wild animal, you, chance. Contact with an alien world.

She changed into shorts and found her notebook, but she couldn't help it: she lay back down. She knew what she should have done, but she couldn't go back to February and do it. *That* was the problem.

Take, for instance, the morning the doorbell rang. A Saturday. Bright and beautiful.

She'd still been asleep, which was why she hadn't answered the door right away. She'd called out several times in a not very patient voice, "Could someone please answer the *door*?" No one had answered her, and the bell rang again. The sofas were empty when she huffed herself out of bed and down the stairs. Sections of the *New York Times* flung over the kitchen island. Coffee cups drained. A single pancake dry at the edges on a sticky plate. Finally she remembered her sister Ted's regatta in Alamitos Bay. That was where everyone had gone.

She opened the front door, and there it was: A fortune cookie on a paper plate. Not in a wrapper but under plastic wrap like when you made cookies yourself and gave them to somebody. When she pulled the plastic off, the cookie smelled of almonds. She scanned the giant hedge between her house and Mrs. J's: nobody there. The Greenbaughs' magnolia trees: nobody. Nothing but lawns, parked cars, and flickering sun.

A gift or a prank? She didn't want someone to drive by and see her in her pajamas, so she bent down (careful not to show cleavage), grabbed the plate, and paused. It might be one of those things she heard about all the time but had never personally experienced, proposal bombs; no, it was some made-up word—*promposals*. Like when the guys from the water polo team had painted one letter per bare chest to spell P-R-O-M-? to ask Emily Jenks to go with . . . was it Bruce Greckenthaler? Thisbe forgot which guy, but maybe this was like that. And the cookie could be for Ted. That was a depressing thought. Ted was only fourteen, and guys hit on her all the time. On Valentine's Day, Mike Rounderman had left roses for her. Red ones. And he was a junior.

Thisbe wanted the fortune cookie to be from Jerome, but that was crazy. Jerome didn't like her. If he did, he would have smiled back at Thisbe in the quad and picked her to be in his small group when Mr. Shao had asked for volunteers to take the pro-Shylock side.

Thisbe stood there holding the plate. Should she set it back down or take it inside? Say something ironic to the empty street? No, that would be dumb. It was normal to take the plate inside even if it wasn't for her. She shut the door behind her and then spied through the peephole in case someone made a run for it, but no one did.

The fortune was actually sticking out. Just a bit. And the seam of the cookie was pretty wide. Thisbe could push the fortune back in if it was meant for Ted, and who could blame her for looking, anyway? The plate had no name on it.

She tugged, and the paper slipped free.

TRUST ME, THISBE, it said.

Thisbe, not *Ted.* The good feeling started small and flared to every corner of the room. It had to be Jerome, because who else would even be worried about whether she trusted him? Two nights earlier, he had come over to study. They had stood together right here, on this very rug. She'd felt bad because of the way the night had ended, with him thinking she thought he was a stoner when she didn't. She'd smiled at him in the quad the next day and he hadn't smiled. Or maybe he hadn't seen her?

TRUST ME.

She'd had no conversations with other guys. Only Jerome.

On the back, under Lucky Numbers, it said: 25 29 66.

The date for prom? Not unless she was going to the prom in the twenty-fifth month of 1966. Maybe they were just random numbers. They probably didn't mean anything at all.

Awesome, she thought. She took pride in never saying

that word, but she thought it now. Because really it was awesome: Jerome Betchman, who was more interesting than Mike Rounderman on every level, was (1) romantic, (2) creative, (3) not mad at her. He'd gone to a lot of trouble to show her that.

She stuck her eye to the peephole again and saw a white car. The sun falling slantwise through the window on her bare feet was even brighter now, and she broke off a tiny piece of cookie to eat. Fortune cookies were the worst dessert in the world, to be honest, worse even than pecan sandies, but this one was sort of buttery, like a crepe, and she had to make herself stop nibbling because she wanted to keep it forever. She took the broken cookie to her room and wrapped it in a tissue and set it in a yellow tin box that said *Sunshine State*. Then she sat down on her bed to tell Jerome that she got the fortune cookie and she loved it so much and she *did* trust him. Of course she did! She was sorry she'd ever worried what her mother thought of him. But what should she do? Call him?

No. Her voice would sound too excited. Quavery. She would talk too fast and say too much. If she texted him, though, she could compose it all first. Think it through. Write and revise. Then send.

Thanks for the cookie, she typed.

Did it need an exclamation point? **Thanks for the cookie!**

Still not that impressive. **Thanks for the amazing cookie!!!!!!!**

No. Too delirious. Just: **Thanks for the cookie!**

Should she add an emoji? She didn't normally use emojis, but Ted said that was why Thisbe always sounded like a cranky old hagball.

Just one. A heart, maybe. Not a red one but a blue one. Or was there a fortune cookie emoji somewhere in her phone? She looked at all the tiny pictures, and although there were a whole bunch of cute ones and a lot of truly weird ones, none of them made sense in this context.

Okay. Just, **Thanks for the cookie!** and heart picture. Deep breath. Send.

There it went.

She sat expectantly for five minutes. Nothing happened. The sun shone. Wind clattered through a palm frond. A bird sang.

She would take a shower and then see if she got a message.

Nothing. Not at 12:30, 1:30, 2:30, 3.

As the hours passed, she did an outline for history, a Spanish assignment, and all of her calc. Practiced the piano. Ate not one but two muffins. The only message she received was from Ted. **Bullet in the third race!**

Bullet as in first place.

Congrats! She typed. The day was eight million years long. All the sunshine was going to waste, but she couldn't think what to do with it. If Jerome had left the cookie for her—if anyone had, really!—he or the random stranger would be wondering if she got it, right? Wondering what she thought. Waiting to hear back from her. But clearly Jerome wasn't.

The answer she was waiting for finally came after dark. Two stony words.

All that Jerome said was, **What cookie?**

She waited a few minutes so it wouldn't seem like she was one of those people who constantly checked their phone. She felt so confused and deflated now. Prickly all over her skin and in her stomach. Something was wrong, obviously. She typed: **The fortune cookie.**

Sorry. Wasn't me.

It wasn't? **Oh. Okay! My mistake.** No heart shape or koala bear or smiley face. There was no emoji for this.

The conversation ended. Sat there like a dead thing. No matter how many times she reread it, she couldn't find any desire on Jerome's part to talk with her. She'd gotten a cookie from someone, and the cookie wasn't from him. Of course he would be terse.

But who *had* sent the cookie? And why? She opened the tin box and picked up the curved shards she hadn't eaten. She bit off another piece and tasted it as if the flavor might provide a clue. It wasn't quite as delicious now. She turned the message over again and read `Lucky Numbers 25 29 66`. There was nothing lucky about them, as far as she could see.

The next fortune cookie appeared in her backpack after lunch on Monday, in the front pocket where she kept her pencils. Jerome was in class as usual, sitting slightly behind her and far to the right. Thisbe stared at the cookie briefly and left it there, straightening herself in the chair. If she unwrapped the cookie on her desk or even in her lap, everyone near her was going to notice, including Jerome and Mr. Shao. She glanced around to see if anyone was watching her lean back down for the second time to take a pencil out of her bag. Jerome wasn't looking right at her, but he seemed to be aware of her self-consciousness, so she turned back to Mr. Shao and listened to the difference between metonymy and synecdoche.

She would have to wait. All through class. She waited and she thought about the cookie wrapped in plastic.

It seemed weird to go to a bathroom stall to unwrap something you might eat, but that's what she did after the bell. Peeled the plastic, broke the cookie open, and slid the paper out. It had the exact same lucky numbers on the back—25 29 66—so they must mean something. And this time the fortune said: YOU ARE SO MYSTERIOUS.

What was she supposed to make of that?

She didn't eat any of it. She was in the bathroom, first of all, and that would be gross. She wrapped the broken halves and tucked them in her backpack and felt distracted the whole rest of the school day, wondering if she was missing something, if someone was watching her.

She stayed after school to make up a physics lab, so it was nearly 3:30 when she went to her bike. Only a few people were walking around when she reached for her helmet and saw it, another cookie, right there in her basket. She froze. A girl in a purple jacket, Wendy something, was walking slowly, so slowly to the gym. Thisbe waited, fiddling with her lock. No one else was nearby. The windows of the classrooms were tinted, so she couldn't see anything in them but reflected palm trees and brick walls. Finally she just picked up the cookie like it was a normal thing and untwisted the plastic and pulled out the fortune.

PLEASURE AWAITS YOU BY THE SEA, it said. Same lucky numbers.

Corny, but in a good way?

No one appeared at a school window. No one stood by a car in the parking lot, waiting for her. The two boys walking with their lacrosse sticks barely noticed her. And yet, riding away from the school, she felt strangely good, as if the messages meant something had changed about her.

Every day that week she reached into her backpack with a little knot of hope in her stomach and looked into her bicycle basket the way you looked under bushes during an Easter egg hunt. Nothing on Tuesday. Nothing on Wednesday. Nothing on Thursday. On Friday she went to her bike at the usual time after school, in a crush of people, and finally, finally there it was: a pale, curved cookie in plastic. She blushed. She couldn't help looking around. People were talking to one another in the usual way. Didn't they see it? A girl from Spanish said hello, but Thisbe didn't move to point out or pick up the cookie because they didn't know each other all that well. She extracted her bicycle in a haze, waited for more space to open up behind her, rolled backward and then forward. She couldn't wait any more, so she picked up the cookie, studied it self-consciously, and stuck it in her pocket. No one said, *What's that?*

Perhaps Clay had been watching from a distance, though, because by the time she'd crossed Orange Avenue and was riding along Seventh Street by the park, he was there. On a bike. Beside her. Jerome's best friend, and surreally handsome. She couldn't even look straight at him without blushing.

"Aren't you going to open it?" he said.

"What?" she said.

"You should open it."

"Why?"

"Because you might want to answer me."

"Okay," she said, though that wasn't what she'd meant to say. She wondered if he meant for her to stop right then, in the street, at the corner where the Catholic kids were standing around in their red shirts and their parents were waiting in a line of shiny idling cars.

"Maybe I will," she said, and she kept riding slowly along. He stayed beside her for another block before he said, "You're killing me."

"Oh, yeah?"

"Yes. The suspense."

"I turn here," she said. She stopped her bicycle, and he stopped his.

"So maybe you should open it now."

"All right." Again, that wasn't what she wanted to say. She needed more time to think. Clay Moorehead had asked her to trust him? Clay Moorehead had sent her a message informing her that pleasure awaited her by the sea? Not love or romance, but pleasure?

She slowly peeled off the sticky plastic. She tried to remember that she was not a bimbo and she didn't need his approval. The kind of thing her mother always tried to tell her when Thisbe's feelings were hurt.

"So do you have a fortune cookie machine at home or what?" she asked. It was hard to breathe because everything was strange. The sky was extra high up and the trees were in sharp focus. She wished she weren't wearing her dorky bike helmet.

"No."

"Do you order them from somewhere?"

"No. I make them. Someone else bakes them and I write the messages."

"Who's the someone?" she asked. She had it all unwrapped now and held the sweet, sticky curve of it in her hand.

"Lourdes."

She raised her eyebrows. People kept streaming past them in cars and on bikes, students from the high school most of them, but none of them, thank God, were Jerome.

"Oh," Clay said vaguely, as if he was embarrassed, "she cooks for all of us."

"Lourdes makes all the cookies for all the girls?" Thisbe said.

She could look at him, she found, right in his dark brown handsome eyes, if she was challenging him in some way.

He frowned and she noticed his dimple. He said, "All what girls?"

She tried to sound jaded and indifferent. "You know. The others."

"What others?"

She was still holding the cookie, but she hadn't opened it.

"The other girls you've"—she searched for the right word, peering at the blossoms on the orchid tree—"been with. Like . . . Penny Wheeler."

"I didn't give her any fortune cookies."

"Serena Tringman?"

"No. Just you."

"Just me. Why did I get fortune cookies?"

He shrugged. "Sometimes you have to pull out the big guns." He smiled at her, and his dimple was deeper when he did that.

"Really." She cracked open the cookie and pulled out the slip of paper. It said, DINNER AT CLAYTON'S TONIGHT? "Clayton's, the coffee shop?" she asked.

"Yeah. Is that bad? We could go somewhere else."

"No! I just didn't know if Clayton was your full name or something." She didn't say she thought he might be asking her to eat at his house while referring to himself in the third person.

"What?" He laughed and seemed a little confused. "No."

She loved the coffee shop. Maybe she could go to dinner with him and see what he was like before she told her mother anything about it. This idea hung in the air like the drowsy blossoms on the orchid tree.

"What's with the lucky numbers?" she asked. They were on the back again: 25 29 66.

"They spell my name."

"How?" she asked.

"Like on a phone keypad. Remember that time in English, freshman year?"

She didn't.

"We had to make up codes like in that one book. You don't remember?"

She did, dimly, but she was studying her phone keypad and the numbers on the slip of paper. *6* equaled *MNO*, so *66* was . . . "CL-AY-*NO*?"

He stood close enough to touch her and shielded her screen from the sunlight with his hand. "Oh my God," he said. "I didn't think of that. Moorehead is too long, so I did my nickname. *Claymo.*" He laughed the way a confident person could laugh at himself and stepped away. "I guess it wasn't the greatest code."

She remembered that whole long day, sitting on her bed, waiting for Jerome to write back. "Depends," she said. "It's great for being hard to crack."

"So will you?" he asked.

A date. With Clay Moorehead. Who had made up a code for her.

"Sure," she said, but she had not ridden a single block before she began to feel unsure.

"Thisbe?" her mother said, her voice buffered by the bedroom door.

Thisbe hated how you couldn't keep feelings in a box the way you kept the stuff that inspired them. All she could do when she relived the fortune cookie morning was wish it had never happened. "Don't come in!" she said.

"Are you okay?"

"I'm fine." She stared in the mirror as she said it, and she didn't look un-fine. Did she look sane? She made the face her mother always made when she was driving late at night and felt herself getting sleepy: mouth open in a huge, arrested scream, eyeballs bulged out.

Her mother spoke again. "Do you want to watch a movie with me?"

Thisbe let her face relax into a fake, lips-only smile, an emoji only she could see. "No. Thank you."

"Do you want to play a game?"

"No, thanks," Thisbe called, watching herself say it with a deceptively normal face. "I'm going to the bay."

"Why?"

Her mother's voice had changed now. Thisbe heard with superdog ears the way her mother paused to take a supposedly centering breath. Everyone believed way too much in the power of breathing, that's what Thisbe noticed.

"I just like it there," Thisbe said. "It's low tide."

Thisbe hadn't actually checked the tide chart, but it didn't matter. You could see a stingray whenever.

"Are you sure? I could make the sauce."

Chocolate poured boiling hot over ice cream. Extremely tempting once upon a time. "No, it's okay. I want to go out for a while."

Her mother was disappointed, as per the norm. Her bare feet thudded down the stairs. She reappeared on the front steps, still worried, when Thisbe crossed the wet grass, to remind Thisbe to turn on the front and back lights of her bicycle even though it wasn't dark yet, even though she'd told Thisbe ten million times to remember the front and back lights, to latch her helmet strap, to be careful. "When will you be home?" her mother called as she rode away.

"I'll text you!"

Summer was pretty, you had to give it that. A few jacarandas were still blooming that crazy purple color, and the flowers that fell down popped under her bicycle tires. White house, blue house, funny little garden with pinwheel birds spinning. The cone-hat roof of the Hotel Del like a cake topper with a paper flag. What if she saw Jerome right now? What would she say? Would he pretend she wasn't there?

She didn't see him, though. The last rays of sunlight were lacquering the rocks when she parked her bike near the Glorietta Bay boat ramp. The tide was high, not low, and the bay was lilac under a lavender sky. Things loosened, flattened out, stilled. The clean white hulls of yachts were like . . . what? Beautiful, anyway. She saw no people, luckily. One heron, three swallows, and an egret.

Her phone was nearly dead, so she turned it off and dropped it in her basket, then picked her way across the pointed boulders until she reached the slab that was nearly flat on top and had thus been perfect for setting up her specimen jars. She stood ankle deep on another familiar rock, one that was lower down and positioned like an underwater stair, feet dry inside her rubber boots, the pink ones Ted said were her nerdaloshes. Instead of watching for a stingray, her eyes went to the boats. She tried to see which, among the boats moored at the yacht club, was the one where Clay Moorehead was probably sitting right then, ignoring every one of her messages, which maybe she should have baked into a pie or rolled into a cigarette or stuffed into a tiny baggie of weed! He'd notice them then, wouldn't he?

Clay was living aboard his parents' powerboat for the summer because his parents had rented out their house and gone to Mexico on business. That meant he was alone a lot. Thisbe wanted to ride her bike into the yacht club parking lot on her way home, walk to the door of the *Surrender,* and knock. If Clay answered, she'd tell him he was a crapping crapper of a human being and she'd never felt one particle of a speck of interest in him because he wasn't *worth* any interest.

Which is why I slept with you and tanked my exams.

She waited until the sky was indigo and she couldn't see the white crowns of owl limpets anymore, let alone a stingray. She steered her bicycle down Glorietta Boulevard, headlight off, helmet unstrapped, and remembered that she didn't have a key to the yacht club gate in her bike basket, so how would she go in there and say, *I hate you and I was just using you too.*

The gate was open, though. Ajar as if to say, *Come in.*

Don't mind if I do. She'd been to the club a million times. Her stepfather had started hauling them on beer can races every Wednesday night once he fell for their mom. After Thisbe showed a consistent tendency to barf in the South Bay, Hugh, her mother, and Ted sailed without her. But Hugh let Thisbe and Ted charge burgers to his account all summer, so nobody would be like, *What are you doing here?*

Thisbe parked her bike and started walking down the ramp with a deliberately pleasant look on her face: composed, serene.

The boats beside her were dark. Yotters who'd gone out for the day were finished now and their cute canvas curtains were closed, dinghies raised, *nighty-night,* a bronze glow here and there where maybe someone was living aboard, as Clay was at the end of D dock. He was in there. When she stood on the deck by the cabin door, knuckles poised, heart racing, breath shallow, she could hear guitar music and the falsetto voice of a singer Clay liked. She rapped on the door, three light taps, and then, too late, she saw them: a red-flowered bag and a pair of girls' flip-flops, yellow Havaianas with pink straps.

MAHALO FOR REMOVING YOUR SLIPPERS, a little hand-painted sign on the door said, the same sign that Thisbe had seen and obeyed a month ago. Whoever it was would think Thisbe was just jealous. Crazy jealous stalker girl. She must get off Clay's boat, walk down the dock like nothing had happened, find her bicycle, say to her brain with her brain that it didn't matter. Compose her face into a nice emoji.

Back when Thisbe never even hung out with anyone, she was expected only to text her mother when she came in at curfew. **I'm home**, she'd type, and her mother would wake up just enough to type, **Good night xo**. Now her mother would be sitting on the couch, waiting for the door to open. One look at Thisbe's face and she'd know Thisbe had not been counting owl limpets and parts per million. She'd say, *What's wrong?* even though she knew what was wrong, and if Ted happened to be awake, Ted would go, *Why are you wearing your nerdaloshes?*

She should hang here awhile. Not where Clay and his girlfriend could see her, obviously, just around. Be a little stingray under the sand. Wait for Ted to lock herself in her room with her headphones on, and then Thisbe would slip in the front door last minute, right at curfew, when her mom was half-asleep; say, *Good night, see you in the morning, love you too.*

Thisbe rolled her bike farther down the parking lot, where it wouldn't be noticed, and wedged it between a couple of FJs, the sailboats the high school team used. Then she lay prone on the carpet of an empty flatbed trailer. When she was little, she had thought stars were gold and silver rocks like mica, each one no bigger than her own body, and she used to imagine herself stepping star to star as in a tide pool. She would do that now: vault her imaginary self up there, leap, pause, leap, pause. A girl in space wearing boots and a hoodie. She was a good leaper, ha ha, traveling light-years in a single bound.

It got darker and later, blacker and cooler, and still she didn't move. She wanted to see who it was, that was the truth of it. Who was in there with him.

"See you tomorrow," a man's voice said into his phone, it sounded like, and then a car door opened and closed. She heard a click and a buzz—someone was opening the gate—and when she sat up to see if it was Clay, she got what she wanted and then it made her sick: she saw Clay Moorehead riding a bike beside Isabel Knapp. Headed to Starbucks, probably, or down to the Del, where the surf hit the rocks over and over and fires burned in little grills set up by the hotel staff, and Clay's friends sat in darkness, pulling smoke into their lungs.

"Hanging out at the *Of*," Thisbe had joked, and Clay said, "The what?"

"The Hotel *del* Coronado. *Del* means 'of.' "

"Right!" he said, not really laughing because of course he spoke Spanish so why was she telling him? But sometimes he *had* laughed. In the beginning he had laughed at everything, and there was something about making Clay laugh that she liked very much. It made her feel like a whole different person.

The gate rolled itself shut, and the streetlights buzzed. They lit the yellow kayak in the boat rack where Clay hid his spare keys: one for the car, one for the door to the boat. "You can take my car anytime," he'd told her when she said her stepfather never wanted her to drive anywhere. "And this key?" he said. "That's for if you ever get locked out after curfew."

"What?"

"Yeah. You're, like, on the golf course, say, and the cops are out. You have a key to the yacht club gate, right?"

She nodded. Her family did, anyway.

"This is the key to our boat."

"So, what," she said, "I'll let myself in when you're not there?"

"Or when I *am* there."

Stay out after curfew, run from cops, and go to a boy's boat? Why did he think she would do that?

Because she would, it turned out. Not the running-from-cops part, but slip out of the house after eleven o'clock and meet him at the boat, stay two hours, sneak back home? Yes.

Ted had caught her in the bathroom afterward, the one that connected their rooms and so gave them pretty much *no* privacy. She said, "*Clay?* Clay *Moorehead*! You know he deals, right?"

"No, he doesn't," Thisbe said, though of course he did.

Thisbe knew where he kept the dealables, too. She could use the spare keys right now, while he was down at the Of with Isabel. She could walk back down the ramp and unlock the door of his now-empty yacht cabin.

Black sky overhead. The stink of wet iron and mud. She found the key under the yellow kayak: simple. Walked down the ramp to the slips, turned right, then left, then right: simple. Stepped onto the deck like she'd been sent there on an errand. Laughed a little and said, "Whoopsy!" when she lost her balance. Turned the lock like she'd been sent back for a lighter or blanket or coat. The yellow Havaianas and the flowered bag were gone, as she'd known they would be. She didn't even have to flip on a light, because he'd left a bulb burning. She could see blankets heaped on the unmade bunk, Clay's hoodie on the deck, unwashed dishes askew in the sink, bits of food—noodles and blobs of steak fat—stuck to them. Two glass cups where chocolate mousse had been scraped out with greedy spoons. Same exact food to do the same exact thing. "You know he has about a million girlfriends a year, right?" Ted had asked. "He's like a serial killer, only with, like, girlfriend changing."

What kind of person fell for a guy like that?

It was now 10:55 p.m., so she had five minutes to make curfew, six percent power on her phone. She could just type, **I'm home**, and hope her mother was upstairs in bed, not on the couch.

Risky.

I'm at Nessa's, she type-lied. **We're watching a movie. Can I stay?**

There it was, the devil's cabbage, ha ha. Hidden in Starbucks bags all lined up like books on a shelf. Just one bag, mahalo. A pound of French roast to go.

Her mother's reply was so gentle that it gave her a stab-and-twist: **Ok. Call me in the morning. Have fun!!**

She was not having fun. People should stop telling her to have it. Still, her mother was so good. She was trying to be nice. Thisbe walked past all the boats with a bag that said *Starbucks* but was light as air. She'd had Clay's permission to drive his car anywhere, anytime, when he so-called loved her, so mahalo, Clay! Mahalo, tiki doll swinging from the mirror! Mahalo, yacht club gate, which opened as she touched the clicker

Clay kept by the gearshift. Maybe she would toss the clicker in a trash can later on. The club made you pay to replace those and it was always a big fat deal, like you'd given away the keys to the White House and *now everyone would get boat-robbed!*

She had no place to go, but that was the whole, entire, total, unchanging problem. She'd killed her chances to leave, and she'd mucked up any chance she had with Jerome. She had to do something with Clay's weeded-up car.

2

TIDELANDS

Frank Le Stang rowed to Coronado Island from the *Sayonara* with his usual supplies: the week's garbage, a clean Hefty bag for any recyclables he might find in the park trash bins, duct tape, stun gun, wallet, canvas sail bag. It was not, however, an ordinary night. The girl in pink boots, the one who came all the time to the boat ramp near Glorietta Bay Park, filling jars with seawater, measuring creatures—she was Julia reborn. Julia was here, on this very island, 229 nautical miles from the place where she died, and he had found her. It was akin to sifting sand every day for forty-eight years and finding, in the very last handful, the pearl that had fallen out of its setting all those years ago, the pearl that he alone—he *alone*—remembered.

The girl in pink boots was Julia, he was sure of it. Her walk, her manner, her eyes were the same! Her concern for creatures. When one dies, another is created. Shiva protects souls until they are ready for rebirth. She knew that, and when she stared into the water, she seemed to be watching for it to happen.

But how could he make the girl see that he was the same

Frank, just older, but that he was different now? That he had been given another chance?

"Do not expect the Lost One to remember you," the Seer had warned. The Seer was very cryptic on this point, and the letters, especially of late, were discouraging. *"The past is present as the moon is present when the earth is turned away, but can the earth make the moon look at her? Yea, it must."*

Frank couldn't go to Julia in daylight, because the ignorant families on the beach, the boaters, the swimmers on the pier would not see the seven signs. They would not see that this girl was his sister come back to life. How could they? He had to approach her in darkness. If he had to be the stronger one for now, it would all be worth it when Julia said, "Yes, I remember now. I remember you." He would tell her why it took him so long to come back to the cave that day and how sorry he was, and how long he'd been preparing for her return.

Frank had seen the new Julia many times, mainly on the rocks where she took notes and pictures, but also on her bike, on the docks at the yacht club where he was not a member, and on a catamaran with another girl, perhaps the sister of her new life. With each glimpse he was more certain and more determined. He didn't want to make another mistake, like he had in Oceano. That girl wasn't Julia, though she shared some traits, a few, enough to fool him.

He had learned from his mistake: Don't be impulsive. Observe. Bide your time. Trust in Shiva.

He had an inflatable Ribcraft he used for fishing in both bays, the big and the little, plus a dinghy for going back and forth from the *Sayonara* to Tidelands Park, where he kept a bike for doing errands in town. He had the stun gun, which he would use only if he had to, if she wouldn't listen.

Initially he had come to this place off Coronado Island to save money, not just because of the girl in Oceano. Mooring in the bay and living aboard would make his percentage of the inheritance last until he found Julia and bought her a little cottage close to Pismo so she could live near Cousin Telma if something happened to him. It wasn't bad living on a boat, and when he needed to get off the water, there was a lot of undergrowth along the bike path and on both sides of the hill where the bridge connected with the island—a forest, really, a small piece of wilderness between the golf course and the park, with all manner of trees and dense acacias. He kept a few things there for safety and convenience, wrapped in plastic so the weather couldn't rot them, buried in the soil so the world wouldn't steal them, and from the forest he saw women and girls go under the bridge. Cycling, laughing, walking. Julia's soul did not shine out, though, until he saw the girl with brown hair and pink boots staring into the water and making notes. If he could only be alone with her the way the Seer had instructed, she would remember.

"Can the earth make the moon look at her? Yea, it must."

Maybe tonight was the night. He would do his circuit in town: sort through the trash bins, take bottles and cans to the machines at Albertsons, withdraw cash, buy supplies, check his camp in the acacias. Keep his eyes open for the seventh sign. On the water or on the earth she would come to him.

3

THE BRIDGE

Thisbe had never noticed before what a lot of streetlights burned around the library, turning the air yellow, particulate, plus there were a surprising number of people walking around—tourists, it looked like—though that guy on the steps was definitely Jake Grossman, and the girl with him was Mandy Shue, both of whom had been at Clay's party three weeks ago. They'd see her get out of Clay's car in her pink rubber boots and remember her lying there on the rocks with her head all bloody. What was she going to say when she got out of Clay's car?

Why aren't you down at the Of, Jake? I think all the cool people are down at the Of.

Better to cruise for a bit down Orange Avenue and find a darker but still conspicuous place to leave the car. Roll down the window and stop inhaling the weed-coconut-tequila smell that was an extension of Clay's body, a unique and powerful drug. She breathed Clay Moorehead out of her lungs and turned right on Ocean Avenue, but the pangs rose like the waves that rose and fell in the dark, one following another following another following another. *You could have waited for Jerome. Once you knew the fortune cookie was not from Jerome, you should have said no to Clay Moorehead.*

She'd tried to tell Jerome it was all a mistake and he could trust her—they could start over—but he wouldn't talk to her. She didn't blame him. Why should he? Why would he even be interested in her now?

You could ask yourself the same questions a million times, but if you didn't know the answers, you didn't know.

The houses along the beach were *grandiferous,* one of Ted's made-up words. Also beautiful. You could hate them and think they cost too much but part of you still wanted one.

She turned Clay's car inland to cruise past normal-er houses that had soccer nets in the yards, minivans in the driveways, wet suits hung up to dry: Ashlynn Myrick's house, Eric Feingold's, and Daisy Koop's, where a banner that hung down from the porch roof said USC. Meaning, *Look where our daughter got in!* Five months ago, all Thisbe had thought about was getting a letter that said *Welcome to the Trojan Family.* She hadn't known Clay at all except as a boy who took easy classes and drank a lot. *Say goodbye to that situation, Thisbe Locke. Grade point average down the toilet. You're not getting into USC with a 3.5.*

These streets were no good. There were no red curbs along here where she could leave Clay's car, and his Starbucks French roast weed sitting out for cops to see when they towed it, just quiet houses, one sleeping block after another until she got to Fourth Street, the Way Out of Coronado via the bridge.

She felt in her hoodie pocket at the red light on Orange and there was her driver's license—so *that*'s where she'd left it—and a little slip of paper, one of the stupid fortunes, probably. The light turned green and she held the slip in her hand—just, like, rolling it in her fingers as she floored it to make the car climb up the bridge. Not the strongest car, this one. Kind of weak. *Tick tick tick* went the streetlights like a picket fence, on and on, up and up, and it felt so different being the driver. When she was a passenger, she could look over the rail at the huge navy ships made small like models in a museum, the water rippling with moonlight and yellow sodium, but she had to concentrate when she was driving and keep Clay's car close but not too close to the concrete zipper that curved down the center line. Where was she going, anyway? It felt good to leave.

The road was like a tunnel to the sky, a ramp that went up and up and up, but really she was just headed for San Diego. What was she going to do? Drive north on the 5 until she ran out of gas? She needed to get off the bridge and think, which meant the Barrio. She turned right where the bridge curled slowly into Cesar Chavez Park. The concrete pylons that supported the end of the bridge were painted all over with the faces and fists of angry women and men, Aztec gods, enormous flowers, the Virgin of Guadalupe. The lights were so bright that she could see every color in all its intensity: purple, green, blue, orange, red, and yellow. The grassy playground was empty, and no one sat at a concrete table painted to look like the Mexican flag. She slowed as she approached a crosswalk and came to a full stop before she realized there was no stop sign. A group of men turned to look at her, wondering why she was here by herself at midnight.

Don't hurt me, she thought racist-ly. Racistentially. She had to go back to Coronado because she didn't belong on this side of the bridge. When she went back, everything would be just as she'd left it: Jerome would never talk to her again, and her grades would be too low for an exceptional future, the one that would allow her high school failures to reveal that all along she'd been a swan, not an ugly duckling. She might even have to stay at home after her senior year and go to a local college if Hugh went on being mad at her. She wasn't smarter than Ted. Not now, maybe not ever, not in the important ways. That was why she had fallen for Clay, maybe. So there would be senior year with homecoming and prom and parties and hanging out at the Del (not the Of) and everyone getting their college acceptances and bragging about it on Facebook and hanging the flags over the doors. She found her way to the place where she could get back on the bridge. She drove more slowly now, as if dread were a huge trailer she pulled behind Clay's car.

It was weird how empty the bridge was. Only one car, a little red truck, appeared behind her, and she slowed down even more, thinking he'd pass her, but he didn't. She stopped; he stopped. *Go away,* she told him with telepathy. *I am going to leave now.* There was no forward and there was no back, so she must go down. Dive like an Olympic swimmer and part the water like an arrow and sink into the Depths. Travel to an underworld of castles and mermaids and turtles like in *The Golden Book of Fairy Tales.* Well, no. She knew better. Under the water were black sea nettles and ruffled sea hares and leopard sharks. As many as 625 sand dollars per square yard, on edge, their purple cilia quivering as they moved captive sea crab larvae to their O-shaped mouths. All the lost sunglasses in the world. Water bottles and dead phones. At least there, though, she wouldn't have to *think.*

She felt in her pocket for the fortune she'd been fiddling

with. Whichever one it was, she would know it was a sign. A harbinger. Synonym: *omen*. From within the car she breathed coconut and it did make her want Clay a little bit. Wind huffed the car and the glass rattled. Still the red truck behind her shone its headlights at the back of her head. She unrolled the paper and read, `I AM CLAY AND YOU ARE HANDS.` Oh, God, the stupidest one of all. It had seemed a sign of his poetic nature at the time. She had snuck out of her bedroom, ridden her bike to the yacht club, knocked on the door of his perfectly named, how-could-you-be-so-stupid boat! Enjoyed most of it, some of it, well, the beginning, but mostly the way he looked at her before. Kissed him the next day in Spreckels Park, middle of the day, people everywhere, even though Clay was acting really weird. She kissed him the second time and looked where he was looking, and they both saw Jerome. "I gotta go," he said, and he practically sprinted across the park, but Jerome didn't let Clay catch up.

Such a fool.

She put the fortune on her tongue and found that it tasted of nothing but sour paper and sour ink. She chewed it a few times to compact it into something small and hard she could spit onto the floor. Then she shifted the gear into park and opened the door and stepped onto the Coronado Bridge.

4

THE RED TRUCK

Fen Harris didn't feel sleepy at all, just euphoric that he was here, at the edge of the Pacific Ocean, driving over the bridge to the island where he'd always wanted to live. There were only two narrow lanes on his side, no shoulder, and the rail was so low it was like being in an airplane. He kept trying to see, in glimpses, the things he remembered from summer visits—the sailboats he had counted from the backseat, the tiny beach where he'd written his name with a stick, spelling the whole thing out, F-E-N-I-M-O-R-E, and lying down beside it in his swimsuit so his mom could take a picture—but he couldn't see much in the dark, plus it was misty out, and he was stuck behind a white Honda that went slower and slower and then, *putter putter,* stopped. He didn't have time to check his blind spot, so he stopped, too. There was no car behind him, no headlights in the rearview mirror yet, but he was afraid to shift lanes. What if he needed to back up first? His truck literally shook in the wind. How high were they? Two hundred feet? Two fifty? High enough for an aircraft carrier to pass underneath, because he'd watched one do that before.

The door to the dirty white Honda opened, and a girl wearing shorts and pink rain boots (well, *that* was odd) stepped out without looking back or shutting her door. She walked to the rail in front of her own car and faced the black bay and the island with her hands in her pockets except when the wind blew her straight brown hair so that it whipped her face. She kept pulling it out of her eyes, which she appeared to be using to take in the view like this was a turnout, not a bridge lane. She picked the hair out of her mouth and kept staring. Crazy-calm or calm-calm. Only one black car—that's all he registered, the color—zinged past in that time, and it didn't stop, though it swerved in a jerk to avoid the open door of the girl's car. The girl turned in Fen's direction and showed him her phone. She used her hand to scoop the air, as if she were directing traffic around an accident, clearly telling him to go on.

Go on?

His uncle Carl had been expecting him for, like, two hours. Carl was a water cop, so he patrolled the harbor in a police boat. He'd know what to do if Fen called him. Should Fen call him? The dashboard clock said 12:09, and two more cars passed in the far lane, racing in the opposite direction, toward the city. Windshield getting misty. Wind whacking car.

The girl scooped the air again. *Go* on, she was saying. She ticktocked the phone like he was a moron who didn't speak Human Sign Language. Overhead, the streetlights formed a blinding, speechless arc.

He backed up a tiny bit, cranked the steering wheel, and eased out, watching his rearview mirror in a state of panic, swinging wide to miss the door she'd left *wide open*—she couldn't even close the door of her broken-down car?—and as he gunned it he gave her a look that said she was a crazy, self-absorbed idiot who could have killed them both, but by then she had turned away.

5

THE MALFUNCTION

The California Highway Patrol's monitor for pylon 19 had been dead for three days now, an electrical short, the result of some bird building a nest, probably. The coastal commission was supposed to get up there and determine if CHP cameras were a threat to nesting falcons or ospreys or seagulls—Graycie Dunn couldn't remember which—but obviously they hadn't figured it out yet. Graycie watched the working screens and picked at a brownie she shouldn't be eating, and when Kyle Jukesson went to the bathroom, she couldn't help it: she got out her phone. Only time you could even act like you had a phone was when Kyle wasn't in the room. The man had no idea why anyone would communicate with the outside world, and she had to say, given his personality, a flip phone was the right choice for him. Nobody was going to follow that dude.

Graycie checked the monitors first, to make sure traffic was flowing in the same monotonous way. Car, car. Caaaaar. Empty lanes. Car. Long gap. She turned to the phone. No new messages, no picture of baby Genna in her pajamas. No word on whether the runny nose was still an issue. Graycie did, however, have one challenge waiting for her on QuizUp. Guy named Splash in Puerto Rico. What time was it in Puerto Rico?

Kyle brought hunting magazines to read on his breaks—including toilet breaks, because she'd seen him carry one in there. This gave her more time, but how much time, she couldn't recall later. Eventually she heard the toilet flush, which startled her and interrupted her game, and she didn't want to lose to Splash in Puerto Rico, so she answered the final-round question (nailing it in the first second), shut down the app while the YOU WIN! picture was still on her screen, and hurried through the braille of muting her phone. She had just tucked it back in her pocket when Kyle set a contaminated copy of *Ducks Unlimited* on her desk—way, way too close to her face. He took a bite of a brownie before he said, "How long has that car been stopped there?"

And that's when she first saw it. Monitor 3, which had a pretty bad angle for pylon 19, showed a definite stoppage.

"It can't have been that long," Graycie said.

"You didn't go anywhere, did you?"

"No." She wanted to say that nobody could take a break if Kyle was reading in the restroom, planning a duck vacation, but she didn't. She was new.

"You *were* watching the screens."

"Yeah." It's funny how lies felt the same when you were grown up. Like you were the child.

"Did you see anybody get out?"

Guilt flowed, spine to fingers. "No."

"So it just stopped? The door didn't open?"

The car was a grainy blob of grainy bits.

"Not that I saw," she said. "I mean, it's the worst camera for that part of the bridge, right? If the one that's supposed to be working were working, we could see what's going on."

He called for patrol cars, saying "incident on the bridge," not "jumper," because jumpers made the news, and when jumpers made the news, more crazies got the idea to haul their desperate selves to the top of the bridge. Plus, maybe it wasn't a jumper at all. Maybe somebody was just sitting there waiting for help. It might be no big deal at all, what had just happened.

An undercarriage scraped the road, a foghorn blew. All the windows reflected the mostly empty room, the desks, herself, Kyle.

Kyle watched the white blob on the screen where nothing moved, so she watched the dots with him. She hoped Kyle wasn't going to tell her again about the tiny red Nike shoe with the clean white laces untied—"no bigger than this," he always said, holding his finger and thumb two inches apart—left on the seat of a taxi the night a man jumped off the bridge holding a baby, but he didn't speak, just finished one of her aunt Estelle's brownies, and Graycie ate hers, too, though her appetite was completely gone.

6

ON THE WATER

Howard Accorso steered the harbor patrol boat with one hand and popped a piece of gum through the foil onto his tongue with the other.

"Why isn't Carl on tonight?" Chrissy Truesdale asked.

"Nephew coming in."

"That's a mistake," she said. She sighed and shook her head, so he asked, "What?"

"Bringing a sixteen-year-old boy into your house to live. Carl just barely got through his own kid's craziness."

"I guess it's his brother's, though. The brother that died."

"That just makes it worse. There'll be, like, suppressed grief."

"Did the Chippies say there'd be a spotter on the bridge?" Howard asked. If an officer didn't stand up there to show where the jumper'd been, you didn't even know where to start. The CHP was in charge of the bridge because it was a state highway, Coronado usually got to the scene first, and then it was group *numero tres,* harbor patrol, on the water. One bridge, three forces. Messy.

"Nobody saw a jumper. There's just the car."

The moon was half-full or half-empty, tooth-colored. Wind blew hard from the southeast. Ahead of them in the water, Howard saw a darker darkness skim by, one tiny red light on the bow, no light on the stern. "Is that Gretchen Ryman again?" he asked, and Chrissy said, "Looks like."

They'd nearly cited Gretchen once for mooring too close to the bridge. Usually only drunks moored like that, where you could be pegged for a terrorist, but Gretchen wasn't drunk, just a sharp-eyed, skinny chick with curly blond hair who hadn't even stood up when he got on the megaphone. She had leaned back on her elbows and stared into the searchlight while two big birds, cockatoos or parrots, flanked her on the rail, squawking.

"What the—" Chrissy said, low down so only Howard could hear. "She used to be on dive patrol."

Howard remembered her, barely. She'd gone on only a few dives and then quit because the bodies freaked her out. The night they first saw her cruising around, Chrissy had told Gretchen, nicely, that she needed to moor back at Glorietta with a three-day or rent a buoy at the flats, and she had moved her boat, no problem, but they still saw her roaming at night, as if she, like them, were working graves.

They were close to the bridge now, and the pylons looked the way Howard's son said they looked: like twenty stone giants with no heads. He slowed way down and began to coast into the black-and-white ripples that when he was young he would touch with the palm of his hand, thinking how soft water was, softer than anything else on earth.

7

OFFICER LORD ON THE BRIDGE

When the bridge call came in, Elaine Lord followed R. P. Skelly's squad car over the bay, descended into the Barrio, shot through the park with its murals of roses and Aztecs, and ascended the westbound ramp to pylon 19, the very tip-top, where Skelly was already getting out of his car.

All the doors were closed and the car was empty. No one in the front, no one in the back, no one standing anywhere in sight.

"Didn't they see anyone?" Elaine asked.

"Nope."

"How did that happen? Somebody called it in while driving?"

"Dunno."

Skelly stood at the rail and looked down, talking into his handheld, and once she shut herself in the car, she couldn't hear his voice, just the wind as it tried to come in. The car was still warm. Not the seat, but the air. Breathed in and out by someone who was not here anymore. At least the driver's side door wasn't open. Jumpers left them wide, the ignition on, the world askew, as if they had no time. The ignition was off, but the key was here. Dangling by her knee was a dirty green plastic key tag, nothing written on the paper inside it, water damage and grime on the paper and the rubbery green edge. Only one other key on the ring.

Nowhere in the car did she see a suicide note.

Skelly opened the passenger door and stuck his head in. "Jukesson says one of the cameras is broken. The good one for this spot. They couldn't see much."

"Who's they?"

"Him and somebody new. I think he said Gracie."

"But they didn't see anyone walking around?"

"No."

"How could that be?"

Skelly shook his head. He was so tall and broad that he made the car seem like a toy. She wanted him to shut the door again so the wind would stop blowing the air of the missing driver into oblivion. "They gotta look," she said. "In case." She meant the dive team, and she knew he understood.

"I'll call," he said, and she saw the tow truck heading east. It would pass them, circle around, and return.

She wrote everything down as she went. No purse/wallet/backpack in the front seat, glove compartment, console, or back. Gas tank half-full. 46,701 miles driven. Sticky Bumps air freshener, tiki doll, two Corona bottle caps under the driver's side seat, a straw wrapper from In-N-Out, a tiny wad of paper she did not pick up, sand, crumbs. She didn't write down that the car smelled like Axe and coconut, but she noted it. She copied down the name on the registration—Renata Moorehead at

714 First Street, Coronado—and then she stood with Skelly beside the back bumper.

"First Street, huh?" Skelly said, leaning down to flick the red duct tape over the broken taillight with his giant index finger. "So, what, a ten-million-dollar house? Plus this car?"

It hadn't seemed like a woman's car, Elaine thought. Wrong kind of messy.

"Tragic lack of automotive priorities," Skelly said.

Skelly was just like her nephews. Money was for buying nice cars, plain and simple. She hadn't wanted to work with him at first because of his various childlike views and because he was a twenty-five-year-old Mormon the size of Sasquatch. It had turned out, though, that he gave her a little of the old hope and ardor. Not a lot of hope and ardor, but a little.

The wind was blowing harder now, cutting into her ears like December, and the vest under her shirt was pinching her stomach again, so she'd probably gained back those five pounds. She didn't go to the rail and look over, but Skelly leaned his torso way out while the tow truck driver cranked away.

"Are they down there?" she had to shout at him.

"Yup," he shouted. He leaned backward over the rail and smiled wickedly at her, waving his hands like he'd lost his balance. Then he stopped kidding around and got on the radio to confirm the location for Howard. A few cars passed on the eastbound side, slowing down to looky-loo. She willed them to keep their windows and mouths shut, shut, shut. "Jump!" people liked to say if it was daytime and they'd been forced to wait for negotiators to arrive and do their stuff. This time there was no one to reason with or be mad at. Just the car like a coat dropped in the forest.

I remember all of mine, Chief Grody had said to Elaine the first time, as if once you witnessed a suicide, it was yours. She had been coming back from the courthouse the day she saw her first, March 2, same day her nephew Mike was born. She was thinking about how fast she could get to the hospital after her shift ended and whether she should get a perm and whether it meant something that the sexy electrician she'd met at the Water's Edge hadn't called yet when she saw a middle-aged woman, ink-black hair, sweatshirt with a picture of a kitten on it, big sunglasses, standing by the rail, her car stopped behind her like it had broken down. It was a red car, she remembered that. Something new and foreign. Elaine had parked in the emergency lane that used to go down the center of the bridge and said, "Hi, I'm Elaine!" So optimistic back then, so chirpy! "You should step back from the rail, okay, ma'am? It's safer inside your vehicle."

March 2, sunny and warm, a perfect spring day. The woman in the kitten shirt took a step closer to the rail and said, "Get away from me or I'll jump."

"Okay, ma'am, I'm stepping back, everything's okay," Elaine said, but the woman still climbed onto the rail with stunning speed, plugged her nose like a child, and bent her knees a little.

It was true, what Chief Grody had said. You did remember all of them, and they were yours.

8

LOOKING

At 1:15 a.m., Elaine stood with Skelly in front of a locked gate on First Street. All the houses on that side of the island faced out, not in, toward the bay and the towers of downtown, as if the only reason their owners lived in Coronado was for the view of somewhere else.

"No party here tonight," Skelly said.

It was quiet and the lawn was clean. The metal panels of the house's front wall—or was it the back?—looked like silver ice. The last time she and Skelly had been here, the gate was ajar because some kid had put duct tape over the latch. The front door had been open, so they could walk right in, right past the red lacquer table and bottles of vodka, tequila, Coke. Kids everywhere, voices loud, skirts short, red cups in hand.

"What was that, a month ago?"

"May seventeenth." Skelly had a weird talent for dates and times. "Boy named Clay."

"His sister bailed him out," Elaine said. "Was she Renata?"

"No. Something similar. Renee."

"Could be short for Renata."

"Yup."

The boy who had thrown the party hadn't been arrested, merely "detained," which was how they did things in Coronado so the kids wouldn't be too traumatized. The detention room in the new police station was nicer than some hotel lobbies, and Clay had certainly not been traumatized. More like indignant, as if he were the one who'd been wronged.

The voice that answered Elaine on the call box was groggy and female. "Hello?"

"This is Elaine Lord of the Coronado Police Department."

"Is something wrong?"

Of course something was wrong. "Could we come up to the house?"

"Jim, it's the—" the woman said, and there was an electronic bleep, a loss of connection.

The heavy man and woman who stood beside the black Foo dog statue looked nothing like the party boy and his sister, but Elaine still hoped.

"We're looking for Renata Moorehead," Elaine said.

The man tightened his wine-colored velour robe and said, "Join the club. I've been trying to call her all day to say that the guy who was supposed to fix the shower never showed up."

So they were renters.

"Twenty thousand dollars a month and I can't get the damned shower to work."

"What did she do?" his wife asked Elaine, excited.

Elaine ignored the question.

"I thought there was something fishy," the man said, talking to Skelly, not her, like most men.

Skelly asked, "Have you ever seen a white Honda Accord parked here? Two-door?"

They shook their heads. "Nope," the guy said. "She drove an Escalade. Newest model."

"Where do you send the rent check?" Elaine asked.

"A PO box," the woman said to Elaine.

"Located where?"

"Here. Coronado."

Elaine asked for the address, wrote it down, and said, "We're sorry to wake you."

"Are they in trouble?" the woman asked, still excited at the prospect, rolling the belt of her terry cloth bathrobe with one hand and making Elaine hate her.

"No," Skelly said. "Just go back to sleep, ma'am."

There was something about the hours after midnight that still brought you back to age seventeen or eighteen, when you were up only to have fun, to be older, to see how far you could go. That feeling still hovered in the fog on First Street, somewhere above the empty lawns and damp streets, but it was out of Elaine's reach. She stood by her car and felt heavy. "Where did they go if they rented out their house?" she asked Skelly. "Did you see the car Clay's sister drove when she picked him up?"

Skelly shook his head, and she thought briefly about driving to the CHP station at the base of the bridge, where she could maybe look at the monitors that showed the bridge lanes and see what the clarity was like. She could ask what kind of a gap there might have been between when they first and last saw the car. Either the newbie or Kyle had looked away, Elaine bet. Doing something besides watching, when watching was the whole job.

"Let's see if Renata Moorehead owns another house," Skelly

said. "Maybe she's living somewhere else on the island and renting the bay house for the big summer bucks."

This seemed more productive than grilling the CHP, so Elaine said okay, and she heard the sound of her door slamming, Skelly's ignition, and two cars making U-turns on the wet street as disturbances, aberrations, minor interruptions to a sleeping world.

9

FRANK LE STANG

Shiva lives on Mount Kailash. He has a thousand names and a thousand faces. He is woven into all that the eye can see: the urban forest, the body of the girl, the bag once used to carry sails.

Frank opened the bag in the acacias, where a sign helpfully said NO TRESPASSING. He settled Julia's head and body first, then her feet in their white socks, dirty now, a hole in one toe. The gun was a terrible thing in the short term but Julia was just sleeping, a heavy sleep, the weight of her body as he pulled her to the trees surprising. If she awakened too soon, she might overturn the dinghy and drown, so he wrapped pieces of an old T-shirt, torn into strips for this purpose, around her ankles and slim wrists. No one passed on the jogging path as he wrapped tape over the ribbons of shirt, once around, twice around. No one but Shiva was watching him in the urban forest. There was a man near the skateboard park sitting on the hood of his cab to have a smoke, but he was too far away. Other side of the bridge. Only Shiva could see Frank and Julia, and Shiva understood.

But Julia's boots. They were too big. No place for them in the bag with Julia. One hand for the boots, one hand to pull the sail bag to the dinghy.

The black man who was smoking on his taxi, what if he could he see the boats from the parking lot and thus would see Frank lifting the bag that held Julia? Frank walked out of the acacias to the chain-link fence, under the bridge, and out to the beach, just a sailor with empty hands, every right to be there, to observe the dark water, inspect the sky. It was normal to turn and face the park, the general direction, normal to see if the man who had sat with his knees raised, skinny as a monk, sat there still.

Nothing, no one, pavement, light.

The time was now. Sweat covered his entire chest, slicked his arms. He carried the sail bag until he reached the sand, then dragged it. The strap tore right off. No good. He needed both hands for the last thirty yards. He laid the pink boots over the bag and hurried: twenty-five yards, twenty yards, fifteen, ten. Achieved. He turned the boat right-side up as he always did. Removed the oars as he always did. Dragged it to the water because the extra weight would be impossible unless the boat was already afloat. Thinking! Always thinking. He was too impatient, though. He thought he could lift the sail bag and balance the boots, but the boots slid off, *kerplunk kerplunk*. One floated and one filled as he arranged the foot end of the sail bag in the dinghy, his eyes dry and over-open, his back tight with panic, the silver light on the white dinghy inhumanly bright, as if disgusted. He felt in the water for the boots, both submerged now. It was high tide. Headlights raked the bay, skimmed the bushes, streaked his hands. He needed to climb in the boat now, look normal, begin to row. Somebody's car turned in the parking lot, toward, then away.

Go. He'd just go. Come back for the boots if he had to.

Row, row, row your boat.

It was simple now. It was a matter of rowing, water, and balance.

Whoever had been in the parking lot was not there now. No one stood on the beach. No one stood on the sidewalk. The *Sayonara* was moored on the far end of the first row, the outer edge, and four of the five nearest boats never had a soul on them, not even on weekends, just parked, collecting slime. Nobody was home as he passed, not even the Parrot Lady, who was out cruising again, probably sailing around in the dark with no lights on, the way she liked to do.

There were flashing lights up on the bridge, something happening up there, a jumper, maybe.

One more stroke, and he was home. All he had to do was carry Julia aboard.

10

WITNESS

Fen Harris was tired but he couldn't sleep. The highway still seemed to be going under him the way it did when you'd been on your skateboard for a long time. You moved, but the bed didn't go anywhere and you couldn't slow your mind down. Again and again he saw the girl on the bridge wave him on, her hair like a flag in the bleaching light, and the poles of the streetlights ticked past uncounted.

"Alea iacta est," his father used to say when they moved to a new town or he bought a new car or signed a check. He even said it when he and Fen did something silly but irreversible, like ascend the first hill of a roller-coaster ride. *Alea iacta est.* "The die is cast."

Moving to a new town was like getting to cast the die again, in Fen's opinion. No matter how disappointing the last town had been, and Las Vegas had been bad even before his father got depressed, Fen had always felt that this time when the die stopped, the number he wanted would be right there on top.

It was easy to feel this, because he was lucky. The second

time he'd broken his arm, his dad asked for a description of what Fen had been doing at the skate park, and when Fen gave him a slightly modified version of the truth, his dad said, "You know what, Fen? You don't weigh the risks. That's your problem. You do what you want, and you think it'll be fine, you'll always be lucky."

"I'm an optimist," Fen said. "Why do you hate that so much?"

"I don't."

"Yes, you do."

"Whether I like it or not doesn't matter. It'll end on its own."

"What will?"

"Optimism. It's a thing that ends with experience. Experience does not breed optimism."

Fen felt sick inside, the way he always did when his dad talked like this.

His dad said, "What, you think it's not true?"

"I don't want it to be true."

"I'm not trying to depress you, Fen. I'm trying to prepare you for real life."

Fen would have preferred his father to say goofy, cheerful stuff like *The world is your clam,* the way his uncle Carl in Coronado did. *Carpe diem,* maybe, if he had to use high-horse Latin. That would have prepared Fen better for things like his father dying by the side of the road. Wasn't it bad enough that his father had been mistaken at first, or so they presumed, for a homeless man under an overpass, car after car driving on while Alan Harris, fighter pilot and father of one, lay gasping in the cold shade until one driver thought, *Why is that guy wearing new shoes and nice shorts?* But by then all hope of reviving him had passed.

Alea iacta est.

Experience does not breed optimism.

He could not find other words to think.

The day after the funeral, Fen had taken a die from the Yahtzee game he and his mother used to play, driven to the bare, sandy edge of Woodlawn Cemetery, walked to his father's grave, which he found easily because of how disturbingly fresh the dirt was, and shaken the die in cupped hands.

"Six," he said out loud. It was hot in the cemetery. There was not a single dark color in the atmosphere, as if everything living had been faded by the sun, even the grass and the tall palm trees. The die was deep red plastic, a beautiful ruby cube with soft edges and white painted dots, and it felt like a caramel in his hands. He visualized the six, the two rows together like buttons on a coat, and he willed the die to give him a sign that his father was wrong. Fen squatted down, shook it a few more times, and let it fall on the powdery dirt. It tumbled toward the grass and stopped. Four white dots. Fen felt disturbed but not defeated. He came back the next day, and the next, and the next, until all the dice from all the games in the house had been used up: Yahtzee, Farkle, Risk, Payday, backgammon, Clue. Sometimes the dice lay where they'd fallen out of his hand until the next time, and sometimes they'd been picked up and set somewhere else, as happened the day that the flat marble tombstone that said ALAN GREGORY HARRIS, BELOVED HUSBAND AND FATHER, NOW FLYING JETS IN HEAVEN lay newly installed, flush with the ground. The headstone installer or whoever it was had set all the dice in a straight line above his father's name, the same way someone had arranged toy cars on the nearby stone of a boy who had died at five years, six months, and thirteen days.

Yesterday, before he drove to Coronado, Fen had taken a die from a friend's Monopoly game and stood by the grave until he was sweating from his scalp and his armpits and the backs of his knees. The dice on the headstone were different shades of white and red and they were all different sizes. The numbers facing the sky were random, not in any order.

"Alea NOT *iacta est,"* Fen said to his father's stone, then visualized a six and tossed the last die. He felt almost psychic as it tumbled over the dirt, as if he could not only see the outcome but control it: James Fenimore Harris the Magician. But no. He got a three.

Normally he walked away at that point, but this time he reached down and turned the die over so the six was on top. He turned the others, too, all twenty-one of them, so that he had a colossal set of sixes, and he raised his hands in mock victory before glancing sheepishly around to check if someone had seen. But it was blazing hot. Baking. No other mourners stood at the edges of the green, shadowless, mown-over graves. He wished all the headstones were sticking up instead of lying flat, so the people's souls or whatever could see out, like invalids propped up on pillows. Then he thought what a stupid, childish idea that was.

"Bye, Dad," he said. "I'm moving to Coronado now."

The thing about visiting people in the cemetery and thinking them back to life was that you left them all alone afterward. You turned your back on them and walked away into the world, free and heartless.

"There won't be anybody here, not for a while, anyway, not *right* here. . . . I'm sorry."

Fen had almost reached out to roll all the dice again and leave them in a more random state, the way the world left things, but he hadn't, and now he was awake in his uncle's house, searching the drawers of his cousin's old desk, pushing aside paper clips, roach clips, pushpins, tarnished pennies, a torn book of matches, broken mechanical pencils, and tangled headphones until he found, at the very back of the bottom drawer, a red-and-white wooden die, which made him feel vaguely hopeful as soon as he cradled it in his palm. "I'm an optimist," he said, but he didn't roll the die to prove it. He set the die—which was chipped and dented, as if someone had idly bitten down on it with pointed teeth—inside the top drawer, deliberately choosing the snake eye instead of the six, and then he lay back in the borrowed bed and wondered if he should have gotten out of his truck to help the girl on the bridge.

11

GRETCHEN RYMAN

The fog on the golf course was waist-high at dawn. Gretchen liked to drop anchor in Glorietta Bay and sleep near the yacht club for a few days because she could use the bathroom in the storage area. Plus, when she woke up every morning, she could stand on the deck of the *Broker* and pretend the eucalyptus trees on the golf course were a forest in a gray mist that she saw from her castle in the middle of a Scottish loch. She was the Lady of the Loch, and Peek a Boo and Roll Again were human princes trapped in the bodies of cockatoos until she finished some impossible task.

"What do you think?" she asked the birds.

"Peekaboo," Peek said, or maybe it was *pickeroo.*

"Roll again," Roll said, or maybe it was *roar again* or *righty then* or *rid of them.*

"Lady," Gretchen said. "Say, *Lady of the Loch,*" and she pulled out their bag of food, which brought them the kind of happiness she wished you could give humans after they grew up, and she hoped Thisbe was sleeping better now, making plans, getting over Clay the way you got over anyone if you waited long enough. That's what Gretchen should have told her: *Just wait, Thisbe. You don't believe it will, but it will. The pain goes away.*

12

TED LOCKE

Two hours after dawn, Ted was coasting facedown on her long board in Glorietta Bay, willing the sun to come out. June was the worst month of the year and the sun wasn't likely to burn through the fog before noon, if at all, but she wished it anyway. It was supposed to be summer.

The foghorn was so loud and low that she felt it thrumming through the board and the palms of her hands. The water was cool and soft, and although she could see its true color—swamp green—below her fingers, in the distance the bay was milk pink and milk lavender, a waveless mirror for the ghostly sky.

When Ted had left the house, her mother had been checking Facebook to see if there'd been a party at Nessa Creevy's last night, scrolling through useless pictures posted by moms, who did, it was true, sometimes tell each other when a party had been rolled. "Why didn't you just say no?" Ted asked. She didn't see why Thisbe should get to have a sleepover if she was still lying about stuff.

"I don't know," her mother said. "She's been avoiding everyone. I thought it would cheer her up."

"It probably did," Ted said. It was Thisbe's problem, this situation, and it was kind of nice, honestly, to be the good daughter for a change. Thisbe had always been the brainy-brain, never doing one thing wrong in their parents' eyes, and then once Hugh had started dating their mom it was even worse because he was obsessed with USC, and so was Thisbe, so it was twisted in a good way that Thisbe had made *Ted* promise not to tell Hugh about the party that got rolled three weeks ago on First Street, and Ted had agreed, but mostly because Ted was the one who had told Thisbe she should go to parties! If Thisbe was a little more normal instead of so stuck-up, if she hung out with people instead of doing homework on Friday nights, she'd be a better judge of boyfriends.

Ted paddled with her arms in cold water until she was beyond the slips, and sure enough, Gretchen's new boat was moored out there, guarded by one of her birds, the green one, which screeched and stuck its chest out in a way that made you wonder where half its feathers went. Gretchen's parrots were named what they supposedly said most of the time, but they didn't speak that clearly (B.J. called them Pick Your Boob and Rogaine) and also did a lot of random shrieking, in Ted's experience, but if Gretchen happened to be on the deck watering her upside-down tomato plants or reading a book or grilling meat, the birds would ride around on her shoulders, which was exactly what Ted would want her pets to do if Hugh would let her have any, which he never would. This time, Rogaine was alone on the top of the mast, watching over the bay, which was turning a summery blue-indigo now that the sun, mahalo-alaylay, had burned through the fog.

Ted was always hoping there'd be a chance to talk to Gretchen, who'd been their neighbor a long time ago, and find out if she had really won the boat in a poker game with that guy who was dying, like people said, which was so cool, and if she liked living on the water, which Ted wanted to do when she grew up. A boat like that was worth, minimum, fifty thousand dollars, so it was pretty weird that someone would bet it away. Didn't that guy have kids? Maybe stepkids who didn't go to the right college, LOL. Ted let her hands float as she passed, trying to spy without openly spying, but Gretchen didn't come out to read a book or water her tomato plants, so Ted paddled on.

13

CLAY MOOREHEAD

Clay Moorehead hadn't seen Thisbe for a week. He hadn't answered her texts or Facebook messages so why did she think he'd take her phone calls? His mother had decided to rent out their house all summer, 20K a month for three months, almost enough for the E-class coupe his sister, Renee, wanted, because it just wouldn't do for her to drive a piece-of-crap Honda and plus she was the one who went to San Miguel for the summer, which their mother had asked Clay over and over again to do, but there was nothing to do down there. So he was flying solo for three months while his mom found folk art for her shops and Renee played perfect daughter and his dad did whatever he did with the hotels. Clay had planned to sleep on the boat, because, hey, as he'd put it once to Jerome while they stared at the *Surrender* from the dock, "What you see before you is a boat and what I see is a floating motel room," but, God, it was loud out there, especially if the Parrot Lady and her freaking birds were moored in the bay for who knew how many nights, and besides, Thisbe didn't understand how pathetic it was to be banging on the door of the cabin when he was in there with someone else.

Because of the parrots and Thisbe, Clay barely slept on the boat at all and stayed instead at Mark's. Mark was okay, but he wasn't much of a wingman. Jerome had a kind of *presence,* almost too much, honestly, for wing duty, which might've been why he'd gotten so cheesed about Thisbe. Anyhow, Mark's parents were never home, never as in never ever, and if Clay absolutely had to come to the boat for clothes or private time with girls, he kept the lights off and used a flashlight and locked the cabin door. He was sure Thisbe had knocked last night, though. Twice. Then the mistake had finally gone away.

14

FEN HARRIS

Morning felt like summer, the night wiped clean. He studied the surfing posters on the wall, the window with its view of white sky bisected by a power line, the unfinished pack of Newport cigarettes his cousin, Paul, had left behind (which Fen might or might not smoke), and tried to remind himself of the unbelievably awesome fact that he lived three blocks from the beach. A beach on an island in California. Perfect added to perfect equals perfect, except maybe he shouldn't have rushed off when that girl was standing by her car.

Fen hadn't even told Carl what had happened. He could have said, *This stupid driver nearly caused an accident,* or *I was late because this car stopped right in front of me,* but he had the feeling he'd done the wrong thing. When he'd been a kid, it was kind of cool seeing his uncle in a police uniform, hearing about weird stuff people did at the marina, but nobody had really wanted Fen to drive from Las Vegas by himself, and it was his uncle who had said, "I trust him. He's got sense!"

Fen started putting his stuff away, shuffling around. Carl stuck his head in and said, "How are you doing?"

"I'm good."

Carl came all the way in, and Fen was glad he wasn't wearing his police stuff. He was dressed for the beach, it looked like. Shorts and a very old T-shirt. His expression was serious, though. Man-to-man talk coming up, that was clear.

"I mean, like, really doing. About your father. All that."

He sat down on the bed and waited.

Fen still didn't say anything.

"Your mom said they screwed up, the police or the hospital, I don't know which."

"Didn't she tell you the whole thing at the funeral?"

"Her view of it, yeah. I meant yours." Carl had come for the funeral, of course. He'd flown in one day and back home the next. It was during that single day that he had offered to take Fen for the year so his mom could use the funding she'd been awarded to do research in Brazil. The "Full Bride," Carl called it, not the Fulbright, even though Carl knew what it was really called.

"Well, yeah, they did screw up." Fen didn't mind, really, going through all that again. There'd been a phone call from the police saying Alan Harris had been in an accident. Not *Alan Harris has had a heart attack and he's dead now,* but *Come to the hospital, there's been an accident.* Two totally different things.

They'd driven to the hospital in a panic and this woman, an old lady at a desk, said his dad was in room 411, and they raced to the fourth floor, the end of a green hall, and the room was . . . empty.

The blanket smooth, the pillow clean. Like nothing had happened there lately. Fen said, "So a woman who was not a doctor came out to talk to us in the waiting room and asked us to come with her to what turned out to be an office, and I knew by the way she said she was Marie LeBeau and asked if I was Fenimore Harris and my mother was Ellen Harris that we weren't in a hurry anymore, you know? She wanted us to sit down, and she looked us both in the eyes, one by one. Then this Marie LeBeau person said, 'I have terrible news.'

"Right after that, this heavy guy in green hospital clothes, he came in, and he took my mom to make the 'identification.' I went on sitting with Marie LeBeau, and we're facing this giant picture on her wall, which was a photo of the ocean with sunlight all over it, the kind that's like wallpaper. She sat beside me with her hand on my arm. She goes, 'You can see him if you want.'

"I didn't, really. I didn't answer her or move my arm, just went on looking at that ocean wallpaper.

" 'I understand he was a pilot,' she goes.

"I didn't tell her he flunked an eye test, so he wasn't a pilot anymore, just a guy working in the command post, hating life.

"She goes, 'It's fine not to talk. I'm going to give you my card in case you want to talk later. Anytime later. Tomorrow, in a month, six months, a year, you can call me.' She kept her cards in a big shell on her desk. It looked like a real shell, and I thought maybe she was obsessed with beaches, which made sense if her job was living in the desert and talking to people about death.

"My dad and I were going to take a trip this month, did he tell you? Just the two of us, to this island he'd read about in the Caribbean that's about thirty yards around. It's just sand, apparently, and one umbrella made of coconut fronds, and the shape of the sandbar changes with the tide and storms and waves, so sometimes it's oval and sometimes it's a circle and sometimes it's kind of a wedge, but it never completely disappears. *'L'île Morpion est un banc de sable,'* it says on the website, which is all in French because a lot of the big islands in that area used to be French colonies. My dad showed me a picture of Lyle Morpion—that's the way we said it: *Lyle Morpion,* like the name of some kid on the debate team—on Christmas morning, and the water surrounding Lyle was the most incredible shade of green. It was awesome. We both made Lyle the background on our computers so we could visualize being there in six months. It was weird because my dad was being optimistic about that. Superoptimistic.

"So I'm sitting there with the social worker, and my mom hasn't come back. I ask Marie if my dad said anything right before he died—you know, like people do in movies. That's when she told me about the underpass, how he had the heart attack and someone stopped, a guy who was or used to be a paramedic, so he knew what to do but it was too late. My dad couldn't say anything to anyone because he was already dead."

Fen paused. "That's it. Finito. The End."

Carl sat for a while on the bed that was way too small for him. He looked heavier and older and Fen felt older and heavier, too. Carl was tanned on his arms and legs but his forehead was white, like he wore a hat most of the time. "Crappy way to handle it. But there's not a good way, most of the time. It's never something people want to hear."

"Do you have to tell people?"

"What?" his uncle asked.

"That their relatives are dead."

"Sometimes. Usually the MEs do it. The medical examiner's office has people."

Fen hoped his uncle didn't tell people there was an accident if really the person was already dead. "That sucks," he said.

"Hey, I've signed you up for a sailing class that starts next week," Carl said. "My friend Barnaby says he can give you a little refresher course on the water today, so what say you put on your suit?"

Refresher didn't seem the right word for a person who'd never sailed, but Carl stood up and hugged Fen really hard and it made Fen want to cry, so he didn't talk. Then his uncle went down the stairs, saying, "Let's get out of here."

The house was tiny and creaky and old. From the front it looked like something in a picture book by Arnold Lobel, the one where the mice flooded the house and the water rose up in little C-shaped waves. It had thick pink shutters and light green window boxes (with dead geraniums now that his aunt Stacy was gone), a pink plank door that was curved on top, and two more windows that stuck out of the roof on the cramped second floor and let him spy on the street if he was lying on Paul's bed. When Fen was little, he'd pretended the three different colors of roof tiles were Necco wafers: pink wintergreen overlapping black licorice overlapping brown chocolate in sugary rows. Now he saw that they had bird poo all over them and the edges were caked with moss, but that did not mean he was a pessimist. It was just a fact about roof tiles, was all.

"Where are we going?" Fen called down the stairs. It was good that all of Stacy's stuff was still there, he thought, such as the yellow-and-orange ruffled curtains in the kitchen, and the bookcase full of mystery novels, and her gardening gloves in a basket by the back door. All the board games were still there, too, a whole stack stuffed into the shelves by the TV, the cardboard lids tattered and split at the corners. *A whole lotta dice in there,* he thought, which made him wonder if he was turning into a freak of some kind.

Carl had left the back door open and was whistling his way, barefoot, to the garage, where he and Fen surveyed five rusty bikes. The air in the garage smelled piney and birds were twittering and cawing and hooing away in the trees, ecstatic about their plans for the day.

"You know they don't have sailing in Nevada, right?" Fen said. "Or New Mexico?"

Carl just said, "Cruiser or a ten-speed?"

"Cruiser, I guess."

Carl pointed Fen toward an old black bike and threw a towel into the rusty basket of a red one that was in even worse shape. The tires were totally flat.

"You sure you don't want me to drive us?" Fen asked. "I've still got gas in the truck." He thought again about the girl on the bridge. Had she been towed to a garage? Did whoever picked her up say, *You know, you should probably* close the door *next time?*

"Nope," Carl said. "It's faster on a bike. Especially in summer." He located a tire pump, spun the front wheel until the stem was where he wanted it, and unscrewed the cap. Nothing about the process appeared to irritate him, and he was clearly in no rush. Fen wondered, but didn't ask, if it was faster only if you didn't count tire-pumping time.

At last they were both on bikes with fully inflated tires. They rode for thirteen blocks, going "off-peest," whatever that meant, so his uncle could buy coffee for himself and a donut for Fen at the ferry landing. "I can't believe this weather," his uncle said.

The clouds had burned off and the day was just what Fen had expected: sunny and warm.

"June is normally like winter," his uncle called back. "Cloudy all day. It's even got a name: June Gloom."

With coffee in one hand, his uncle pedaled slowly down the wide sidewalk that curved along the bay, weaving around little kids on scooters and trikes at the edge of Tidelands Park, around whole families walking slowly in clumps and stopping to take pictures in front of the blue water and the blue bridge. Fen rode slowly past the skate park he'd gone to once when he was about seven, before he could even flip his board, then past the dinghies beached upside down on the shore, not far from the little neighborhood of sailboats moored in straight lines, the sparkly water slapping them, rocking them, tugging at their hulls, and then he and his uncle passed under the bridge itself to the snap of tires on metal seams cracking like an endless roller coaster overhead. His uncle pointed to the golf course and called back to him, "Maybe we'll hit a bucket of balls later!" and Fen said, "Yeah!" though he'd never golfed in his life, and Carl said the same thing about the tennis courts, which were full of cheerful women, little kids, and a pretty intense guy his age who was killing balls spat at him by a machine while a Doberman leashed to the chain link slept in the shade.

15

JEROME BETCHMAN

If only everything were like a ball machine. It never stopped to see if you were getting tired, if you wished you had a sandwich, if you wondered where Thisbe was and what she was doing. The ball machine was heartless, and heartless was good.

Crosscourt, alley, crosscourt, alley, Jerome thought, on and on, stroke after stroke, and if now and then the sound of the ball leaving his racket was *Thisbe,* there was another ball coming up fast behind it to be struck without cognition until he fell back into the part of himself that had nobody and nothing in it except his racket and the next ball.

16

FEN

The gate opened at the click of Carl's remote and they coasted under a blue-and-white wooden arch that said CORONADO YACHT CLUB. Ahead of them in the lapping water floated rows and rows of big white beautiful boats with jokey names painted on their hulls: *Liquid Assets, Reely Hooked, Vitamin Sea, Job Site*. "What's your boat called?" Fen asked.

"Stacy Mae."

Fen was trying to decide which boat he'd choose if someone said, *Pick one!* when a girl on a shiny red board paddled into view. She had blond hair braided like Rapunzel's. Black sunglasses. She lay flat out and skimmed across the water with the flicking of her long brown arms.

"Can I see your boat from here?" Fen asked Carl, watching the girl appraise him or at least the general area where he stood, and he willed himself to look like the kind of guy who could appraise her, which meant he clenched his jaw a little tighter and tried to look bored.

"No."

The girl reached the dock, stepped off her board like someone who never lost her balance, and said, "Hey, Barnaby." She got a "Hey, Ted," from a tough-looking guy who had his head in a tiny wooden boat, so Fen learned her name, not that he needed it.

The Ted girl lifted her board out and slid it into a rack of other long, skinny boards and kayaks. She was wearing a bikini top and tight board shorts, and to distract himself, Fen asked his uncle when they could take the *Stacy Mae* out. His uncle said, "Soon, pretty soon," and kept walking until they were standing next to the Barnaby guy, who still had his head down and was doing something to a metal pulley. He wore a white veneer of unabsorbed Zinka sunscreen, sunglasses, and shorts that looked like they'd been dredged up from the sea and dried on a bush.

"Hey, Barn," his uncle said. "Why are the police here? Did somebody's boat get robbed again?"

They all looked at the police car parked in the red zone by the club door. "Don't know," the Barn guy said. "Thought you might tell me. They've been there awhile."

His uncle stared a second longer at the police car, then turned back around, introducing Barnaby as an Olympian, which made Fen dread the lesson even more. "I hear you like to sail," Barnaby said.

On a grassy place by the ramp, Ted was rinsing her tanned feet and long brown legs with a hose.

"What's your favorite boat?" Barnaby asked.

"I don't know," Fen said, hoping Ted couldn't hear a thing over the splashing hose.

"Did you start in sabots?"

Fen looked to his uncle for guidance about what a sabbit

might be, but Carl was moving off toward the yacht club, saying something about paying for the lesson. "No."

"How about Lasers?"

"Not those, either."

Barnaby had been very intense with the pulley, but he came to a full stop. "You *can* sail, right?"

"My uncle may have oversold that. A tad."

Barnaby didn't say anything. He just rolled the dolly to the edge of the dock and showed Fen how to thread the sail onto the mast, talking the whole time about where to put this and tighten that. Vang and leeboard and rudder and tiller were pointed out to Fen, and he knew Barnaby saw he didn't know what anything was and couldn't remember half of it two seconds later—rudder, maybe, but not vang. He had no idea which part was the vang. Barnaby said, "You're going to want to sit athwart most of the time" (*athwart?*), and handed him a sawed-off plastic AriZona tea jug, saying, "That's your best friend," and Fen wondered if he was supposed to pee in it. When Barnaby said, "Ready?" Fen lied and said he was.

17

TED

Ted was aware of the boy on the dock, who was about her age, she guessed, and was idly curious about how moronically he would sail. He was probably a Zonie, one of a zillion tourists who came every summer from Phoenix, but even so he was cute. If she ate a breakfast burrito from the snack bar, she could take the Bic out while Barn and the Zonie were still on the water and avoid being home when Thisbe walked in (would she be hungover?) and her mom went apocalyptic.

Ted ducked her head to get closer to the window and said, "Extra bacon, no cheese."

She sat down at one of the picnic tables with a cup and a straw and pushed her sunglasses closer to her eyes, as if getting ready for a 3-D movie. She didn't look in her Torka bag for her phone because Ashlynn was the only person she felt like talking to and she was at sleepover volleyball camp, where you couldn't use your phone during the day.

18

CARL HARRIS

Carl sat at the bar, drinking a fresh coffee, staring out at Fen on the dock and hoping he'd done the right thing. Fen was not sarcastically aloof, as Paul and his friends had been from fifth grade on, surfing or playing full-contact sports and sneering a lot. "He skates" was the only answer Ellen had given him about Fen's hobbies. Then there was the stuff, revealed by Ellen at the last minute, about Fen cutting class to snorkel in the swimming pool of the Isle of Capri Deluxe Apartments, which was actually just some run-down housing complex, where apparently some mother had turned him in as a truant, which was why his latest grades were anything but stellar. Cutting class to snorkel in a germy swimming pool was either (A) a normal reaction to your dad dying of a heart attack under an overpass or (B) the first sign of maladjustment to a world in which you preferred not to play your assigned role. Carl thought it was probably option A, but the one thing he'd learned firsthand as a father was you didn't know and you couldn't predict.

Sailing was the only sport Carl could think of that had cachet but very little public exposure. Maybe Fen was one of those people who did better on water than on land, who knew? But Barnaby would never have agreed to give lessons to somebody who'd never touched a boat before. He'd have fobbed Fen off on one of the kids on the high school team, who would have made Fen nervous, and it would have ruined Fen's chances to make a decent impression on kids his own age.

"Hey, Carl," a woman said. It was Elaine Lord in her uniform, heavier than she'd been in high school but with the same friendly, forgiving face, the same slight overlap of her two front teeth, like someone crossing her fingers for luck.

She looked over his head at the nearest drinkers, then led him to the patio where a crumpled napkin rested in a glass of ice. She went through it all: how the registered owner of the car on the bridge was a member of the club but out of town, how she'd called the number in Mexico (no answer), checked the boat (nobody on it).

He didn't know Renata Moorehead.

"Husband's name is George. Or maybe Hor-hey."

Again he shook his head. "Nope. But then, I don't hobnob that much." He smiled. "Need a fresh cuppa?"

"Nah, I gotta go."

"Did Howard find anything?" Carl asked.

"No."

An egret stood in the mud below the deck, perfectly white, as if it had just come from a wedding. Stacy always used to say it was a shame Carl's job ruined so many beautiful mornings.

"Nice seeing you," he said to Elaine, and she started to shake his hand, which was not like her, and then she pulled him into an awkward hug.

"God, I'm sorry," she said. "I heard about Stacy."

"No big deal," he said.

19

FEN

If you pointed a bicycle west, you went west, but if you wanted to *sail* west, evidently you had to go north, then south, then north, then south, and half the time you still weren't west enough to round the buoy that Barnaby called the mark. Plus, Fen kept tipping over while the Ted girl watched. She'd gotten into a boat with a bright orange-and-silver sail and zoomed past him like a wasp.

He trimmed poorly and he didn't pinch enough, apparently. He still didn't know what the hell *reach* meant. Barnaby stayed nearby in a motorboat the whole time, circling him like a killer bee, telling him things he didn't understand until finally Fen had to say flat out that he'd never sailed before, which he was pretty sure came as no surprise whatsoever to Barnaby.

Far off at the edge of the golf course, where the bay opened out and started flowing toward the bridge, the girl sailed back and forth.

When they finally got back to the dock, Barnaby was forced

(because it was his job) to show Fen how to wash the boat Fen couldn't sail, then wheel the boat in a dolly to a parking spot, and Fen was forced to shake hands, say sailing was very, very fun, awesome, in fact, and thank you very much. Only then could he sit alone at a snack bar table.

"Fen-omenal!" his uncle said. His face was always so cheerful. An annoying characteristic just now.

"Hey."

"How was it?"

"Horrible."

"Really?"

"Why did you say I knew how to sail?"

"I thought you'd be a natural."

"I'm not." All those times he'd counted sailboats from the shore or the backseat of his parents' car. It had looked like the most incredible thing in the world, the coolest and richest and awesomest. *What a crock,* he thought. Then, *I am an optimist an optimist an optimist.*

Silence. "Want a cheeseburger?"

"No."

"I'll get a couple."

You know who the optimist was? Carl. "Okay," Fen said. The girl was back. If she tied up her boat, she might come this way. His fear that she'd say something about his sailing (or refuse to talk at all) made him want to run, but then he might not see her again.

"I'll get us some cheeseburgers, Fensterman," his uncle said. "You'll do great next time. You're a natural."

Despite the crappy thing that sailing turned out to be, the water rocked everything, even the floating piers, and what rocked in it gleamed. People wheeled little yellow carts to yachts they probably knew how to sail, even if he didn't. And now the Ted girl was coming toward them with her finely cut, sunlit shoulders. She definitely was. Or toward the snack bar. One or the other.

20

KNOWN

"Let's go over the things we know," R. P. Skelly said. "The awesome party house is rented to people with ugly pajamas. The Mooreheads are in Mexico, not answering the phone. Or we have the wrong number." He was looking at the computer screen, not at Elaine.

"So that doesn't even count as a thing we know."

Skelly went on. "Clay sometimes lives aboard a boat called the *Surrender,* but not always, and not right now. So he's either in Mexico or somewhere else—we have no idea where—or he took the tackiest car in the family fleet and jumped without leaving a note."

"He wasn't the jumper type," Elaine said. "More like a nascent international playboy."

"Nascent?"

"Beetdigger Word of the Day," Elaine said. Skelly had made the mistake of telling Elaine once that his high school mascot in Utah had been Digger Dan the Beetdigger.

Skelly tapped his lip with a pencil. He was a habitual lip

tapper. "Who do you know at the Yotta Yotta Yot Club? Any old prom dates who might do raft-ups with the Mooreheads?"

"Just Carl Harris," she said. "And I already asked."

Tap tap.

"Maybe someone stole the car," Elaine said.

"And then the poor guy thought, *Why didn't I steal a better one?* and jumped?"

"The girl at the front office said you can't open the auto gate without a clicker or a key. Can't get out of the parking lot."

"Wouldn't the clicker or key be in the car?"

"I checked the front pretty well," Elaine said. "What did the Chippies say when you asked why they never saw a person? Did they run back the video?"

"It's not video you run back, remember? It's just you watch, you see. You don't watch, you don't see." He paused. "Or it's busted and you don't see."

"So they're going with the busted-camera defense."

"Yeah."

Elaine couldn't decide whether she wanted to drink more coffee or lie prone in a dark room. "Let's go look in the car some more."

It was easy to miss stuff in the dark, but she didn't think she could have missed a clicker. The car was cold now, and the grime stood out more. "I'll do the back," Skelly said, and Elaine kept sticking her hands in disgusting crevices until she found, pressed up against the lowest part of the console, the driver's license of a pretty girl with long brown hair and dark brown eyes that were probably not bad at brooding. Or maybe it was her lips that made her look pensive. They looked swollen, almost. *Thisbe Jessica Locke,* the license said.

On the floor between the brake and the gas pedal she saw again the tiny ball of paper, like a spitball, with red printing on it. She picked it up, prying an edge until she saw the word `Luck` printed in red, and carefully spread the thin slip of white paper on her knee: `Lucky Numbers 25 29 66` on one side, `I AM CLAY AND YOU ARE HANDS` on the other.

Skelly stopped what he was doing to look at the fortune. "I never get fortunes like that."

"Me neither," Elaine said.

"Kind of weird that it's the same name."

"If you found your name by chance in a fortune cookie," Elaine asked, "would you wad it up afterwards?"

"If I found a cookie that said `I AM R.P. AND YOU ARE HANDS`, I'd frame it and put it on my desk. Or yours."

Elaine kept squatting beside the car, the girl's driver's license in her hand. "When do you take just your license in the car, without your wallet?"

"When I'm going running."

"You run?"

"Hypothetically. Also when I go to the beach."

"So when you're going to drive a car but you don't need money."

Elaine was pretty sure they both filled in the blank the same way: you wouldn't need money if you were going to jump off a bridge, but you wouldn't need your license, either. "Goddamn it," Elaine said. She stood up and felt her head drain like a bottle held upside down.

"The girl might have dropped her license in the car a long time ago," Skelly said. "I dropped my house key between the seats once and found it a century later." He went back to searching the rear compartment, and she watched him lift a lid that fit over a spare tire. Smashed flat over the tire was a brown Starbucks bag. Inside the bag, ten little plastic bags of weed. Priced. Little labels on them, white stickers, handwritten. *$12* in ballpoint pen.

Jesus, her vest felt tight. That's what happened when you took a week off from running and allowed yourself salt-and-vinegar chips at lunch.

"Intent to distribute," Skelly said.

Elaine had to take off all her gear to pee, the whole gun belt, and it always felt a little like getting undressed for bed, which cleared her mind. "I have to go to the bathroom. Why don't you take that up and log it."

Maybe the license had been dropped there months ago and been replaced. Maybe the driver wasn't a seventeen-year-old girl. They just had to find the girl and see what she knew.

21

GRAYCIE DUNN

"No," Graycie said when the Coronado police officer who said she was Elaine asked whether she had seen a girl with long brown hair on the bridge.

"I found a girl's license in the car," Elaine said. "Seventeen years old. Tall."

"I didn't see anyone."

"You guys were watching the monitors the whole time, right?"

It always felt so bad to lie. If she didn't lie, though, what would happen to her job? What would happen to Genna? "The camera that's really close to that spot, it's broken. So the only view we had was far away."

Graycie was glad it was a woman who had called. Though maybe a woman would be even harder on her.

The Elaine person started in again: "You didn't get distracted by something and miss a person getting out of the car, did you? I mean, what's hard to figure out here is how a car got on the bridge without anybody driving it. So somebody drove up there, and if the car was empty when we got to it, somebody got out, and somebody went somewhere, and we both know that normally where they go is over the side. Or they dither a lot. You didn't see any dithering. So maybe they went straight over, and you didn't see it because it happened so fast."

"That's what I think, too," Graycie said. She would never look at her phone while she was at work again. She would tell Estelle or her mother to handle it, whatever it was. If Genna was sick, they could do whatever they decided. Meanwhile, Graycie would delete stuff, QuizUp and everything, on her phone, as a personal punishment.

"Kyle said he was in the bathroom," Elaine said. "So you were watching by yourself for a while."

It had a cold color, the light that was falling on her counter just now. The room felt bugged. Genna was quiet, hunched up against Graycie's chest. If they decided to check Graycie's phone, would it all be there in little codes? Dates and times and what she had done at that exact second? The trivia game with Splash in Puerto Rico, it was in there. All they had to do was demand to see her phone.

"I might have checked my text messages," Graycie said. "I have a baby. I'm a single mom. She had a cold."

Silence. People were silent when they were judging you.

"So someone could have gone over the side of the bridge while you were checking on that."

"Yes."

Elaine said nothing.

It didn't mean Graycie was the reason the girl jumped. You couldn't always stop them. Not if they were fast.

"How long do you think you weren't watching?" Elaine said.

"I don't know."

This was a mess. A big mess. A girl had gone over, and they couldn't find her, so the parents would not believe. It was a hard thing to believe even when you saw it, that's what Kyle said.

"I'll keep in touch," Elaine said.

"I'm sorry," Graycie said.

"I know."

22

THISBE LOCKE

The pain is worst in Thisbe's left arm. The arm feels cut open when she wakes in a tiny room with a low ceiling and a cushion. She's on her back, and her hands are stuck together underneath her, which also hurts. Something is tied around her head, her mouth, her tongue. Those are her legs far down, dirty legs, dirty socks. Silver duct tape round and round her ankles and calves. Through the hole in one sock, her big toe is sticking out. Naked. Bright red. Not blood but the red nail polish she picked out when her mother said *I know what will cheer you up* and she took Thisbe downtown to sit in the chair that rubbed little baseballs up and down your back.

It seems like she should be able to free herself. Rub one foot against the other, point her toes, point them harder, slide her right ankle over the left, then left over the right—but no matter how she turns her legs, the loop is too tight, and when she pulls, she rolls back and forth over her stuck-tight hands, and it's like pushing a sharp thing farther into her arm. Panic forms a band around her chest that tightens as she twists and fails at getting her hands unstuck. She can't get enough air or space. The harder she sucks on the wet gag, the less air there seems to be.

Lie still and think.

The plastic ceiling is three feet above her face and smooth. Light comes through a little window, the kind on a boat: therefore a porthole. The porthole is scratched and grimy but through the grime the color is blue. Blue: therefore day. She tries to sit up, but that hurts more, and she cries but it comes out a gurgle.

The way beams of light roll and bubble on the ceiling, the slosh of water, the mildew smell—she knows this. She's slept in a place like this: the aft cabin of a boat. In Hugh's aft cabin, a tiny fan could be switched on. The window could be popped open to let in fresh air. She and Ted had slept in the cabin once when their mother first met Hugh, when they were both little enough to think it would be fun. But this boat is a lot older. There's no fan. The gag in her mouth is disgustingly wet and cold. She rolls back and forth, kicks her naked toe on the slats of the small cabin door. She's a mouse stuck in a box, a beetle upside down. She scoots herself down so she can reach the door with her heels. She makes the gurgling scream and bangs with her heels on the wood.

Only when she hears a click and footsteps does it occur to her that someone coming could be worse than being alone.

The door at her feet swings out to reveal a man, hunched over, elfish, nearly bald, dirty. "You're awake," he says as if pleased. The dirty elf says, "I'm sorry, Julia. It was the only way."

He doesn't move to touch her but she scoots back. Her toe feels disgustingly naked, the nail red and glistening outside the sock.

"Do you remember what happened?" His eyes are full of psycho gentleness. He has a blue spot on his lip and brown spots all over his walnut face. She doesn't know him.

She remembers standing on the bridge. A car. Running with her arms around her boots. A gun. The elf-man shot her with a gun.

"Don't worry. This is temporary. Until we get under way."

Under way is the last thing she wants. The tears make her face feel sticky. If she could put her toe back in the sock, she would do that before she wiped her nose.

"Wheah awh whe?" she asks. She sounds like a baby.

"Going home," he says. He leans in as if it's an oven she's inside.

"Wheah?"

"Pismo."

That can't be. Pismo Beach is hours away, in central California. Way past Los Angeles and Santa Barbara. How many days would it take to sail there? Days and days. She says *no* but he doesn't listen and the boat rocks in a world made entirely of water: edgeless, harborless, shoreless, bottomless. Her head aches and her arm aches and she wants to put her toe back in the sock. The snot in her nose globes into a bubble, and he tries to reach in and touch her face with something but she writhes away from him, so the spotted man with the spotted lip turns his back, says he'll check on her again soon, and shuts the aft cabin door.

23

TED

By noon, Ted still hadn't checked her phone, not a single time, though she knew the messages might be piling up, as they always did when she forgot.

The Zonie was sitting with Mr. Harris, so maybe he was a Zonie with native ties. "Greetings, Mr. Harris," she said. She liked Mr. Harris because he didn't say creepy things to the sailing girls and he remembered not to call her Teddy and that one time she and Thisbe had slept out on the Getaway near Stingray Point and they were moored in the wrong place, he was cool about it and towed them closer into shore instead of calling their parents. He said he'd keep an eye on them because all kinds of lunatics could be out there.

The boy was sopping wet and looked extremely mad, which was natural given how truly terrible his sailing was. She felt sorry for him but not repulsed. He was still kind of cool-looking and manly, like maybe he was good at something else. Surfing, say.

She thought she was going to have to say something adult-ish like, "And who's this young man you've got with you today?" but Mr. Harris finally said this was his nephew, Fin, and he was starting high school here in the fall and he'd narrowly missed exile to Rio, where his mother had a Fulbright, whatever that was.

"Why Rio?" she asked.

Mr. Harris waited for the Fin boy to answer. "She's writing a book," the Fin boy said.

"About what?"

"Some lady," he said, still pissed, clearly, about nearly sinking the boat. She was glad Thisbe wasn't here to lecture him on how *lady* was a hierarchical term used to value some women over others.

"Why didn't you want to go live in Brazil? The sailing is supposed to be awesome there."

"I thought I'd like it here."

His eyebrows were all squinched. They were cute eyebrows. Bushy.

"Do you?"

"Yeah," he said, not at all sincerely.

Mr. Harris went to the window to pick up cheeseburgers and she still didn't want to go home, so she stayed where she was and the day stayed where it was, unspoiled, expectant, bright blue.

24

SUN SALUTATIONS

Not a single one of Anne Locke's increasingly angry texts to Thisbe had been answered. Was Thisbe's phone dead again? It was noon, and Thisbe should be home now. She had a piano lesson at two o'clock in Clairemont Mesa. The essay she was supposed to write for her college counselor, the one Hugh said he was about ready to stop paying for, was due tonight. Why had Anne not called Nessa's mother to ask if she could send Thisbe home at nine a.m.? Of course, Anne would have needed Nessa's mother's phone number to do that, and she didn't have it.

Maybe Thisbe hadn't even been at Nessa's house. Maybe she'd stayed with Clay on his boat. What, dear God, had happened to the old Thisbe, and how could they bring her back?

Ted was ignoring Anne's messages, too, but that was normal. Ted barely considered herself part of the family. She needed sun and water, yes, and to get sun and water you needed money from somewhere, but not conversation with the people who funded you. The kind of talk that you engaged in to show people you cared about them and were interested in their well-being was not the kind of talk that interested Ted.

When Anne felt crazy and lost—which she had since the day she'd found blood on Thisbe's towels and her pillowcase and demanded that Thisbe take off the beret she'd been wearing inside and outside the house for two days, whereupon she'd seen a jagged red cut two inches in length that could not have been made (as Thisbe claimed) by a chain-link fence—Anne tried to go someplace in the house and do sun salutations. Anne didn't do yoga class on the beach anymore because Hugh made fun of the way Desiree told them all to focus their third eyes, but sun salutations still felt good when Anne did them alone. She stood in the center of the living room, faced the window and the sun-bleached couch, then moved slightly off center so that she wasn't visible from the street, and raised her hands and pointed them like a steeple at the ceiling, arched her back, closed her eyes, then arched a little more, took a deep breath, and thought of what she was going to do to Thisbe's phone with a hammer when Thisbe finally walked through the door, smelling like rotten wine. *Just be present,* she told her herself. *Take a deep breath. Exhale and stretch down to your toes,* saying it to herself the way Desiree did. Anne leaned over and pointed the steeple of her fingers at her toenails, perceiving with her first, second, and third eyes that the nail polish Thisbe had picked for both of them was peeling off and would need to be stripped, and as she was wondering if she should do that now or later, the doorbell rang.

The dark shape through the glass might be a Jehovah's Witness, but it could also be FedEx with a package.

A middle-aged woman stood on the step. No FedEx uniform. No Jehovah's Witness pamphlet. Long hair like a folksinger, slacks and clogs and a plain green shirt with cuffed sleeves. A lanyard of some kind, as if she were a camp counselor. Behind her, a milk-skinned man with a light brown mustache and his own photo ID on a cord. "Mrs. Locke?" the woman said.

The things on their cords were badges of some kind. A sick feeling spread across Anne's skin and seized her throat.

"I'm Mary Price from the medical examiner's office, and this is Gordon White. Is Thisbe Locke here?"

The water that flowed one direction, strong and fast, for all the years of your life changed direction and flowed the other way. "Why are you here?"

"May we come in?" The man stepped up behind the folk-singer type but Anne didn't move to let them in.

"It's probably nothing," the woman added, "but I'd prefer we all sat down."

Medical examiners. Where had she heard the term before?

She let them in, and the woman named Mary said she was here because the Coronado Police Department had found Thisbe's driver's license in a car. "Is Thisbe here?" she asked.

Anne shook her head. The window behind Mary's head framed the unaltered summer street. As recently as yesterday, she'd looked at that view and felt that things had gone well at dinner, that Thisbe had joked and eaten a whole taco so maybe she would play a board game later or watch a movie and things would be normal.

The woman took a driver's license out of her purse. "Here it is."

Thisbe's.

"We found it in a car parked on the bridge. The keys were in the ignition.

Not the bridge. Not a thing that involved the bridge.

"Do you know Renata or Clay Moorehead?"

Anne nodded.

"The car was registered to Renata Moorehead, but it seems it was his car. Generally, when a car is found on the bridge like that it means something."

Anne didn't want them to tell her what it meant. She saw Thisbe on her bicycle, her face either sad or defiant—hard to tell anymore—hair loose over her shoulders, long legs in shorts that were a little too short but Anne had decided not to fight about that, just let her go out the back door to fetch her green-and-white bicycle, on which she'd coasted out of the garage and flicked on the lights only because Anne had come to the steps and said, "Lights."

"Are you going to hang out with somebody?" Anne had asked. Touchy subject lately. To ask it was to imply that Thisbe *should* be hanging out with somebody. They wanted Thisbe to do that, the hanging out, but not if that person was Clay, or if the hangers-out were drinking themselves into oblivion in the dunes or having a party (for the sole purpose of drinking into oblivion) in a house where the parents weren't home. So it had been a relief, a good sign, when Thisbe had texted later to say that she'd gone over to a friend's house after all, the house of that new friend, Nessa Creevy, whose mother was a nurse.

"I'm just going down to the bay," Thisbe had said before that, in her room, through the door she didn't open.

"But it's almost dark. I thought you were finished with the tide project, anyway."

"I just like it there."

Thisbe had not seemed upset. Her eyes had not been red; her face had not been puffy.

Anne looked at the woman from the medical examiner's

office and wished that she hadn't started to cry, because if she was crying, Mary Price and the silent guy would think they were right, and they couldn't be right. "She was riding her bike when she left here," Anne said. "She was going to check on the marine life she'd been monitoring for a while. Then she went to a friend's to spend the night."

"Are you sure?" The woman waited with so much calm sadness that Anne wanted to kill her. "What time did you see her last?" Mary asked Anne.

"Around sunset. It was still light."

"Could she have gone out with this Clay person instead?"

The tears were still undermining her confidence. "No, she's not seeing him anymore."

"We haven't been able to reach him or his parents."

"They're out of town a lot."

"Maybe we could call the friend. If that's where you think she might be."

Anywhere on the entire island, that's where she might be. On the ground, walking, two legs and two arms, beautiful long hair, sweet brown eyes. Passed out in the dunes, even, would be preferable. In Clay Moorehead's fancy house. Not on the bridge, though, not ever beside a car on the bridge.

"Did Thisbe call or text anyone else in your family since you last saw her?" the man asked.

"Ted, maybe."

"Is that your husband?" he asked.

"Our other daughter. It's short for Theodora."

"Where is she?" Mary asked.

"Sailing. The phones, they just . . ."

"Maybe we could check with her?" the man asked.

She could explode. She could implode. That's what she wanted but couldn't do. Her mind ate everything in its path like Lady Pac-Man. It rode over the woman on the sofa and the man on the sofa and the phones in her daughters' hands and she took them away and said, *From now on you are grounded,* but everything she didn't want to see anymore stayed there, and Thisbe didn't call.

25

FEN

When Carl came back with two cheeseburgers, he acted like one of them was for Ted and one was for Fen, and then Carl said, "Hey, I've got to go return a phone call, but Fen's going to be in Bronze on Wednesday, Ted, so . . ."

"Bronze?" Fen said.

"Bronze Lasers."

"They have bronze ones?"

"It's the starter class."

Fen was done feeling stupid about boats. "Let me spare you," he told Ted, not daring to look at his uncle. "I won't be there."

"You're not quitting, are you?" Ted said. "You did fine. I'm teaching that class—well, like, co-teaching it. It will be awesome."

"It will not be awesome."

"You should give it, like, a year."

"A year?"

Ted shrugged. "Nobody's good at it the first time."

"You're saying that was a normal first-time experience that showed raw talent."

"Normal first time."

Fen noticed that she said nothing about raw talent.

"Exactly!" Carl said. "I'll be back, Fen. Tell your mother I said hi, Ted."

Fen ate clumps of French fries in silence and saw that a preppy guy their age or older was walking toward them through the parking lot. He was one of those guys who didn't have acne at all. Besides being absurdly handsome, he was pretending not to notice them, heading straight for the snack bar window and digging his wallet out of his jeans pocket.

"I'll have a suicide," Ted said, deepening her voice so she sounded like a girl pretending to be a guy.

"What?"

"That's what he's ordering. Every soda flavor mixed. It's like he's eight."

When the guy walked past them with a giant soda, Ted swiveled her head in an owly way. To Fen she said in a louder voice, "I told Barnaby that we need to do that at the work party for sure and he totally agreed with me and I said you could come and help, but I don't know about the others. Did you get the wax?"

"Yeeaah," Fen said slowly. "I got the wax."

Then it was like she reversed tactics. She called after the guy, "You coming to the work party, Clay?"

Clay stopped. He had to pretend he'd just noticed humans were sitting at the picnic table. "What? I don't know. Maybe."

"I'll tell Barn to let you know the time," she said.

"Awesome," he said.

When Fen heard the heavy club door suction-close behind him, he said, "So who was that?"

"Clay Moorehead."

"Boyfriend?"

"God, no."

Clearly a defensive pose. She loved him.

Ted scowled. "You don't believe me, do you? I *loathe* him, okay? I only talked to him because he tries to pretend he didn't destroy my sister."

"Destroy?"

"It's too hard to explain." She reached into a red vinyl bag with the word TORKA printed in white over a drawing of a Viking head, pulled out a phone, studied it for a few seconds, and swore. Maybe she was one of those bizarrely uninhibited girls, like Hillary Tieran with her tattoos and her tongue spike.

A woman in a white linen shirt and a huge scarf was striding toward their table. She wore big sunglasses and kept spinning a key chain around one finger.

"Hey, Mrs. Vicks," Ted said, extracting herself in stages, the way you had to when you were folded into a picnic bench. "Fin Harris, Mrs. Vicks." She said his name wrong but he didn't correct her. "Fin just moved here instead of to Brazil."

Mrs. Vicks smiled oddly, as if smiling was very difficult for her, and then she said to Ted, "Honey, your mom sent me over here."

"Don't worry, I'm going."

"I'll take you."

"I was, like, on the water. That's why I didn't call her back."

"It'll be faster."

"What's wrong?"

"Nothing," the lady in the big scarf said.

"Did Thisbe come home from Nessa's?" Ted asked.

It was the first time Fen had heard Thisbe's name. The woman who was not Ted's mother said no and didn't smile.

"Sheesh," Ted said, and rolled her eyes. "Sorry about not finishing the cheeseburger. Tell your uncle thanks, okay?"

"Okay," Fen said.

Two white gulls circled the low-tide mud. Ted, walking away barefoot, was a lot taller than Mrs. Vicks was in heels, and also slower. Ted didn't turn around to look at him, but he could tell that she knew he was watching her, so he strolled over to where the grass dissolved into mud, and flakes of rust came to life in the wet cracks and shallows. The flakes of rust turned out to be crabs. "Tack," he said to one that was giving him an angry stare. It stayed put. "Jibe," he said. It scuttled sideways into a cliff hole of mud and didn't come back out.

26

TED

Riding in Mrs. Vicks's car, Ted read her phone again: **It's Mom. You need to come home right now.**

Then, **This is mom again mrs vicks is coming to find you.**

"Why is my mom freaking out?" Ted asked Mrs. Vicks.

"They're looking for Thisbe" was all she said.

"Who's they?"

"I don't know," she said. "Don't worry."

As they drove past the tennis courts, Ted saw Jerome Betchman with his bike. He was standing still, waiting to cross. He recognized her for sure, locked his eyes right on her eyeballs so hard she blushed. What was it with these guys Thisbe kept pissing off? Was it true what Thisbe had said, that she'd ruined everything with Jerome because of what she did with Clay? If a guy with eyes like that—you thought he was shy and mousy until he laid a stare on you and you saw his eyeballs were light green over white sand—had come over to study with *Ted,* she would have made sure there was a second time and a third and a fourth and not just studying, either. It wasn't so much that Jerome was handsome but that he was so hungry-looking, which Ted wouldn't even have known except Thisbe had made her go along one time to watch Jerome play tennis (Ted had thought it would bore her brains out, watching two guys do the most boring unit in PE), but *playing* was not what Jerome did on a tennis court. He hit the tennis ball the way you might aim an arrow at someone you wanted to kill, and then he killed him. It was electrifying.

"This isn't about Clay, is it?" Ted asked. Thisbe had truly no sense about guys.

"I don't think so," Mrs. Vicks said. Was she crying?

"What's wrong, Mrs. Vicks?"

"It's going to be okay," Mrs. Vicks said, though clearly she didn't believe this, and that's when the fear started.

27

JEROME

He didn't smile at Thisbe's sister but he felt bad afterward. She was nice enough. When he thought of Thisbe, his insides clenched, and when he thought of Clay, he understood why his mother never smiled at his dad when he picked up Jerome for a tournament or dropped off a forgotten sweatshirt. If you trusted someone and they turned on you, it changed everything, not just that one person.

Jerome had met Clay in fifth grade, the year Jerome's parents got divorced and he and his mom moved to an apartment on the island. She said it would be fun; they could walk to the beach on weekends and he could go to the tennis courts all by himself when she was at work, take lessons from a terrific coach his dad found, and the schools would be so much better, she said, but it seemed to Jerome like they were worse because no one would give Jerome the ball when they played football at lunch. They wouldn't throw the ball to Clay, either, so Jerome and Clay sat together. Clay gave him a nickname the second week of school—Romey—and invited him to his birthday party, the biggest, fanciest party Jerome had ever seen, like a wedding in a scene from a movie, with an ice sculpture and a guy playing the piano on the grass. Clay's mom had light brown hair and white skin but she spoke Spanish and called Jerome Hairr-oh-nee-mo, the *r* in *Hairr-oh* a sound he couldn't replicate in Spanish class or anywhere else, and she insisted on kissing him—both cheeks—every single time she saw him, hugging him to her breasts, and when she introduced Jerome to her relatives, she called him Clay's best friend and they all kissed him, too. It was so much more affection than anyone in his family showed that he couldn't help feeling like he belonged there.

Jerome's mom, on the other hand, never smiled when she said hi to Clay, and she never hugged him, certainly, and she hardly ever baked or bought the kinds of snacks you could offer a normal person, so Jerome went to Clay's house after school all the time.

"It's because we're not rich enough, isn't it?" Jerome's mother said.

"No," Jerome said, wondering if that was true, starting to realize, even then, that it would become true. What was he going to say? *It's because you're not friendly? Because we have nothing to eat but pumpkin seeds and Craisins?*

After Jerome's mother met Clay's mother at back-to-school night, his mother said, "What do Clay's parents do, anyway?" and when Jerome said he didn't know, she said, "They live where?" and he didn't want to show her, but he told her where to turn until they were parked outside 714 First Street. She not only parked but turned off the ignition. Jerome was worried the whole time that one of the Mooreheads would drive up and see them staring out the car windows at the green grass and the gleaming metal wall.

"Here?" she said.

"Yeah," he said, proud of Clay, almost, for having something that impressed his mom.

"*That* one." She started to laugh.

"What?"

"Nothing," she said. "Just be careful."

"Can we go now? Before they come back?"

She pulled away from the curb, and he asked her what he needed to be careful about, and she said, "Don't worry about it. I got you into this by moving here. I just mean that you're something, too. You don't have to think they're better than you because they have more money."

It hadn't occurred to Jerome to feel inferior until she said it, but he and Clay stayed friends, mostly because Clay didn't care that Jerome always came to his house rather than the other way around and because Jerome was so busy with tennis lessons and tournaments that he never made friends with laxers or basketball players or guys on the water polo team. On Jerome's sixteenth birthday, Clay gave him a fake ID. "See? Two copies!" Clay said. "If one gets confiscated, you still got your backup."

"But this is a picture of Reggie Toksun," Jerome said.

"No. It's Reggie Toksun's older brother. People are always saying you and Reggie look alike."

Other people thought this; Jerome didn't.

"They're not going to look that close, man," Clay said. "Some aren't going to look at all."

"This doesn't mean I have to be your mule, does it?"

"It's for fun, dude! Aren't you excited? Aren't you gonna thank me for my awesome gift?"

"Thank you for your awesome gift."

Jerome barely ever used it—just that one time in Imperial

Beach over winter break when he passed out for three hours and threw up in a girl's shoes. He felt so awful the next morning that he lost in the first round of the Norwood Classic, and his dad said, "What the hell is the matter with you?" It was a kid he never should have lost to, a total dweeb who kept saying, "Let's go!" every time Jerome made a fricking unforced fricking error. Never again, he decided. The tournaments were far away lots of times, anyway, in Ventura and Palm Springs and Las Vegas, so he and his dad left on Friday nights. Weekends were not for lying around with friends, taking hits on somebody's bong, but for killing kids who said, "Let's go!" in the round of sixty-four to make the round of thirty-two to make the round of sixteen to make the round of eight and so on to the finals, to be ranked and recruited, to play Division I tennis, to live, ad infinitum, where the green court smelled like hot paint and the ball kept coming at you like a thing you thought you had already killed. For this his mother had brought them to live in the Deckerling Arms on Fourth Street, grilling chicken on a crappy balcony and taking care of old, sick people in the Shores, though tennis was not a game she understood or liked or even came to watch when the high school had a home match. It was his fault, in a way, because when he was still playing in under-twelves, he had lost when she was watching and he screamed at her not to watch him anymore and she said, "Okay, I won't." She didn't. Not ever again. Plus, she had her job.

Kids who hated Clay said that anyone who was friends with him was in it for the bling, but those same people were the first ones to show up when Clay threw a party, because his sister was happy to buy the booze. The Mooreheads' house was right on the water, and sitting in any part of it, you could see the

Hyatt and Seaport Village across the bay, "the whole toolbox," as Clay's father had called it one time, showing Jerome how the Hyatt was shaped like a flathead screwdriver, Emerald Plaza was a set of Allen wrenches, and the One America building was a pointy-cross-shaped Phillips head. In the blue current that was deep enough for container ships and aircraft carriers but narrow enough that you could fantasize about swimming across it someday, an endless parade of boats went by. It mesmerized Jerome to sit there on those weekends when he lost in the round of thirty-two or sixteen and came home scared and Clay said, *You're the best, man. Don't worry about it.* The bayfront walls of the Mooreheads' living room were made of thick glass, hooked together by hinges in a slot that allowed you to fold the whole house open, and when you did that, the living room extended to a lawn planted somehow on a platform that hovered right over the rocks and slabs of broken concrete that rose from the mud at low tide. It was there you could feel for whole seconds at a time that you were on the way to the best, that you certainly had the best in front of you, so there was no need at all to worry. This was the feeling money could buy.

28

THISBE

She points her toes to touch the wooden door and tries to stretch the duct tape. She smells disgusting. When did this happen? When he shot her with the gun? She's like a goat penned at the fair. Black diarrhea on its trembling legs.

She calls out, "I half do pee," and "Leth be outh," twice, three times. The boat rocks, the gag crushes her cheeks against her teeth. Finally she hears the click of the outer door, his heavy feet, the scrape.

There he is with his turtle skin and his spotted lip.

In his hands he holds a white blouse that's yellowy tan at the collar, a knitted poncho in pink acrylic. Small clothes, like for a child. "Remember these?" he asks her, and his eyes are trying to be soft but they scare her to her very core. The fear that keeps her from nodding or shaking her head is that he used to have sex with Julia. She closes her eyes and holds her bladder tight in the stinking, hot cabin of the crazy man's boat. Seven signs, he says. Sand dollars are one of the seven signs. He puts aside the ancient blouse and the stained poncho so he can hold up a jar of sand dollars packed in sand. "For you," he says. "I wrote the date on the bottom and the number it is in the collection. They're good luck, you know."

She has to pee. In an effort to make him listen, she makes what sounds like a goat's grunting. A goat's choking. He takes hold of her legs and pulls her toward the main cabin, which is toward himself. Her feet touch the floor and she feels the grit of sand on polished wood. He says, "If you sit up, I'll take off the gag, Julia," and somehow she sits up even though pain streaks up her throbbing arm, and he puts his disgusting hands behind her head and she holds her bladder tight like a balloon she's filled for a water fight.

"We're going home now," the crazy man says. "The Seer says it's the only way."

"Wheah awh whe?" she says, and suddenly retches. All is feverish, smelly, choking. The sand dollars in jars that ring the hull—all the way around one side and down the other, on a high shelf—are yellow in the bone-gold light, so it's afternoon, maybe. The cushion beside her, speckled black from mildew, torn at the corner and thready, expands and contracts in her blurred vision. She retches against the gag again, her whole body prickling with nausea and fear.

"Let me help," he says. "Mustn't choke," and his root-brown fingers come at her. They touch her hair. It's repulsive to have those fingers on her head, to see two inches away the grime on his sweatshirt, white paint, drops of oil, the slick denim of jeans that have been worn forever, it looks like.

"Almost," he says, struggling with the knot behind her head, pulling out what feels like clumps of her hair, when, like a tooth from a socket, the gag pops out of her mouth. He drops it on the floor and uses a dish towel to wipe her chin. Like she's a baby, he swabs at her lips. Every time she spits she's revoltingly swabbed.

"Wheah awh whe?" she says, her tongue still thick.

"On our way home," he says.

"I *wath* home!"

"It won't be long."

"I half do pee."

"Of course, Julia. Of course that's right. Go to the bathroom. That's right, only fair. Who doesn't help his sister?"

He brings a steak knife and cuts the tape around her wrists. Her arms noodle painfully apart and he cuts through the tape around her ankles. So simple. One swipe.

"Back here," he says.

She sways and falls to the right when she reaches to pull her sock free of the toe, throws her hand out for support, then does it, makes the sock bloom out and hold all the toes inside it. The smell gets worse as they walk, but boat toilets always stank. They were the worst part about sailing, so she always peed in the yot club bathroom one more time right before they launched. Or she hiked her bare bum over the water in the dark and peed into the bay while Ted pretended she was going to turn on the flashlight.

"I gould pee oudside," she says, the consonants thick, like she's an alien German or a German alien. She would never actually pee in front of him. She would jump overboard.

"Too dangerous," he says.

"Why?" she says, hoping he'll say where they are, but he doesn't. They've reached the bathroom now, and the need to pee is the strongest thing in the world, stronger than hunger or fear or shame, a snake biting her deep inside. The man's claw, clamped on her shoulder, lets go of her once she reaches the tiny compartment, and she flings the door shut, yanks at her zipper, gets herself over the metal bowl from which the stink of waste is rising, and feels relief. Tremendous relief.

And then, almost as soon as it comes, the joy goes. Same fouled underwear, same dirty shorts. Same legs. Tissues are not good enough to wipe her legs clean, just falling apart and tearing off.

"Es-cuse be," she says.

No answer.

"Can I half sub clea panz?"

He doesn't answer right away, and maybe he can't understand her. She hears him rustling, snapping, the slide of wooden doors. He knocks. Sticks his arm through the little gap she makes with the door, as if decency existed, as if she were trying on clothes in a store: *Here you go, miss, the size you wanted.*

In his turtle-ish hand he holds a pair of faded jeans. No underwear, but this is not a store. This is not her room. This is not the day before. When she lets the folded jeans fall open, the smell of mildew plumes, but it's just the scent of towels that have been folded still wet. How she'd hated that smell back when she was stupid! When she could throw a sour towel back into the dirty clothes basket unused.

Thisbe studies a grayish rag balled up and dry in the tiny stall shower. Fossilized there. She picks it up and holds it to the showerhead, creaks the handle. Only a trickle of water spills out.

"What are you doing, Julia?" the man asks.

"Wathing."

"The shower doesn't work right."

She can see that. But there's a little water, a shard of old soap. She uses it and puts on the old jeans. It's not good but it's better.

When she leaves the bathroom, he holds the duct tape and strips of cloth. The knife is right beside him on the table.

He says he's sorry to tape her wrists again, but he isn't sorry. The tears she meant not to cry are oozing out of her eyes again. "It will all come back," he says, "and then we'll be together again, like we used to be," and she stiffens with the fear that the man used to have sex with Julia. Only when she's lying once again in the aft cabin behind the locked door does she permit herself to move her hands against each other to see if the tape can be stretched this time.

In the silence she hears water. Lapping, flowing, lapping. The water might be moving around the boat or the boat might be moving through the water. If they're sailing, how far have they gone? How many miles a day, and for how many days? An engine starts, then sputters, starts again, and holds. All she can see through the porthole is sky, and the sky is blue-green, a trick of the glass or the time of day, she can't tell, so she rubs her wrists together slowly, the way you might rub the edge of a bandage that has been glued to your skin for too long, the way she used to rub the stickers on the spines of library books that said, in red letters, *14-Day Book,* knowing that eventually the edge of the sticker would dry up and curl away because she couldn't let it alone.

29

JEROME

Jerome dropped his tennis bag by the front door, where it basically blocked the whole entrance to the kitchen, as his mother had many times pointed out, and took Maddy out on her leash. The sun on his skin was perfect, dry but not hot, weather his mother said he should learn to appreciate because his dad was emphasizing small liberal arts colleges now, especially DePauw. Friendly coach, full scholarship, midwestern values, his dad's relatives within range for dinner, especially Thanksgiving, because it would be too far to come home, and never mind that it was Division III, which just meant, according to his dad, that Jerome could play every match and win some. Jerome knew the truth was he hadn't panned out. At ten he had seemed headed for the highest high-holy teams, the kind his dad hadn't been able to play on, but the better Jerome got and the higher he climbed in the rankings, the more kids he faced who practiced like he practiced and played like he played, who had also been competing, since six or eight or ten, for the highest high-holy teams, and who maybe had something he didn't.

The text that came through as Maddy sniffed a telephone pole said, **Jerome?**

He didn't want to answer it or even show that he was there. He let Maddy go to the end of the extending cord and then tugged her back. He typed, **Who's this?**

Thisbes sister Ted.

He allowed part of himself, a small part, to hope that Thisbe's sister, who thought he was a beast, was texting him secret information about Thisbe, who regretted her association with Clay and was in love with Jerome, spent her nights crying about it, actually, and Ted wanted Jerome to know that.

Hi, he said.

But it wasn't like that. It never was. All Ted said was, **Have you seen Thisbe today or last night?**

No, he said. Of course Thisbe wasn't crying in her room over the stupid choice she'd made. Who wanted Jerome, anyway? Probably not even DePauw. He thought about adding, **Did you check with the stoners because they'd probably know.** He didn't, though. He walked up the steps with Maddy and left the door open so she could sit on the threshold, half in, half out, while he made a sandwich that he ate in four bites because he didn't want to taste it.

30

THISBE

What the crazy man is doing she has no idea. They are definitely anchored somewhere. It can't be the open sea because she'd be seasick, wouldn't she? Or is the sea calm right now? She should tell him she gets seasick. She might barf again while she's locked in the cupboard and die.

A splashing sound. Scraping. Through the porthole she sees nothing but sky. The same blue-green color. It's impossible to tell what time it is, or to feel that time will pass.

She lies on her side, knees bent, and thinks. A yellow taxi pulled over in front of her, she remembers that. Yellow with black letters that said *Eritrea* on the trunk. The driver was a black man with bony shoulders who told her to get in. The taxi driver is or is not a part of what is happening now? She got into the taxi, and the backseat had no padding, so you felt the round springs. "My phone died," she said to him, by way of explanation. The thought came to her, too late, that she was in a taxi without her purse. Like a dream of being at school in your underwear. She asked the man from Eritrea with the long, slender hands to pull over right at the end of the bridge, in Tidelands Park, and she told him she was sorry, so sorry, that she had no purse. She promised to send him the money. He said no. He said it was nothing. She said *please give me your address and I'll send you money.* He wrote it down on a piece of paper he tore from a book. Did he have something to do with Julia? He stayed in the taxi and she walked toward the bay, across the wide lawns of Tidelands Park. The boots were bugging her, slowing her down, so she stopped and took them off. Where was she going? Home. She was planning to walk home under the bridge.

But when she turned the corner at the golf course, where the bike path ran straight like a gray ribbon, a man came out from the bushes. "Julia," he said. The bristly beard, the tanned skin like the neck of a tortoise, the blue spot on his lip. He wore a beanie and a stained sweatshirt, the look of scary imploring.

"I'm not Julia," she said, and kept walking, but the man followed her, his feet scraping gravel on the asphalt path.

"Julia," he said again. "Forgive me."

If only she'd had money, she could have paid the man from Eritrea to drive her home. She walked faster, but the man followed.

"I saw them all, Julia," he said. "The seven signs."

She started to run with her boots clutched hard against her chest, awkward running, sharp stones underfoot. She heard him ask forgiveness one more time before she felt the pain in her arm, a violent shuddering that spread and stiffened in all her bones at once, and before she fell like a dropped puppet, the trees on the golf course grew whiter, taller, almost human with their muscled arms reaching upward in the empty air.

31

JEROME

On the night of what Clay called his Spring Fiestathon, Clay's older sister, Renee, was supposed to be in charge, which was a laugh. "Be good," she said before she left. There were already fifty or sixty people there.

Even when the house was full of kids drinking out of red cups and making out, you could sit and stare at the water flowing past like a river. That's what Jerome usually did: sat in one of the ultramodern chairs with immaculate white upholstery (they somehow never got stained or grimy like the chairs on the balconies of the Deckerling Arms) with a rum and Coke that he dumped out in the bathroom sink when the ice melted so he could refill. This way he never felt more than a slight buzz, which he would have gotten anyway from sitting on that lawn by the bay as it turned cobalt, then lilac, then flickered in the dark like a black-and-white movie.

It wasn't like he spent a lot of time with Clay at the parties now. The parties were places for Clay to circulate, sexually speaking. The girls he'd had in the past still came to the fiestathons—Clay couldn't really stop them, because once the word got around, all the juniors and any underclassmen who thought they could enter unchallenged would show up—but Clay wouldn't talk to conquered *facilones* (which even Jerome with his mediocre Spanish knew meant "the easy ones"), no matter what they wore or said or did. The girls never seemed to learn from each other. Didn't they think the same thing could happen to them? Was it just Clay's looks, or was it the house?

Until Clay had started fishing for Thisbe Locke, not one girl had ever been hard to catch. Thisbe was smarter than the girls Clay usually liked, for one thing. She took multiple AP classes, which is why Jerome knew her. She didn't go to parties. She didn't (though he sort of wished she would) post pictures of herself in a bikini so her girlfriends would write, *you r so gorgeous girl!!!* She was beautiful, in Jerome's opinion, with a narrow, intelligent face. Her lips were naturally dark and full, like lips in a painting, and her eyes were the exact shade of brown as his Doberman Maddy's eyes, which would have been a weird comparison except that no one looked at you the way that dog did: the steady, confused, worried response to being stared at. If you looked into Maddy's eyes, she looked back with a sweet, unnerving doubt that always made him say, "Relax, Maddy, you're the predator here." Maddy didn't seem to know her own power, and neither did Thisbe.

Thisbe's legs were long and she didn't have a narrow waist or wide hips; she just went straight up. He'd see her walk in and sit down and he'd forget to notice what they were talking about in English because his whole mind was now occupied by the nearness of her. One time on his way to a tennis lesson, he saw her walking down the sidewalk in pink rubber boots and shorts and a tank top. Rain boots, even though the rain had stopped so long ago that Jerome was positive the courts were dry. "Hi, Thisbe," he said, turning around so he could see the way the tank top was tight on her breasts. "Hi, Jerome," she said, which was the first time she uttered his name.

The worst, most soul-corroding part was that Clay never would have noticed her if Jerome hadn't pointed to Thisbe (crossing the quad in a white skirt, arms folded, hair in a pony-tail) and said, "Her," when Clay said, "Come on, Jeronimo, who would you pick? First choice, I mean, not who could you *get*."

Thisbe walked, Jerome pointed.

"Frisbee?"

Jerome had forgotten that people used to call her that, and Clay sounded incredulous.

"Forget it," Jerome said. He didn't want to hear why she was inferior to girls Clay picked up.

"Awesome taste, bro. You should do it," Clay said. "Make a move."

"Nah."

"Come on, Hairr-oh-nee-mo. I thought you said you liked her."

"Forget I said anything." He liked her but he didn't want to talk to Clay about it.

"You're a junior, bro! You never get any, and it's disturbing. I've seen how you work on the courts—you like to be the dark horse. Maybe that's your problem."

"I don't even know what that means."

"You have to be four down before you try to win."

"That's not true," Jerome said, though for a second it flattered him that Clay knew his game so well. Clay had seen more of Jerome's matches than anyone except Jerome's dad, and he always knew the score, which was more than you could say for the other four people in the stands, usually the mothers of freshmen. Ask Clay after a match if that kid had hooked you in the second game of the first set, and he'd know.

The winter went on, bright blue and cold in the morning, balmy all afternoon, rain falling seldom, though it was the season for it. Jerome went on going to class and hitting with Rolf and not doing anything about Thisbe until he got the flu and missed two days of English. He thought about texting her, **Did you get the notes in Shao's class?** but he didn't have her number. That Friday night he was doing homework because he had a tournament in Palm Springs, and Clay was lying on his bed, telling Jerome to get done already because Clay wanted to get MTO, and it took Jerome a second to remember that MTO wasn't a drug or a sex thing but Mexican takeout. Suddenly Clay said, "Look who's posting helpful homework hints on a Friday night! She's your total soul mate, man."

Clay held out his phone to show Jerome the name beside a tiny picture of what looked like a painting of squiggly vases: **Thisbe Locke.**

"What the hell is that?" Jerome asked.

"She says it's the painting in the poem."

They stared at the picture together. Vases, bowls, a strange blue blob. This was going to be one horrible essay assignment.

"Dude," Clay said. "I'm getting a headache because you're taking so long! Do you have any Motrin?"

Jerome shouldn't have left his computer behind, since he was logged on to Facebook, but the Motrin was in his mother's bathroom, and then he had to wash a glass because his mom hadn't done the dishes in a while, and then he went to the trouble to get fresh ice cubes out of a tray because one time Clay had said, "Why does your ice taste so weird, man?" and Jerome didn't say it was because the Mooreheads probably had springwater piped from Switzerland to their giant freezer's ice-cube maker. Jerome's extra effort allowed Clay to have a pretty long chat with Thisbe on Jerome's computer.

When Jerome came back with the bottle of pills and the ice water, Clay was looking very amused.

"What?" Jerome said.

"Laying the groundwork, man. Laying it down."

"What are you talking about?"

Clay showed him the speech bubbles:

"*Crackadilic*?" Jerome said, practically exploding. "What the hell does that mean? Did you have to pretend to be me *and* talk like a total imbecile?"

" 'You have a large and interesting vocabulary,' " Clay said, quoting one of their English teachers.

"In which the word *crackadilic* does not appear."

Clay just laughed while Jerome started typing in a mad rush to tell Thisbe that wasn't really him a minute ago, and she said, **Sayonara, you crackadilic pranksters.** That was sort of funny but it was hard to tell if she thought he was a jerk, so when Clay left by himself to get MTO for both of them and Jerome saw she still had a green light by her name, he said, **Hi again.**

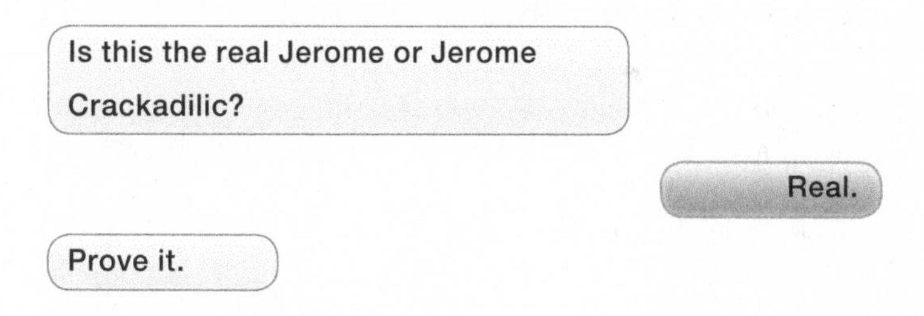

He could have taken a picture of himself but he always looked stupid in that camera's little eye, like his nose was a foot wide and his eyes were closed. The poetry handout was nearby, flipped open to the poem Jerome was writing a bunch of nonsense about, something called "Angel Surrounded by Paysans," so he skimmed it for the lines he'd sort of liked when Mr. Shao had read it aloud: *I am one of you and being one of you / Is being and knowing what I am and know.* God, no, not that. It would sound like he wanted carnal knowledge or something.

I am the angel of reality, he typed.

Aloha, Jerome.

It was like being kissed on the cheek by Señora Moorehead. Sexier, though. God, he was deprived.

To keep things going, he said, **So that's the painting, huh? The picture you posted.** He could see the vases and blobs better on the computer than he could on Clay's phone, but it was still nothing like he'd thought the painting would be when Mr. Shao said the poet was writing about some picture he'd bought. Jerome thought a painting called "Angel Surrounded by Paysans" would at least have an angel in it, something you'd see in church over the altar, where flat-faced women held flat-faced babies under flat-winged doves. **I don't get it,** he said.

The bowl on the left is the angel, she said.

He wanted to say something about what he liked so she wouldn't think he was stupid, but it would take too long to do that and he wasn't sure what he liked except for the part about being one of you and knowing what you know.

I don't get the poem at all, he said.

She didn't say anything back, and he didn't want to go on and on about his inability to understand poems that were like a cross between the Bible and Dr. Seuss, so he changed the subject. **Did you get the notes in history? I had early release today.** He already had the notes from Gabe Friesen but she didn't have to know that.

Sure.

A photo appeared. Her notes were a billion times more detailed than his, and her handwriting, dark and limber, could be a type font called Thisbe. Her fingertips showed at the edge of one page, the little half-moons white above her cuticles. He printed the pages even though he could see the words better on the screen, where he could (and did) zoom in and out (feeling more deprived and depraved), and said, **Thanks. I owe you.**

Yes, you do, she said, and he floated on that all evening, pathetically.

For the next four school days, he looked at her empty chair in English and his empty in-box at home, slowly accepting that she thought he was too stupid for further communication, and then a message came during dinnertime, while his mother was reading the newspaper and he was reading an old *Entertainment Weekly,* a routine they'd developed because she was so tired of pretending to be cheerful with her dying clients that she didn't want to talk at dinner.

Excuse me, Jerome, but do you have any notes from Shao? I had the flu.

His mother was engrossed in some article about vacationing

in Greece, her glasses low on her nose, her Stouffer's lasagna half-finished and cold.

> Yah. My handwriting's kind of sketchy, tho.
> Hold on while I get to my desk.

Standing up got his mother's attention, and she studied the look on his face (he knew he was grinning but he didn't care) and, to his surprise, she smiled. A big, wide, happy smile. "Huh," she said. "You never look like that when you're making plans with Clay."

He just waited and held on to his phone.

"What's her name?"

"May I be excused?" His lasagna was all gone and his glass was empty.

"Sure. Tell her I said hi."

He sent Thisbe his clumsy picture of his crappy notes, and she wrote, Um . . . .

He waited a few seconds and then said he knew they were confusing but he could get together with her in a few minutes, if she wanted, and he could explain it better in person. There was such a long pause he thought he'd been a fool. Then finally she said her stepdad wouldn't let her meet guys at Panera or anywhere like that, to which he said that was cool, no problem. Probably she didn't want to meet with him at all, it was just an excuse, but then she said it had to be at her house, sorry, it's so embarrassing. Would he like to come over?

An invitation. To Thisbe's house. Would he like to come over? On my way.

He already knew where she lived. Five blocks away, but a much nicer street, where it was all wide houses and wide yards and little picket fences. Hers was a two-story reddish-brown wooden house, tall and serious, just like her, with black shutters and a wicker sofa on the front porch and a Ping-Pong table in the side yard. The front door had a black iron thing on it he remembered from trick-or-treating years ago: a disembodied hand holding an orange, which was the door knocker. Coolest Halloween decoration ever, he'd thought then, but it was still there, so obviously it was not for Halloween. He stood in the dark beside the wicker sofa and an empty stone bowl full of water. Did they have a giant dog?

Her hair looked shiny when she opened the door. Maybe she'd changed her clothes and put on lip gloss for him. After she stopped smiling, though, she got that Maddy-ish look in her eyes: concerned and doubting. Everything else was confident: the way she walked, the way she said, "We can sit in here," and led him to the dining room, where a girl—Thisbe's sister, he guessed—sat doing her math until Thisbe said, "I told you to move." The girl said, "Are you Jerome?" and when he said yes, she said, "I saw you playing tennis. Thisbe made us stand outside the fence like spies so you wouldn't notice us."

He blushed, and Thisbe went scarlet. She looked at her sister with a loathing he didn't share. He'd never been so grateful to anyone's sister before, and he liked her very much. "Get out," Thisbe said. The sister thumped her book shut and gathered her pencils and her calculator and made a face.

"Bye, Jerome," she said.

Thisbe couldn't or wouldn't look at him when they sat down. He had time to study the wood grain of the dining room table, the leaves pressed against the window glass, the painting of a yellow beach beside an orange sea.

"So that was you," he said. "I saw your legs." The green mesh at the high school courts started about two feet up, so you could see the ground, old tennis balls, leaves, legs.

"You did?"

"Yeah."

"Did you think we were the biggest dorks ever?"

"No." He thought they were watching Juan Carlos, actually, who was playing on the next court. Juan's nickname was Sexi Mexi.

Thisbe tapped her pencil a couple of times and said, "I just didn't want to make a big thing about it. Like have the whole team see we were there."

"It's okay. Thanks for coming to watch."

"People said you were good. They've always said that. It's the only thing I've ever heard about you. But I hate basketball and football. And oh my God don't get me started on watching soccer."

He waited. He hoped she wasn't going to ruin what he'd felt after her sister said they'd spied on him through the fence.

"Jesus," she said. "It's incredible, the way you play."

He looked down. He didn't want her to see that it meant so much or that he was freakishly happy. "Depends," he said. "I guess you came on a good day."

"I guess. My sister said you were a beast."

"Thanks."

"It reminded me of—don't think this is weird—it reminded me of how, like—" She stopped and looked embarrassed. "Never mind."

"No, tell me."

"It's, like. I don't know. When I'm playing Beethoven or Bach or anything fast and really complicated and it's crashing up to this really hard part with a million sharps in a row and you think, *Don't miss, don't miss, don't miss,* and you don't, you know? You get it all right to the last note."

Silence as she looked at him, her cheeks pink, her rounded lips pressed uncertainly together, as if to stop herself from saying what she'd already said. "That was probably the dumbest thing anyone has ever said to you about tennis. God."

"No," he said. "It's not." The part about not missing, about everything being in a row and really fast, that made sense. "It *is* like that."

She nodded and they didn't look directly at each other for very long but it was long enough.

Somehow they found their way to the homework. It was a way of not talking about how he felt sitting near her, which was like a hovercraft. He heard himself saying, "I just wrote down what Shao said about the poem and I circled some stuff. I have no idea what I'm going to say in the paper."

She had perfect skin. No zits. Not one. He studied her cheek while she told him that in the poem, the angel of reality was the real world presenting itself to you. He said he didn't know what she meant by that and she said *it's like when you're at the beach and you're obsessing about where you should go to college and your chem homework and what would happen if you didn't get a 4.5 and you're barely even seeing the beach or the ocean and then a dolphin leaps out of the waves, you know?*

She had a 4.5? Jerome had to do well to play tennis for a decent school, but not that well.

"You know how everything stops?" she asked, her lips mesmerizing, the most beautiful color he'd ever seen. "You just wait for the dolphin to surface again?"

He made himself think of what she was saying. It *was* nice when that happened at the beach. When you were looking at the water and a wild animal showed up. "I don't see where he calls the dolphin an angel, though," Jerome said.

"Well, he's not talking about a dolphin per se. That's my example."

Per se. He would have thought it was pretentious if some guy his age said that, but she was sitting close to him and her bare arms were a millimeter away. "See where he says, *I am the necessary angel of earth*? Where he says that if you see him, you see the earth again? The dolphin makes you look outward at nature, reality, earth, the world. See *it*. Not yourself. That's how it saves you."

For a second, it was all connected like a string of beads. When she was sitting beside him and reading the words, the poem made sense in the way a dolphin rising up in the waves made sense.

He was wondering if there was any chance that her breast would accidentally touch part of his arm while she was leaning over him to point at phrases in the poem. It was then that Clay rode by the window the first time.

He never should have told Clay where he was going when Clay asked—it must have been some competitive part of him, just like Clay said—though he never could have dreamed that Clay would ride by Thisbe's house on a skateboard, grinning in at them where they sat at the dining room table. At first Thisbe didn't notice, because her back was to the window, but then she saw Jerome's frozen face and she said, "What?" and turned to look.

"Nothing." He could still hear Clay's skateboard *ka-thud*ding over cracks.

"Was that Clay Moorehead?" Thisbe asked. She looked a little too excited, honestly.

Jerome pretended he wasn't sure, but in a few seconds the *ka-thud ka-thud* and the scraping wheels returned, and she turned and saw the full drive-by, Clay Moorehead balanced on a skateboard, facing the window, this time not only grinning but holding a paper sign that said WAY TO GO, ROMEY.

"*Romey*?"

"He used to call me that."

"Cute."

She went back to reading or at least staring at his notes, but she was smiling to herself. Was she smiling because of Clay? Did she *like* him, which was something you could say about a million other girls?

"Can we close the curtains, maybe?"

"I'm kind of curious what else he'll say." Clay was rich and handsome, and she wanted to keep looking at him. *Clay's weird power strikes again.*

"Please let's not find out," Jerome said. She didn't move to close the curtains, and the next time Clay went past, he held up a sign that said CRAAAACKADILIC, BABY! And he gave them a thumbs-up with a big Clay Moorehead clowning-around smile.

"Are you guys best friends?"

"Yeah," he said, though at that moment he hated Clay a little bit.

"You're kind of different from each other."

"Yeah. So?"

"Nothing," she said. "Forget I said it."

"His family's got, like, a billion dollars, you mean?"

"He's different from just about everybody in that way, right? There are the rich people, and then there are the crazy-rich people." Jerome noticed she left out the poor people. Middle people, too. "It's just—never mind."

"What?"

"I don't want you to take it the wrong way."

"I think I'm taking it the wrong way."

"Sorry. Okay. When I told my mom you were going to come over here and study, she said, 'Jerome Betchman? Isn't he a stoner?' "

No air flowed into or out of the room. Not only was she interested in Clay, but she thought Jerome was the one she needed to watch out for. "Why did she say that?"

"I don't know. Maybe because you hang out with Clay."

"He's not a stoner."

"He's not?"

Jerome thought about it. "If you're a total idiot and you smoke weed, you're a stoner. If you're smart and you smoke, you're not."

"That makes *no* sense!"

"Yes, it does."

"But he throws those big parties by the bay."

"That's not being a stoner."

"They drink there, right? And smoke. When his parents aren't there. My mom"—she turned around to see if her mother was still in the kitchen, but the room looked empty now—

"obsessively keeps track of everybody and who they hang out with and whether their parents go out of town a lot and who goes to the parties where there's drinking. I said you didn't seem like that type."

"I'm not!"

"But you go to Clay's parties?"

"I go because he's my friend. When I'm not at tournaments. But I don't get drunk."

"Good. Getting drunk is the stupidest thing on earth."

That had been the way it had felt in Imperial Beach. But it was death to talk like that around certain people at school. Most of them. Was she tone-deaf? Really good at poetry but couldn't figure people out? Not that he cared. He didn't care if she hated drinking. "So how come I still get to be here?" he asked.

"I told her you take AP classes and have been recruited for tennis."

"Oh. Excellent." Though it wasn't, quite. He paused an absurdly long time, rolling his pencil back and forth over the shiny table. And then he just went for it. He wanted to know if she was interested in him or not, once and for all. "Would she, um, let you do anything else?"

Clay rode by again with a sign that said JERONIMO!!! but Jerome didn't smile this time.

"Jeronimo?"

"Spanish for *Jerome.*"

"Would my mother let me do anything else like what?"

"I don't know." He rubbed at the edges of his notebook, thumbed them so they fluttered. He said, "Like, you know, go out somewhere with me."

She pinkened. She turned her face and read the poem again or maybe pretended to read, and, without looking up, she said, "Probably not, to be honest. She's scared of my stepdad. If we don't do everything perfectly, he thinks it's her fault."

"But you *do* everything perfectly, right? You did get the 4.5, didn't you? The one you were worried about on the beach when you saw the dolphin?"

"I got it. But it's an ongoing thing, right? You do one thing and then you have to do more. And more. And more. And still you might not make it."

"Yeah. Like tennis. You win one point but then you have to win the next one. You win a game but then comes the next one."

She nodded, and then she went back to studying what she'd written. She typed something, held her hands still. He desperately wanted to see her again, so he said, "I'm totally boring, to be honest. Ask anyone. Even Clay. I'm the most boring person you can imagine."

"I sense that. I sense your boringness." She smiled; then her face went sort of blank. "I just don't know if he'd think that."

"Who?"

"My stepdad."

"And that's because I'm friends with Clay."

"Yeah."

It made him angry and a little defensive. Clay wasn't that bad—as a friend, actually, he was very loyal—and the parties were not that terrible, either. If Clay didn't throw fiestas, as he called them, some other kid would. If no kid threw a party, the ones who wanted to drink would fill water bottles with vodka, walk down to the dunes or Stingray, and get just as wrecked. More importantly, Jerome could not possibly be anyone's idea of a stoner. He had a 3.8, for God's sake. He'd played number one varsity singles the last three years. You could not be stoned and do that.

He tried to concentrate on the poem again and write stuff about the angel of reality because he didn't want her to see that he was angry. He typed: **Am I not, / Myself, only half of a figure of a sort.**

What did that mean? He could ask her, but he didn't feel like it. "I have to go," he said.

"Now?"

"Yeah. I have chem, too. And Spanish."

"Okay." She looked miserable but she said, "Thanks for coming over."

"You helped me a lot more than I helped you."

"No," she said. "Your notes helped me. Also, you know, talking it out. It's easier than just writing it cold."

She could feel it, he knew, the heaviness. It was like an anvil hanging from the dining room chandelier. He was going to tell Clay the next morning what a cheesing stoner he was and how his terrible reputation was wrecking Jerome's chances with girls, but what really wrecked them was that Jerome didn't know how to talk to girls. A girl liked you or she didn't, and Thisbe didn't like him. "See you later," he told Thisbe, and it was over.

The first thing Clay said the next day was, "Did you bang her?"

Jerome didn't even answer, just locked his skateboard into a rack and walked into the quad.

"Did you set up some more poetry jams, then?"

"No, I didn't."

"Word on the street is you did."

"Word on the street, actually, is she isn't interested."

"What?"

"Yeah."

"Why not?"

"She thinks I'm a stoner. You too, actually."

"No."

"Yes."

"That hurts, man."

"Hurts you or hurts me?"

"Both. Hey, I'll talk to her. Tell her you're the man."

"Please don't, okay?"

"Why not?"

Jerome paused, and then he said something untrue: "I don't care that much."

By the beginning of March, Jerome had three matches a week plus practice plus lessons with his private coach at Barnes, and he found himself looking obsessively through the green mesh before home matches, hoping to see Thisbe standing there, but she never was. Jerome's father took time off work and drove over the bridge and watched, and Clay watched, and the mothers of the other players chatted and kept their faces more or less facing the courts, and that was it. After tennis, Jerome went home and did hours of calculus and English and chem and Spanish, and on free weekends when he would have been at Clay's house, sitting on the green lawn, looking at the bay flow by like a river, eating the crab cakes the Mooreheads' housekeeper, Lourdes, made on Saturday nights, he stayed home because he thought maybe if he did like her and he got the courage to try again, she'd be able to tell her parents he was not a party guy at all.

On April 1, Clay started razzing him about getting a date to prom so they could double, even though Clay hadn't asked anybody, either. "Who would you ask if you *did* ask someone?" Clay said.

"I wouldn't."

"But if you did."

"I wouldn't," Jerome said.

"Just pick somebody. How about that hot girl from Belgium?"

"No."

"Tell me, bro, because I really want to ask somebody."

"Who?" Jerome was curious. Clay never took anyone to a dance.

"You first." Clay was acting weird. Nervous, almost.

"Okay," Jerome said. "You really want to know?"

"Yeah. I really do."

"Same girl."

The look on Clay's face was odd. Surprised. "What do you mean?"

"Same girl I said the last time we had this stupid conversation."

"Really?" Clay said. "This is not an April Fools' joke, right?"

"No. Why would it be?"

"Thisbe?" Clay said.

"Yeah."

"I thought you stopped liking her, bro. You said you didn't care."

"Well, I was wrong. Or I lied to get you off my back. What difference does it make?"

"None," Clay said, and Jerome left it at that.

The very next day somebody was talking about how they never would have thunk it. Not Frisbee Locke and Clay Moorehead! She was out on his boat, somebody said. After curfew, no less. Jerome couldn't find Clay anywhere when it was time to go to lunch, so Jerome got a protein bar and was eating in Spreckels Park when he saw the two of them on a bench by the swings. Broad daylight, lunch, but there she was, kissing Clay on a bench. You were never more than two feet from someone who knew your mother in Coronado, so not only did Thisbe not care what her parents thought, but Clay didn't care what Jerome thought.

Jerome turned around and walked back to school without eating the rest of the protein bar, which he threw into the trash on his way to English. He thought about cutting class so he wouldn't have to see her, but his feet carried him up the stairs. When Thisbe slipped into her seat across the room, he stared stone-faced at the whiteboard, and he didn't look at her until Shao called on her. Thisbe's eyes slid sideways—dark, scared—to meet his after she answered the question, so Jerome stared at her as if to say, *Yes, I saw you,* and she opened her mouth as if to say something, but he looked immediately and deliberately away and refused to move his head in her direction for the remainder of the lecture, on which he took no notes. When the bell rang, he was the first person out the door. All the way across the quad he imagined her chasing after him, tapping him on the shoulder to say, *It's not what you think,* but no one chased after him and if anyone else spoke to him, he didn't notice. Clay called him later, and texted, and then came by, but Jerome managed to elude him until the day of the party, May 17.

32

CLAY

Clay only answered the phone because he thought it was Rite Aid calling about his Solodyn. He'd already gone a week without taking it because he was always forgetting to renew the prescription, which only lasted thirty days, and the last time he called it in, they'd said the price would be $1,125 for thirty pills. Thirty pills! The trial period during which he could pay $35 a month to not have disgusting acne was over. "Are you sure?" he'd said, and the pharmacy woman said she'd check and call him back.

But when he answered, it was not Rite Aid. It was the police. The police! They'd towed his car, which was unbelievable.

"I was going to pay the renewal fee," he said, thinking the old bag who parked her Mercedes right next to him at the club and liked to give him coupons for Sparkle-Shine Car Wash must have ratted on him. She'd complained once already about his sticker being expired—he hadn't wanted to ask his mom if she'd taken care of it because it would give her a chance, again, to say he had no idea how many things she did for him every single day and how expensive he was—but you'd think the club could just give him a reminder or something, not call the police. He started ripping through the cabinets on the *Surrender* in search of a clean button-down shirt and an unwrinkled pair of pants to wear to the police station, thinking what he would say to pruney old Marni or Larni or whatever her name was. Then the policeman said they'd towed the car because it had been found on the bridge. Parked and abandoned.

"No way," he said, but it was his, all right. A white Honda Accord registered to Renata Moorehead. "Okay. Yeah, I'll be right down there. As soon as I change."

How would he convince the police that the car *must* have been stolen right out of the yacht club parking lot? No way was he paying an impound fee of five hundred dollars for *not* parking his car on the bridge, but he'd been with Isabel, smoking weed in the dunes, last night. Not a supergood alibi. Problem number two was getting the car out of the police station before they felt the need to search it for evidence of who took it and why, because although he certainly wanted to know that information and was definitely going to track that down, he thought there was a fifty-fifty chance that weed he'd once carried or maybe was still carrying in his car could be detected by a drug-sniffing dog, unless it was all bullshit what the cops said in those Say No to Drugs assemblies. Had he cleaned it all out last time? Had he felt under both seats?

He hadn't heard a word from Jerome since the party, so he was glad to see Jerome's name on his phone even though the message was, **did you hear about thisbe?**

Jerome must mean how Thisbe had made out with that total dickwad from Point Loma and then fallen down because she was too drunk to walk, and cut her head open right when the cops were rolling the party. Jerome must have heard about that, finally, and wanted to hear what Clay thought. But he had no time to go through it now.

Bro, I'm done with her. I'm sorry.

Jerome didn't answer.

Clay found a pair of pants that didn't show the wrinkles too bad and a white shirt with a small ink stain on the cuff, which would have to do. He took a Prozac with the rest of his Gutter Water Gush and combed his hair and hoped to God Teddy Locke wasn't still sitting at the snack bar when he left.

33

GRETCHEN

Gretchen had known Clay Moorehead's routine by the time he came in with Thisbe. All the girls who worked with her at the coffee shop had filled her in.

"His family has, like, a plane," one of the girls told Gretchen. "He throws parties when his parents are in Acapulco running hotels."

"It's not Acapulco."

"It isn't?"

"I don't know. Somewhere."

When Clay brought in a girl, he always ordered the same thing and played the same corny song on the corny jukeboxes that stood on the tables in every booth and at intervals along the counter: "Unchained Melody," which was a weird song for someone his age to know, but all of the songs were ancient so it's not like he could pick something current. He got the chocolate milkshake with no cherry, an order the counter girls made crude jokes about (*the cherries he's already gotten are enough,* ha ha). Stared into the girl's eyes and barely ate his food. Held her hands in a sweet old-fashioned way.

It was a sweet old-fashioned place, so Gretchen could see why the girls fell for it. People came to Clayton's for the not-foodie food: grilled cheese and fries, meatloaf and mashed potatoes, pie à la mode, burgers and shakes. They came for jukeboxes, red vinyl booths, and the waitresses, who, whether they were seventeen or forty, wore tight striped dresses, red lipstick, and saucy ponytails. This all helped people pretend, while they were sipping hot coffee out of thick white china mugs, that they were in a play or a movie or maybe, if they were really good at pretending, the past. Even Gretchen fell under the sway of this illusion at certain times of day, usually in the evenings when the light came in like liquid gold and struck a full milkshake glass that had just been topped with whipped cream and a cherry, and the cool, salty air floated in through the propped-open door and even the cars rolling by on the street seemed like props. These moments of delusion didn't keep Gretchen from feeling sad. Just because the place was tricky-good at fooling you into a romantic vision of your life didn't mean the spell lasted through the end of the shift, when she got on her bike in the dark, feeling grimy, tired, and old, and went back to life on a cramped boat with her inheritance: two talking birds.

Clay didn't bring the same girl in more than twice. According to Lauren Davis, who was a senior at the high school, date *numero tres* with Clay Moorehead usually took place on his yacht. "He makes her dinner," she said. "Steak and chocolate mousse."

"Does he cook it?" Gretchen asked, intrigued.

"I don't know. The girls act like he does."

"Then what?"

"What do you think? The boat's called the *Surrender*."

"You're kidding."

"I'm not."

It had seemed impossible at first. Why did girls fall for him if it was a cycle? But he was handsome, he really was. The forehead smooth and wide, the hair black and just the right amount of shaggy, the white teeth blocky and strong, the dimple on one side making his smile seem even more sincere. He could really do a number on you, just sitting at the counter, smiling at you, saying, "Nice dress today, Ms. Ryman," in a way that was innocent but somehow sexual because he looked frankly at her breasts and made her think about how sometimes women her age and boys his age . . . It made her ashamed to have even thought it. She wasn't that way. It was just her maternal instinct gone crooked or an animal response to a handsome male by a not-quite-past-childbearing-years female or the way Clayton's made it hard to remember what decade it was.

Which was why Gretchen hadn't liked seeing Thisbe Locke come in one afternoon before sunset, on a glorious spring day when the light might as well have been champagne.

"Now, that," Lauren Davis said, filling two flared glasses with ice, "makes no sense at all."

"Do you think he drugs them?" Mandy Shue said. "She should know better."

"How would she know?" Lauren said. "She's too stuck-up to go to anything."

"Come on. I know her. She's really nice," Gretchen said.

Lauren snorted. "Depends on what kind of nice you mean."

"I mean *nice* nice."

"She thinks she's so much better than everyone else," Lauren said, and went to take an order, so Gretchen didn't say that Thisbe's mother, Anne, had been a little that way, honestly. Anne of Green Gables, as she had been known then, went away to college somewhere back east—Vassar, maybe—and married a rich guy who died in a plane crash, so Green Gables moved back to the island with her two girls, renting, as it happened, the house next door to Gretchen's mom at about the same time Gretchen came back from Hawaii to take care of her. To Gretchen's surprise, Green Gables was always sending over cake or cookies or soup or bread that she thought might tempt Gretchen's mom to eat. The girls brought it over on what looked like the good china. Thisbe was the older one, lying on a towel in the backyard, reading fat books, or playing classical stuff on the upright piano, her mother's daughter to a tee, and Ted was the wild one, it looked like, and was always heading off in a wet suit or a life jacket. Then Green Gables started dating Rich Guy #2, the lawyer, and Gretchen was happy for Anne, she really was, even though he seemed kind of pushy and critical the few times Gretchen heard him in the backyard. He had a big old house on B, so when they got married, Anne and the girls moved over there, no more than six blocks away but six blocks was like thirty miles on the island, especially if you weren't really friends.

"Hi, Thisbe," Gretchen said. "Hello, Clay."

Thisbe smiled incandescently. "Hi, Gretchen! I didn't know you worked here! I thought you were doing, like, scuba diving for the police. My stepdad told me. That is so amazing!"

"I was."

"Search and rescue, right?"

"Yeah."

"But you didn't like it?"

Thisbe and Clay waited for Gretchen to explain why she would give up an amazing job. "Diving is one of those things you have to do for fun or it gets ruined," Gretchen said.

"Oh," Thisbe said. "But you're living on a boat, right? Ted is so jealous!"

The Lockes were members of the yacht club Gretchen couldn't afford to join. Gretchen felt bad for wondering, but maybe Anne or her snobby new husband had been among those who had helped decide that Gretchen could not be grandfathered in and given a slip, which forced Gretchen to moor at Tidelands instead, where you didn't have any amenities, and every time you needed to go ashore, you rowed your dinghy from the boat and back again and dragged whatever you were carrying—water, groceries, laundry—across the mudflats.

"I hear Ted's sailing a lot," Gretchen said.

Thisbe nodded. "She's so into it. Clay sails, did you know that?"

"No!" Gretchen looked right into Clay's face, which she honestly tried not to do anymore, and he flashed his dimple. He shrugged. He tried to look modest.

"He offered to let Ted crew for him in some big regatta but she wouldn't. She's obsessed with being skipper. Which is cool."

Clay shrugged his handsome shrug. Gretchen was heartened, somehow, that Ted could resist him. "Well, you've gotta hand it to her," Gretchen said, and the way Clay was holding the menu she knew he was ready to order now and stop all the chitchat.

Gretchen wanted to take Thisbe aside before she left with Clay and ask if she knew what she was doing, but there was no chance. Thisbe went to the bathroom after the cheeseburgers, the hand-holding, the melody unchained, so Gretchen found herself standing there with the check, saying, "Thank you," and then she just went for it. "You wouldn't break her heart, would you, Clay?"

"Who, me?"

"Yeah. Seriously."

Amber light touched the edges of the little flip-down names of songs in the miniature jukebox, the crumpled edges of napkins, uneaten fries. Even the dirty milkshake glass, coated with dried foam, gleamed.

"Thisbe's a very unusual girl," Gretchen said, not even sure what she meant by that. Her voice came out a little severe, like she was insane or something. "She's very innocent."

"I know," he said. "Don't worry."

"Consider me worried."

"It's all good," he said. His smile seemed a little anxious, and for a minute she wondered if she was listening to too much gossip. Maybe Lauren and the other girls were jealous, so they spread stories that weren't true. Nobody said you couldn't bring more than one girl to a diner when you were in high school, or that you couldn't play the Righteous Brothers for all of them.

Thisbe had come back from the bathroom, wearing freshly applied lip balm and smelling of the hand lotion she was still rubbing into her hands. Clay had hustled her out as Thisbe was smiling and saying, "Bye, Gretchen! Thanks so much! I miss you! Take care."

34

CARL

Carl Harris was sitting in the backyard, feet up, beer in hand, when he saw that he had two voice mails. Stacy had always accused Carl of leaving the ringer off all the time on purpose to avoid her but it wasn't true. He just forgot to turn it back on, or he couldn't figure out why he couldn't hear it ring, and he hated cell phones, so he never wanted to spend any time learning what he didn't know. This was not the same as hating to hear from Stacy. Before he could punch in his code and get the messages, his phone lit up again.

"Carl?"

"Yes?"

"It's Anne Locke."

The voice was strained, not normal, something wrong. He thought at first that something had happened to his boat. To Stacy. To Paul. He'd known Anne since high school but they'd never called one another.

"You still work for the harbor patrol, right?"

"Yes."

"Did you hear about a car on the bridge last night?"

"I was off," he said. "I heard about it this morning."

"The medical examiner came."

He pulled a dead bougainvillea blossom off a branch that was poking his thigh and rubbed it between two fingers. "The examiner?"

"Someone from the office."

An investigator. Someone charged with notifying next of kin.

"I'm sorry, Anne. What happened?"

"They think it was . . ." She didn't finish the sentence. Then she said, "Thisbe."

He knew there were two girls. It was odd that he'd seen Ted that morning. He hadn't seen the other girl since they had camped out on a catamaran one night, not the craziest stunt he'd ever seen and on the sweet end of the spectrum once he saw they were just camping, not hooking up with guys.

"If they didn't find her, she didn't jump. Right?" Anne was saying.

It didn't mean that. Bodies drifted. Sank. Got stuck in places you couldn't see. None of which he could say. "Was there a witness?"

She said something about a camera, but her voice was getting harder and harder to understand. Maybe the Chippies watching the monitors had seen a pedestrian, so they'd called the dispatcher, and the officers—it must have been Elaine—had gotten there too late.

He asked, "But not a witness? Another driver on the bridge?"

"No."

The search and rescue team could only search for a couple

of hours on the surface near the probable point of entry, and then they would have to give up. Wait to see if she refloated. It didn't help to tell families that San Diego Bay was forty to sixty feet deep, depending on the tide, or that the bridge was two miles long, or that the current was fast, or that cargo ships the size of skyscrapers passed through those channels, or that the pylons, though they were solid above water, rested on dozens of subpylons between which bodies could be trapped. Pylons 19, 20, and 21 rested on forty-four subpylons, each of them four feet thick, and to swim between them looking for a body was like swimming through a forest in the dark. Sometimes visibility even in the daytime was zero because of the silt. It could be twenty feet on a really clear day but it was usually about five. You hoped when you were looking for a body that you wouldn't swim right into the face.

He felt the sun on his feet, the dry grass pricking his heels because he hadn't been watering the lawn enough. "When did they find the car?" he asked, and she told him about the boyfriend from the yacht club, which clicked now with what Elaine had said. Each word was hard for Anne Locke to say, so he strained to listen, to push the stuttered words back together.

She said, "We told her to—to stop seeing him. He throws a lot—a lot of parties. He drinks."

The sky was very blue between the eucalyptus trees. Paul had gone to parties, and Paul drank. It was impossible not to know about it and impossible to prevent. He'd tried.

"But it doesn't make—make sense," she said. "Does it?"

"Which part?"

"There wasn't a note or anything. The woman at the police department said they do: they leave a note in the car or on the table at home or they text a bunch of people. Right before. So it seems like searching the water is premature, and if they didn't find her, it might be something else, like she ran away. Or someone picked her up."

"What did they say when you asked that?" he asked. The sun was warm on the dry grass and a dove rested on the power line.

"That it didn't fit the profile."

"Well, there aren't any rules to this," he said. Not about who jumped and how good their reasons were. He used to think there was a rule: that the truly serious jumped right away. The ones who sat on the rail or the hoods of their cars, who dropped cigarettes over the side to watch them fall, or who shouted at officers to get back were not serious. They were lonely, desperate, crazy, and afraid. They wanted someone to talk to them, fix them, beg them to live. And then one day a man broke that rule. He dallied and threatened and reconsidered for an hour and a half, and then, while Carl watched, his hands empty, the man sprang for the rail and vaulted over it into empty space.

"Even if she jumped she could have"—long pause—"survived, right?"

He hated this question. Those who were alive when you reached them in the water had massive injuries. They often floated in pools of blood. The force of hitting the water ripped their clothes off or printed the weave of the fabric into their skin. Sometimes they were still conscious, but incoherent, and they babbled. They waved grotesquely broken arms in shock. It wasn't like they were capable of swimming to shore, if that's what Anne was thinking. "It's very unlikely" was all he said.

He was thinking of the crisis guys. They were trained to help people process things. What they said, he didn't really know.

What did you say to the mother of a seventeen-year-old girl? "I'll call this guy, his name is Tim Ladow, and he'll call you. Or you can talk in person."

She said she had Tim's name. "I'm sorry to"—long pause—"bother you," she said.

"It's not a bother," he said. He didn't want to leave the sunny warmth of the lifeless backyard, so simple in its state of decay. He could fix it in a matter of days or leave it alone, it didn't matter. "Tell me where you are," he said. "Are you home?"

"Yes."

"Tell me where you live and I'll come over in an hour or so."

The vegetable garden was a tangled mess of dead tomato vines and rusty hoops. It had been Stacy's project, something she did for the planet, with "the planet" in air quotes in his mind. Stacy had all kinds of uninformed suspicions about the food supply, but he'd stopped arguing with her because the food she'd grown had been beautiful to look at from this chair: the shiny red cherry tomatoes, the dark bouquets of lettuce.

The peppertree dropped dead curls into the webs of tent spiders all around the Victorian gazing ball: a big pink mirrored globe on a pedestal that cast back his reflection as a fat, lonely dwarf.

He finished the beer, now warm, and wondered if he should call the sergeant of the dive team first and ask what he thought of the situation. He closed his eyes and saw the man who had not seemed serious falling headfirst from the bridge, arms reaching out for what was already gone.

35

GRAYCIE

Graycie's aunt Estelle did not approve of a single mother working for the highway patrol. Before she agreed to help babysit, she asked Graycie a thousand times: Did Graycie want to leave Genna a motherless orphan? Get shot by a crazy on the I-15? But Graycie was good by then at not listening. Unsolicited scriptures had been raining down since Day One. What did her mother and Aunt Estelle know about life outside the chapel? Graycie could have forged her own way with Danny, moved away from San Diego, even, but Danny had turned out to be exactly what her mother called him: a flight risk. What was Graycie going to do now? Turn down every meal offered by Aunt Estelle, who lived within three miles of Graycie's apartment and was a full-on baby hypnotist? When Genna started crying for no reason and arching her little spine in a rage, which happened almost every day, Graycie would walk her for a while, outside or inside, depending on the hour, then set Genna down in her crib, then pick her up, then set her down in the living room with some toys, but after a couple of hours of that she always thought of Estelle. Estelle could take over, fix things, let Graycie sleep. So Graycie would force Genna into her car seat (were you abusing a child when you made her stop arching her spine so you could strap on the seat belt?) and drive over to Estelle's house. Genna would cry and the stoplights would turn red as if to hinder them, and Graycie would will time to collapse like it did in movies, *cut cut cut, scene over,* but Genna would keep on crying, no deliverance, until Graycie was standing with Genna on Aunt Estelle's porch and the door opened. The second Aunt Estelle held out her skinny arms, Genna was cured. Blessed peace. Nothing but hiccups in Genna's tiny chest.

"It's like you're a witch," Graycie said.

"Hold your tongue," Estelle said. "Nothing but God ruling over this world."

Peace came at a price, though. When you went to Aunt Estelle's house, anytime, day or night, you were going to meet Real Africans. Aunt Estelle's mission, revealed to her in a waking dream, was to minister to the diaspora. She gave no end of help to the recently arrived Eritrean and Somalian Christians who attended her church, the Hand of the Living God. When Graycie accepted an invitation to dinner at Aunt Estelle's, she always asked, under the pretense of buying the right amount of cake to share (not that Aunt Estelle liked or even ate a single bite of your store-bought cake, but Graycie's mother said she didn't care if the hostess told you you didn't have to bring anything. You did. *Bring something*), how many mouths to buy for. Aunt Estelle would say it could be any number God saw fit to send, so Graycie got to the point where she just bought one of those big old bundt cakes, one time cinnamon cream, the next time chocolate swirl.

On Monday, June 8, when Graycie was still worrying herself to a nub about what would happen if the girl who had jumped off the bridge had a lawyer for a dad, someone who might sue and make Graycie testify in court about what she had been doing when she was supposed to be watching the bridge, Graycie decided that the last thing she needed was a long chat with Real Africans in Aunt Estelle's red velvet living room, so she stayed home with Genna. She fed Genna sweet potatoes and rice with the little spoon that was all covered in rubber so Genna could chew on it between bites and not cut her mouth. Graycie took Genna for a long walk even though she was ex*haust*ed, because sometimes when you carried Genna through the pastel streets of Paradise Hills she went quiet as a nailhead. She even pushed Genna in the swing at the park where that homeless guy gave her the creeps, because swings were the only other Genna Hypnotist. Yes, Graycie ate two entire Danishes when she got home, and she felt terrible, but at least Genna stayed asleep when Graycie set her down, and that was a full-on miracle. Maybe Graycie shouldn't have called up Kyle Jukesson on his cell before she lay down on her own bed, but she did. She couldn't help it. "Did they find a body?" she said.

"Nope," he said.

"So maybe she didn't jump."

Kyle made a sound that might have been a sigh.

"Did that woman from the Coronado police call you?" she asked him.

"No."

That was good. A piece of good news, finally. It meant she wasn't digging around some more.

"I have been half in love with easeful Death," Kyle said.

Was he drunk? Since when did Kyle quote poetry to her? Since when did Kyle even *know* poetry? When she didn't answer him, he made a weird laughing sound.

"What?"

"Keats, Graycie. The po-et." He dragged it out like she might not know the term.

"I'm not stupid. I know who Keats is. I just don't see the relevance."

"Oh, sorry."

Long silence in which she hated him.

"People who want to die want to die," Kyle said. "They found a letter from her stepdad. He gave her some sort of ultimatum, I guess. And that was her boyfriend's car. He broke up with her."

She felt bad for the girl. She felt bad for the family. What could Graycie have done, though, if she'd seen someone step out of that car and climb up on the rail? It's not like she could have run out of the building and driven a patrol car up there and shouted, "Stop!"

"I'm going to sleep now," Graycie said.

"Good idea," he said. "This isn't over."

"What do you mean?" He really knew how to stoke up the fear, get it good and hot.

"Until they find the body, I mean. The parents are in denial."

"Yeah, I get that," she said, and when she hung up the phone, it was a long while before she fell into an uneasy sleep.

36

THISBE

The living sand dollar looks like a disc of sodden purple velvet, and the velvet traps prey for passage to the mouth. Inside the mouth, the sand dollar has jaws and even teeth for chewing plants and animals. She's stopped rubbing her wrists together, because she's hungry and it doesn't make the tape come off. When she passes out or falls asleep, the sticker on the spine of the library book falls off and becomes a stingray moving gently over rocks. She dreams she is up on the bridge again, and the wind on the bridge is so hard it would take her upward if she were a plastic bag. It flings her hair into her mouth and flays her eyeballs, and the water miles and miles below the bridge is hard. You can tell by the way the ripples catch the light that they have sharp edges, like flakes of broken glass. Yellow taxi, blond satin edge of the stingray, *I don't have my purse,* the man coming out of the shadows and saying, *Julia!*

It is not yesterday or the day before, and it never can be again.

She and Ted used to try to hold their breath the whole length of the bridge. Ted almost always won, as she won everything that required friends, balance, sails, or paddles. Thisbe was better only at memorizing, math, and words. When they were eight and eleven, Hugh had promised them perfect little wooden sabots if they could learn all the signal flags by Christmas Eve (not just the letters, either, but the messages each one represented). Thisbe learned them all in three days, not because she wanted a boat but because she liked to ace tests. Ted, on the other hand, had cried nightly at the dining room table as Christmas lights twinkled outside the window, red and green, red and blue, flashing Santa, flashing palm, standing deer. Thisbe bought Ted a pack of nautical playing cards that showed all the flags on one side, their meanings on the other:

I am maneuvering with difficulty; keep clear.

I have a diver down; keep well clear at slow speed.

I require a pilot.

Still Ted flunked. Flunked again. After the fifth or sixth failure, Thisbe asked Hugh, "Couldn't she just send up a flare or something? I mean, is she going to carry twenty-six flags in the sailboat every time she goes out?"

"It's good for her. It's good for both of you," Hugh said. "You have to earn the right to be on the water by yourself."

Their mother went upstairs. She always just went upstairs.

"I am on fire and have dangerous cargo?" Ted said as Thisbe held up, again, the flag card that meant *All personnel return to ship.* All personnel return to ship! Under what circumstances would a little girl in a sabot need to send that message? Under what circumstances, for that matter, would a girl in Glorietta Bay find her sabot to be on fire? Still Hugh insisted. A-plus or no sabot.

When Ted finally passed the test late on Christmas Day (and they ate their French toast soggy-cold), they all walked down to the yacht club. The world before them was blue and pink, more Easter- than Christmas-colored, the sky dipped in blue Paas dye and the water warm when you stuck your toe in. Ted, her eyes puffy, climbed into her little vermilion sabot and forgot—it was annoying, really—all the crying and slamming of doors. Thisbe posed for a picture in her own sabot, too, but she would hate hers once she learned what it was like to try to steer it. Another way they were different.

Thisbe had told this story to Clay on his boat the night she snuck out. Went down to the yacht club after curfew like she wasn't afraid of anything, and she thought no one had seen her, not a soul except Clay. He'd asked her why she didn't sail and she told him the whole story while they were lying next to each other in the little boat bed.

"So you know what all the flags mean, huh?"

"Yeah," she said. "If they put them on the SAT, I'm ready. I will *ace* the signal flag section."

"Say them to me," Clay said as he undid her buttons. "Recite them to me and I'll give you a prize."

Alfa, Bravo, Charlie, Delta.

Echo, Foxtrot, Golf, Hotel.

As she recited, he turned all the warnings into double entendres.

I am on fire and have dangerous cargo.

Coming alongside.

Man overboard.

But then the very next day, after she kissed him in Spreckels Park, *poof.* "I think this was a mistake," he said. "I didn't know Jerome liked you."

"What?" she asked.

Jerome was watching them, and then Clay was running after him. Jerome had liked her when? Had liked her then but didn't like her now? Should she have known? Should she have waited? Was she a different kind of person now? She waited to see if Jerome would talk to her, but he didn't. Clay cut her off completely. She should have put it all out of her mind, but she couldn't. The exams came one after the other and she kept blanking out in the middle. Fell asleep instead of studying. Answered adults' questions with a blank stare. *What's gotten into you?* What indeed?

In the aft cabin of the boat, her toe is naked again, outside the sock, and the gag is wet on the side where her cheek touches the cushion, the low point of her mouth. She can't swallow anymore, just click. It was like when the dentist had two hands and a tool in your mouth to suck out the spit and you kept throat-clicking. Like a bird waiting for a mother that didn't come. *Click click.*

37

CLAY

The cop behind the desk said, "Driver's license?"

Clay kept the real one in the front of his wallet, behind the yellowish transparent panel. The fake one was tucked in with the money.

His hand was trembling a little when he double-checked the age really fast, because how dumb would that be if he handed his fake ID to a police officer? The officer was a big, cranky-looking guy with curly hair and a mustache and freckles all over his cheeks. He didn't act like he noticed the trembling but he did what clerks at skate parks did (and liquor store workers almost never did): he compared the face in the picture to Clay's face. He tapped the keyboard without saying a word.

"Did your car break down on the bridge?"

"No, sir. Like I said on the phone, it must have been stolen."

"You didn't notice it was gone?"

"No, sir."

"Why not?"

"I left it parked like I always do at the yacht club. I don't drive it that much. I ride my bike, mostly."

"The yacht club?"

"I'm living on our family's boat for the summer."

He could feel the guy's disgust. Any minute now he'd make some sort of crack about what a hard life kids have these days. *Tap tap* on the keyboard. The cop let his chair rock back a little more.

There was nothing illegal about living on your boat, was there? He was pretty sure you didn't have to be an adult to sleep on your own boat without your parents, but maybe there was some weird rule, so he hoped he wouldn't have to get into that part. He needed to use the bathroom right now because he'd drunk the whole Gutter Water Gush.

"Should I call a lawyer or something?" he said.

"I'm not arresting you, Mr. Moorehead."

Mr. Moorehead. Okay, fine. Who cared about attitude as long as he was not being arrested? He was only here in the police station because his car had been found on the bridge, a thing that had been done *to,* not *by,* him. His bladder was going to pop. "I don't mean to be rude, sir, but if we're going to talk some more I could really use a bathroom."

"Down the hall to the right, Mr. Moorehead. I'll wait right here."

"Thanks."

The bathroom was enormous. A lot nicer than the yacht club's, actually. He couldn't see any cameras but he felt like he was on one.

A woman officer in a black uniform and a fancy gun belt, the whole cop regalia, was waiting for him in the lobby when he came back. "Clay Moorehead?"

He nodded.

"Can I ask you some questions?"

"What about?"

"Come on in here," she said.

It was the same place he'd had to wait on the night of the bad party, the room that was like where you waited to be called into the principal's office, except here they had a glass wall so you could see the cops working on computers and saying stuff about you that you couldn't hear. Renee took like an hour to come and get him and he had to sit there the whole time with nothing to do.

The lady officer looked familiar. Maybe she was the same one from that night. Freckly face, pale eyes, crinkled skin. She walked him into the carpeted glass room with the ugly hotel ballroom chairs and waved him into one. "When will your mom be back?" she said.

"August," he said.

"How about your dad?"

"Same."

"Do you have any other relatives who could come over here for a chat?"

"No offense, but why are you acting like I'm in trouble? I'm the victim here. Someone totally stole my car."

"What about your sister, the one I met before?"

"She's in Mexico."

Clay's phone vibrated in his pocket. He didn't answer it.

"You know what we found in the car, right?"

Stomach dropped all the way to the basement. Dry lips, wet palms. So they did search it. And he hadn't cleaned it out.

"Pretty serious stuff we've got going here, Clay."

Clay looked her in the eye and said he had no idea what she was talking about.

"Possession. Intent to distribute."

"Whoever stole the car must have put it there."

"That could be. We'll check into that."

"Did you call my mother?"

"Yes."

"Is she coming?"

"We haven't reached her yet. Maybe you should call her."

"Now?" He got out his phone. He was thinking he should really call his father about this one.

"In a minute."

He waited stiffly in the chair. The screen said **Missed call.**

"Do you have any idea where Thisbe Locke is right now?"

"Why do people keep asking me that? I have no idea."

"When was the last time you saw her?"

"I don't know. A while."

"A week, two weeks?"

"More like four."

"Was she upset for any reason that you know of?"

He knew a few reasons, but they didn't seem like good ones to bring up now. "No."

"Do you know why her driver's license might have been in your car?"

He thought back. No. "That doesn't make any sense."

"Did she have a key to your car?"

"No. She knew where I kept it, though." That was what had happened. He felt it. Thisbe couldn't get him to open the door on the boat so she went to the boat rack and stole his car keys and parked his car somewhere that would get him in huge trouble. To punish him because he said he couldn't see her anymore. "She stole my car," he said. "And she must have planted stuff in it."

"Why would she do that?"

"To get me in trouble."

It was like he was a germ the police lady saw through a microscope. She was pretty disgusted with what she saw.

"Did Thisbe ever tell you that she felt suicidal?"

Something was wrong here and it was bigger than he'd thought. If Thisbe had parked the car on the bridge, how had she gotten down? "What is this about?" he asked.

"What do *you* think it's about?"

He thought about Thisbe staring at him from the patio chair that night. Just sitting there drinking and staring for a long time, and then asking him if he was going to talk to her. No, he wasn't. Jerome liked her, and that was that. Yes, Clay should have told her to go home when she'd snuck out and come knocking at the boat, but she smelled so good and looked so pretty and he just couldn't help himself.

"Do you have any idea what her state of mind was last night?" she asked.

He shook his head. She was looking into his eyes like she could see Thisbe if she looked hard enough, see a tiny movie of her knocking on the door of the boat. "I have no idea," he said. "I don't know why she would leave her license in my car or why she would take it."

"You didn't see her."

"I told you. I didn't. I haven't seen her in a long time."

"She didn't leave you any messages last night, did she?"

"No."

She waited.

"What happened to her?" Clay asked. He was very scared to hear the answer to that question.

"It's possible that she jumped off the bridge."

That's what he thought.

He looked at the floor. The lobby felt hollow and slick and merciless. "Why do you say *possible*?"

"The body's not been found, but she's gone."

"What should I do?"

"You can call your parents."

He touched the screen. He felt sick.

"You could do one little thing for me first," she said.

He wanted this not to be happening and not to be as bad as it seemed. "What's that?" he asked, sick and sicker.

She was folding a clean sheet of paper in two; then she handed it to him along with a pencil. "Write something down."

He took the pencil. "What?"

"Just a number," she said. "Write four slash fourteen."

He could feel her eyes on him as he rolled the pencil on his knee. *4/14*. His little system for numbering the bags. "Four slash fourteen?" he repeated. He tried to look confused.

She nodded, studying him.

"Like April fourteenth?" he said.

She nodded again.

He wrote the numbers, but he made the fours the way everybody and his brother made a four: right angle over a vertical line.

"Funny," she said when he handed it over to her.

"What's that?"

She looked up from the paper. "When you wrote your address earlier"—she waved the index card he'd written on for the first cop—"and you wrote *714 1st Street*"—she waited a long beat—"you made your four different."

They stared at each other a long time. She had a sad smile on her face and he tried to smile back but he felt sick about everything.

"So," she said, "go ahead and call. I'll be in there."

She pointed to the room where two male officers with expressionless faces were typing into computers.

Before he dialed his father, he saw that he had a voice mail from someone he didn't know, and it was a girl's voice saying, "This is Ted. I need to talk to you very, very much. You need to tell the whole story and help us find her. Okay? Call me back."

How could he help find her? And after what he'd said at the party, who would think anything but that it was all his fault?

He didn't answer Ted. The only thing he was going to do was call his father and see if he could come and get him and fix things, the way he was good at doing. That was all.

38

FEN

Through the window Fen could see his uncle sitting in the backyard, holding his phone and an empty green beer bottle. Same brand his father liked: Heineken. "Hey," Fen said.

"Oh, hey," Carl said. "Have a seat."

Fen dragged a rusty chair through the weeds.

"What's your plan for this afternoon?" Carl said. "Still want to snorkel?"

"Maybe." When Fen had mentioned his plan to take the snorkeling gear his dad had given him for Christmas to the beach, Carl had said the visibility would be bad. He said *you'll be rolled in the waves a lot*. He said *you should probably wear a wet suit because you'll freeze. Don't go, basically, because it'll be terrible.*

Carl seemed different, the way he was sitting there, looking at the weird pink gazing ball and the dead garden. "Maybe I could go snorkeling in the bay," Fen said. "Where I sailed this morning. Is the visibility better there?"

"No!" his uncle said, like that was a crazy idea. "Why don't you wait? I could take you out in the boat instead."

"I'd love that."

"But I can't today. There's a work thing I need to do."

There was definitely something bothering him.

"Okay." Fen had hoped Carl might go with him, wherever he went. "I thought you had the day off."

"I did. Something came up."

"I might go to the beach," Fen said.

"Okay," his uncle said.

In the past, when Fen had visited, his uncle had always gone to the beach with him. Always. Carl could boogie board for hours while Fen's dad and his mom and Stacy sat and talked in their beach chairs. Carl never got tired or cold or bored of playing with Fen. He was like a porpoise or something.

"Well, okay, bye," Fen said, and his uncle barely responded. It felt, for a depressing second, like the sunny Saturdays in Las Vegas, blank and wide, when his mom was locked in her room, working on the biography of the Brazilian lady, and his dad was out running, and Fen's best friend (make that *only* friend) was playing club soccer. Saturdays in Las Vegas were lit by the same hard light as the days that followed his father's death, when Fen was supposed to be back in class but instead was shoving open the metal doors of the gym, the sound like a cocked gun, slipping out the gate behind the handball courts, riding his skateboard home, stirring up a Carnation Instant Breakfast, and taking his snorkeling mask to the Isle of Capri Deluxe Apartments swimming pool. There he floated facedown, arms lank, his skin wet as if he were floating in the Caribbean. He pretended he was just offshore of the little island made of sand, l'île Morpion, with a dive boat somewhere behind him, out of sight but ready, and that his father was not dead but swimming nearby, observing the same creatures that Fen imagined, bright bodies that flickered and darted, and they would talk about them when they took off their masks, when they sat together in the sun.

39

THISBE

The crazy man is in. He pulls Thisbe forward by the ankles and says it's time to eat. It isn't dark but it isn't bright. Muddy light in the cabin of polished wood, which smells of tomato soup.

This time he unties the gag without tearing out any of her hair. Then she can move her arms. She doesn't care that he leaves her ankles taped, because she can sit, and he hands her a bowl of soup.

"I knew you were Julia that time I saw you by Stingray Point. With the other girl."

One bite, two bites, three bites. The spoon's too slow so she decides to drink it instead.

"I see that girl more than I seen you. In her boat."

Stingray Point was in Glorietta Bay. The edge of the golf course. You could only get there in a boat or by running across the course at night, when no one was golfing. Parties were held there on weekends, parties where everyone drank and smoked. Ted went sometimes, but Thisbe didn't.

"Blond girl," he says. "Little red boat."

He knows *Ted*. He's saying he knows Ted. A grotesque fear replaces, for a second, the greed for soup: the crazy man watched Ted sail with his creepy turtle eyes and his creepy turtle thoughts and Ted didn't know, like Thisbe hadn't. Did he want to shoot Ted, too, and tape her hands and call her another girl's name?

"That one night," he says. "I saw you both that one night."

Thisbe and Ted had camped in the dark aboard the Getaway, Hugh's little catamaran that had a webbed floor just big enough for two sleeping bags and a cooler and their bags of junk. Ted had rigged up a tent with a giant tarp and some rope, and it felt like forts they used to make in the backyard in Connecticut, when their dad was alive.

"Did you see me?" the man asks.

The soup is all gone.

"More?" he asks.

She nods but he doesn't get more soup. She holds up the bowl and at least he goes to get it then.

She tries to think if she saw any other boats that night on the Getaway. She and Ted ate Pop-Tarts with their feet dangling in the water. They were not that far from the golf course, not that far from the bridge. Ted was happy to the point of smug, saying, "Told you it would be fun." Later on, when they were in their sleeping bags with the tarp tent all snug around them, Mr. Harris cruised up and scared them to death with his megaphone, saying he was going to Breathalyze them and tow them home, but Ted said, "It's *me,* Mr. Harris! Ted-not-Teddy-Theodora! Remember?"

Mr. Harris said it wasn't safe but he didn't make them go home, and he didn't call Hugh, and every time a wake lifted their boat up and down, Thisbe woke up and saw the bright light of the harbor patrol boat. Mr. Harris watching over them. Or maybe this man.

"Ben died, you know."

If this man killed Ben, she should not be slurping his soup. But she slurps it, drinks it down.

"Ben Crames. The one we played with all the time. He was there that day. Helped look for you."

What day is he talking about?

"Cancer. A few years ago."

Thisbe sits with the bowl. Nothing he says makes any sense.

"Do you want some water, Julia?"

She wants gallons of water. To swim in to bathe in to drink up to guzzle.

He finds a cup in his messy cupboards and fills it from a jug, not the faucet. Fills it again without her asking. When she stops drinking, he says, "Do you remember the cliffs?"

She neither nods nor shakes her head, because she doesn't know the right answer and there are no cliffs in Coronado.

He sits down across from her and laces his gingerroot fingers. He appears to think. A wake lifts the boat, and jars clink together. The wood creaks and groans, something metal pings in the air outside. A little bulb in the galley gleams. She wants a toothbrush, her bedroom, the backyard, the day before, the day before, the day before. Who cared about Clay? He was nothing. Nothing! How wrong she'd been about problems before. To live in her house and go up and down the stairs to her kitchen to her own bed to the kitchen to her own bed was plenty. She didn't care what college she went to. She would get in somewhere perfectly fine. She would show Hugh she could be trusted, and she still had her whole senior year to show him she was smart.

Thisbe keeps her lips together. She reaches down and pulls the baggy sock so her toe is back inside. The hole is wide and stiff like a mouth and getting wider. She looks at the hole and not the man.

He startles her when he moves toward her and she presses herself back so he won't touch her but he's messing with something on a high shelf. He hands her something, just a photograph, brown and cream, thin and shiny. A white frame all around the edge, like old photos have. He clicks on another lightbulb, and she can make out that it's a boy and a girl on a beach somewhere with cliffs behind them. The girl is smaller than the boy, and she's wearing a pair of boyish shorts, rumpled and cuffed and way too big, and a ruffly top that ties around her neck and behind her back like a bikini. Her hair is nearly the same beige as the sky. Ink-brown lips, a serious expression, not smiling. The boy is skinny and older, ten maybe, with a round chin, round nose, a dirty T-shirt, and one leg blurred by movement at the time of exposure. His hair is shaved short the way they did back then.

The man points to the boy with a yellow fingernail so thick it seems inhuman and says, "That's me. Frankie." Then he points to the girl and says, "You. Julia."

She is not the girl. She knows she is not this girl in the boyish shorts and bikini top on a beach.

"This is right after Mom left," he says. "Remember?"

Remembering seems dangerous. Not remembering seems dangerous.

"The boots," he says, tapping the picture. "It's one of the seven signs. It's how I found you."

The faded little girl is wearing boots. Black ones. Nerdaloshes. Those are not Thisbe's boots and she doesn't have any now. Just the socks, the hole wide open.

"Do you remember the boots?"

Thisbe nods.

"That's us," he says. "Do you remember me? Frankie. Everyone called me that. Still do, back home."

Frankie and Julia. Brother and sister? She feels it again, the need to pee. "Can I go to the bathroom?" she asks. She can't go anywhere like this. With the tape around her ankles, around her dirty socks.

"I had to do it this way. To remind you. The Seer said."

She has no idea what he means. "Please," she says. "I have to." She doesn't say *pee,* because she doesn't want him to think of her pants down.

"Of course, Julia. Of course."

She reaches for her ankles and starts trying to unstick the tape because he doesn't move and she has to go. If she says his name, maybe he'll let her go outside. "I could do it outside, Frankie," she says.

"Outside?"

"The bathroom. Since the water doesn't work." She points as if to show him where the outside is.

"No, no. No. Not till we get home, Julia."

She can see the steak knife. It's too far for her to reach, lying on the fold-up table near the galley. If he brings it to cut the duct tape around her ankles, she'll grab it and stick it right into his reptile neck.

"I can't get it," she says, meaning the tape. Her fingers aren't working right.

He walks to the table and she sees how thin he is. Did he kill

Julia? His own sister, that little girl in the picture? She should get the knife from him when he's bent over, cutting the tape.

"We tried to dig you out," he says. "We all did. But it was too late. I have the article. I'll show you!"

He saws at the tape and she wills herself to grab the knife but she doesn't. Not yet. Not until her legs are free.

"All the stones fell down when you were waiting for the ransom. We didn't expect that. No one did. It was a cave-in. Me and Ben went for the ransom, like you said, and it was your idea to be tied up, make it more *real,* you said. You always wanted it to be real, remember?"

The tape splits under the knife he holds and her legs are separated. She could grab the knife, stab it into his neck, and walk away.

"Nobody goes to Harlow's Cove anymore, not anybody that's smart. Too many rock slides. But we didn't know that then."

She stands up and he backs away, puts the knife in a drawer, shuts the drawer.

"We didn't know. It was a pirate game," he says. "We always played it in the summer, down by the rocks."

The knife is too far away and she has to go. She has to go to the bathroom and then think.

"Do you remember?" he asks.

She nods so he'll let her go.

"What do you remember?"

"The boots," she says. She moves slowly so he won't touch her and she shuts the bathroom door.

40

CARL

Fen was gone. To the beach with some fins and a snorkel. Carl felt the way he'd always felt when he told Stacy or Paul he was too busy to do something they'd asked him to do on a beautiful sunny day: lunch or brunch or the beach or paddleboards. The emptiness of the house, a wide pool of regret. But what he also felt—staring out the living room window at Fen's truck, which had been Carl's brother's, a piece-of-junk Ford with no air-conditioning and no air bags, not really the ideal thing for Fen to be driving on interstates in aggressive traffic—was dread of going over to Anne Locke's house without knowing what the police were thinking and why they were thinking it.

He picked up his phone and looked for Elaine Lord's number. "Hey, Elaine," he said. "I just got a call from Anne Locke."

"Are you guys friends?" she asked.

"Not really," he said. "I knew her at school."

"Yeah, me too. More like knew of her. She was younger than me by a year. What did she want you to do?"

"Oh . . . to tell her that her daughter isn't dead."

No answer immediately came. He knew that was a bad sign.

"What am I walking into if I go over there?" Carl asked. "I said I would come by."

"I'm headed over there now," Elaine said.

"She said the MEs were there already. So you must be sure."

"As sure as you can be without the body."

"So what have you got?"

"At first it was all kind of sketchy, stuff that could be explained away, like maybe the girl dropped her license in the car some other time. But she's missing, and the ex-boyfriend is very much alive. He says he doesn't know why she would take his car, but she knew where the keys were. We got a call placing a girl next to the car in question, the one that was on the bridge, and the girl was standing near the rail."

"Someone just phoned that in?"

"A guy called and said he saw someone standing up there but didn't call it in at the time."

"Why not?"

"He said there was already another car stopped behind the first one. So there was the white car, the one we towed, and a girl with long hair like Thisbe's standing at the rail, and behind that, a red pickup truck. Solo driver sitting in that, the caller said. He didn't see anything else."

"What made him call today?"

"He said he told his wife and she had a bad feeling about it."

On the street in front of Carl's house, framed by his living room window, sat Fen's truck. Red. Fen had driven it over the bridge around midnight, but he hadn't said he'd seen a jumper. And he would, wouldn't he? It was the kind of thing you mentioned. Especially if you were a new driver.

"Thanks, Elaine. I'll see you in a bit."

It didn't take long for Carl to find Fen at Central Beach. Crumpled at the waterline was the purple orchid towel Stacy had brought home from their only trip to Hawaii, already layered with sand. Wind caught a beach umbrella and started flinging it down the dunes. A hairless man in a Speedo chased it down, caught it, laughed, and said something in Dutch or German. Carl thought he could see Fen's snorkeled head out there in the waves among the kids on boogie boards, the dark floating birds. "Fen!" he shouted. Fen didn't turn, just ducked under a wave.

Carl strapped Paul's old fins to his knobby feet, pulled the mask down over his eyes, and stuffed the mouthpiece in. It tasted of salt and childhood.

He waddled in, then plunged, felt the cold like he was a turkey in fresh brine. His skin got used to it in seconds—that was the good thing about body fat—and he did his modified American crawl to the smooth belt of water beyond the waves everyone else was catching. It was Fen, all right, and he grinned around his mouthpiece when Carl touched him on the shoulder.

Fen spat out the mouthpiece and said, "This is awesome!"

"It is?"

"You can't see much, but still, you know?" Fen's teeth were chattering and his lips were white.

"Aren't you freezing?" Carl said.

"Nah."

"So the visibility's okay?" He could hear, far in the distance, a helicopter, and it made him think of the divers and spotters, their masks and binoculars. The ocean where he and Fen were treading water was miles from where the girl would have been when she jumped off the bridge, all the way around the other side of the island, but now the water felt tainted anyway.

"It's not that bad," Fen said.

"Yeah?"

Fen stuck his mouthpiece in and waved for Carl to follow him. Carl felt a vague, suppressed need to hurry and wondered how he should ask Fen if he'd seen anything when he was driving over the bridge. If Fen had seen the girl and didn't mention it, maybe it was because it was so upsetting, a thing like that after his father died. Carl should tell Fen they needed to get out of the water, but first he dived under a wave and swallowed water so salty it made him cough, a taste he always underestimated, and when Fen put his head down and stretched out, Carl let himself do the same. He floated like a dead man and stared into the cold, billion-mile Pacific. At first all he could see through the mask was whirling, pummeling silt. But as the building waves moved him up and down, the silt became its own kind of show, the top layer lit by the sun and swirled by the currents in an endless, glittery explosion. Strings of rippled kelp jerked forward, hung back. Then the silt cleared and he could see five feet down, could see plainly, as if through a magnifying glass, the ripples on the sandy floor and a stingray shooting away from him like a puck in a hockey game. He tried not to think about Thisbe Locke in the bay, the same water. A fish darted past him, slim as a pipe. A few feet away, at the surface, Fen's body floated and pulsed, his hands hanging down like wings in mid-flight, beautifully alive.

When Fen stuck his head up again and spat out his mouthpiece, Carl did, too. "Amazing, isn't it?" Fen asked, grinning.

"I love it."

"Yeah, me too."

"I gotta go to somebody's house, though."

"Now?"

"It's kind of an emergency."

"What kind?"

He didn't want it to seem like a trap, but it did, the way he was presenting it. Like when he would say to Paul, *I heard a party was rolled on the Strand last night,* to see if Paul would admit to having been there. "I'll tell you in the car."

It was a long walk across the beach, but Fen didn't ask where Carl was going. He just trudged along the way you had to in sand. Not until they were strapping themselves into the seats of Carl's car, half-wet, cleaned and pickled by the ocean, families all around them dragging boogie boards and towels on sidewalks, rubbing sunscreen onto the faces of children who held up their cheeks and closed their eyes, did Fen say, "So what are we doing?" and Carl couldn't see another way to do it now, so he laid out the basic facts: a car, a girl, a witness who saw a red truck.

"That was me," Fen said.

Carl drove slowly, but he still had to concentrate on traffic. A kid in a swim vest was standing by his mother on the curb, but then he got too excited, so he jumped off, and the mother, holding a baby with one arm and a wagon with the other, raced out, jerked him back, and said, "I told you to stay!" Carl stopped the car and waved them across.

"A white Honda, right?" Fen asked.

"I think so. I don't remember the make." The little boy ran on his tiptoes and the mother scurried behind, her face full of worry.

There was a long enough pause on Fen's side that Carl drove all the way around Star Park Circle—the round green park where he'd first kissed Stacy and where he had come to pick up Paul the night he'd been too drunk to ride his skateboard home—before Fen spoke again.

"Was she wearing pink boots?" Fen asked.

"I don't know that, either."

"I *saw* her! I thought she was having car trouble. Oh my God."

By now Carl was stopped for the millionth time in his life at a red light on Orange Avenue, across from Clayton's with its clean white plaster walls and the painted red letters promising coffee. He could see the lines of gleaming new bicycles for sale outside Holland's; the clumps of tourists on all four corners mystified by the order in which the lights turned green and how long it took for their turn to arrive; the cars idling with windows down and kids in the backseats looking innocent and excited, the sun shining on their brand-new vacations; the edges of roofs up and down the street clean and sharp against a summer sky they'd done nothing to earn and could do nothing to keep. Everything and everyone was just waiting.

"What did you see?" Carl asked Fen. *Let it not be the girl jumping off the bridge right in front of him.* That's what he thought.

"I saw her standing there. She, like, waved and told me to go around her. It was like she was pissed at me for even stopping. I thought she was having car trouble. I just left!"

"So she waved?" Carl said.

"She waved her phone at me. Like, *I've got this*."

Now the light was green. Cars and people moved, so he rolled through the intersection.

"I just kept driving," Fen said. He sounded panicked. He looked panicked. Like he was thinking he could have done something.

"Look," Carl said. "You didn't know. You thought it would be dangerous to get out of your car, and it would have been. You did what she told you to do."

A block later, Carl slowed to pass a family cycling on a surrey, laughing and pedaling like cartoon characters, their progress comically slow despite the number of legs pumping up and down. He turned onto the Lockes' street, a beautiful road on a beautiful day. Magnolia limbs touched overhead. When he reached the corner, he saw two police cars in front of a dark red wooden house. No one was outside except a boy who was standing still across the street, spinning the blade of his scooter around and around under his raised foot, waiting for something interesting to happen.

"It's okay, Fen," Carl said. He studied the red house. Green lawn. Ping-Pong table. Maybe the girl's body had been found by now. If she had waved Fen on, Elaine was right. She had probably meant to jump. To get on with her plan.

"Listen," Carl said. "You can stay in the car if you want."

"I should have stopped, right? People are going to wonder why I didn't help her. Like, talk her out of it."

"That would be a big stretch. Not even professionals can do that all the time. If you want, I'll tell them. I'll tell them what you saw, and you can talk to the police later. You don't have to come in."

Carl walked halfway to the house, then turned around. It wouldn't look right. The parents would notice Fen sitting there in the car and wonder. Once they knew that Fen had seen their daughter, perhaps had been the *last* to see her, it would mark him. Everyone connected to a suicide was unhinged enough to see offenses everywhere.

"It'd be better if you came in with me," Carl said. "Don't worry. You're just a witness. You didn't cause it."

When Fen got out of the car, he looked smaller and thinner than he had at the beach, and it reminded Carl of how Fen had stood squinting in the sun at the Las Vegas cemetery, lost and uncomfortable and too small inside his new dress clothes. "It's okay," Carl said, but Fen didn't answer.

41

TED

Ted saw them park across the street, where Billy Greenbaugh had been watching her house for at least thirty minutes. Billy probably had a cell phone in his pocket even though he was only about eight, and she bet he'd already told all his friends the cops were at her house. She didn't turn around to face Ashlynn's mom or Katie's mom when she told them, "Mr. Harris is here. With his nephew."

Weird how the nephew kept sitting in the car like he didn't want to get out. Then Mr. Harris opened the car door and talked to him for a while and the boy got out of the car the way Ted did when her mom made her go be nice to someone. Well, that was a bad idea. She didn't want to talk about Thisbe to a boy she barely knew. The only people she'd contacted were Jerome and Clay, and that was because they could know something. Clay hadn't answered, and Jerome said he hadn't seen Thisbe. They were worthless.

"I have to go to the bathroom," she said, and went upstairs so she wouldn't have to listen to him being nice to her.

She meant to go in Thisbe's room but two police officers, their torsos thickened by what had to be bulletproof vests, which seemed so weird in Coronado, were standing in there talking to her mom. She heard them say they were looking for a note.

Ted said again, "Mr. Harris is here. He brought his nephew."

Her mother asked what nephew but Ted left so she wouldn't have to answer, closed her door, and lay facedown on her bed. She heard her mother's footsteps going down the stairs, the squeal-thud of Thisbe's desk drawers, the scrape of hangers. She tried to pretend it was Thisbe cleaning her room, which Thisbe did all the time, deliberately making Ted's messiness stand out more.

Hugh was on a plane. He was leaving Chicago even though he hadn't finished his meetings, her mother had said. That meant her mother thought Thisbe might be dead, because if she thought Thisbe had just spent the night somewhere, she would never tell Hugh while he was on a business trip, and Hugh would never come home early. They'd found Thisbe's bike at the yacht club, not parked in the racks like all the other bikes, but over by the tennis courts, leaning on somebody's catamaran trailer. Everybody guessed that meant Thisbe really had taken Clay's car. And if she'd taken his car, then—

Maybe Ted could fall asleep, and when she woke up there'd be a text from Jerome saying, **I saw her she's at Amy's**, or a text from Thisbe saying, **I need your help**, like that time Ted had needed Thisbe to bail her out because Ted had stupidly sent a text to her mom saying, **I'm home**, right at curfew even though she wasn't, and when Ted really got home a half hour later, their mother was sitting wide-awake and vulture-ish in the living room with Hugh, so Ted texted Thisbe and Thisbe distracted their parents so that Ted could sneak upstairs.

Maybe Thisbe had left her bike at the yacht club because Nessa had a car and Thisbe was with her when her phone died, and maybe wherever they were hanging out, people got drunk, and Thisbe fell asleep and now she didn't want to come home because she knew she would get in trouble.

Ted was looking forward to telling Thisbe how epic the mess was that she'd caused, much, *much* worse than the curfew thing Ted had done, but Ted would help her anyway and Thisbe would see that being street-smart was almost as good as being in the honor society. *Ma hay-lo,* Thisbe would say, twirling her finger in a circle over her head, their old joke from that visit to Hawaii when they were, like, six and four and their dad was still alive. *Ma hay-lo,* he would say every time they saw another sign that said *thank you* in Hawaiian. *Do you see ma halo? Mahalo-alay-lay.*

Even with her door closed and her pillow over her head, she could hear Mr. Harris's deep voice. The boy's full name might be Phineas, which was just as stupid as Theodora. Imagine your nickname being Phin. It was crazy letting grown-ups name their children. They were terrible at it. Consider Thisbe. A couple of years ago she'd read some book for English and found out that Thisbe was a girl in a myth who pretended to get killed by a lion or something weird like that, and her boyfriend thought she was dead, so he killed himself, so then *she* killed herself. Thisbe asked their mom, *What the hell?* (Only not swearing.) And their mom said that back when she was in high school, she'd played the part of Thisbe in a play that was Shakespeare's or somebody's and it was just a unique name in a funny play, a beautiful and completely original name, so don't be silly. *I didn't name you after* that *Thisbe,* their mom said.

If Ted had a girl, she was going to name her Margaret. If she had a boy, she was going to name him Jack.

She hadn't changed out of her board shorts or her bathing suit, and she felt grimy and disgusting. She should have taken a shower sooner because now the Phin guy was here and her mom might say, "Ted's in the shower," and when you heard the word *shower,* you saw someone naked in your mind.

Someone was knocking on the door. Mrs. Vicks wouldn't send the boy upstairs, would she?

"Who is it?" Let him hear that she was annoyed. She didn't care.

"It's Officer Lord. Can I talk to you for a second?"

Could you say no to police? She wanted to say no. She walked slowly to the door and opened it.

"Hi," she said. The goofy man with the bald spot stayed in the open doorway, looking overly tall.

Ted stared. They came in with all their black shiny stuff in their black poly uniforms. They looked wrong and she wanted them out. "I need to ask some questions about your sister," the woman said.

Ted waited.

"Did she ever talk about killing herself?"

"No."

"Was she unhappy about anything?"

Pause to think about lying. To decide she couldn't lie. "Yeah."

"What?"

"This stupid guy."

Officer Lord was not going away. She sat on Ted's desk chair, which had a bunch of clothes thrown over the back. There were more clothes on the floor. Also a pair of sailing boots, which stank. Ted hadn't put the pillows on her bed the way her mom liked or even pulled the blanket back up this morning. It was half-dark because she didn't want to raise the window shade.

"So what happened with the guy?"

"He was her first boyfriend."

Still not moving. Just sitting in Ted's chair with her big black orthopedic shoes and her gun belt. "Go on."

"He was just a mistake."

"Why?"

It was hard to explain. "He's very popular. His family's rich."

The giant guy stood like a tree in her room, waiting for her to make sense of Thisbe. Who could ever make sense of her?

"They're also, like, gone a lot. So Thisbe would go over to his house or, like, his boat and there wouldn't be any parents. My stepdad said they were . . . I forget the word." Thisbe and Hugh were so annoying when they used big words like they were the smartest people on earth, if not the universe.

"My stepdad didn't like that Clay threw parties and stuff. And Thisbe didn't get how guys work."

"How do guys work?"

"Thisbe thought he loved her, but it was just for fun."

The tall guy was looking at Ted's bulletin board and tapping his lip. She could tell he was still listening, though.

Ted didn't know how much she was supposed to say about her sister's life. She thought Thisbe had probably slept with Clay, because otherwise Clay wouldn't have gone out with her more than once or twice, and if they had just been kissing or something, Thisbe wouldn't have been so freaked out when he dropped her. "She, like, went to one of his parties after they broke up and she was still trying to get him to talk to her about it. Texting him and stuff."

"When was the party?"

"Like, the last month of school."

"What happened at the party?"

"You guys came."

The lady nodded. "Did something happen at the party?" she asked. "To Thisbe, I mean?"

"Yeah."

"What?"

"She told me not to tell."

The giant man was no longer studying Ted's sailing trophies. He was looking at her with his doughy face that maybe wasn't as dumb as she'd thought.

"Did Thisbe sail, too?" he asked.

"Only with our family. Like, when she was younger. She didn't like it."

"Why did she collect fortune cookie messages?"

"What?"

"Fortunes. Like when you get Chinese food."

When they got Chinese food as a family, which wasn't that often because Hugh didn't like it, she and Thisbe always read the fortunes aloud. Didn't everyone?

"These," the giant cop guy said, and he went out of Ted's room for a second and he came back holding the tin *Sunshine State* box Thisbe had bought at a garage sale. He opened it, and there were four slips of paper, fortunes that looked slightly greasy but otherwise normal, and a stale-looking, broken fortune cookie. Ted didn't like that there was some weird habit of her sister's that she didn't even know about. They watched her while she read them: TRUST ME, THISBE. YOU ARE SO MYSTERIOUS. PLEASURE AWAITS YOU BY THE SEA. DINNER AT CLAYTON'S TONIGHT? They were from a boy, probably, but this didn't seem like something Clay would do. And yet. *Pleasure by the sea.* That was definitely Clay's idea of romance.

Officer Lord said, "I didn't want to rat on my sisters, either, Ted, so I get why you don't want to break her confidence. But this is a really serious situation. We need to piece things together."

"I've never seen these before."

"You're sure?"

"I'm sure."

"What about a letter from your stepdad?"

Ted didn't know what they were talking about.

"Did she mention that he was talking about not sending her to college if she kept seeing Clay?"

"No."

"So, the party. What happened?"

"I just know she got drunk."

"That's it?"

"She got drunk and made out with some guy she didn't like and passed out. For her, that was like, I don't know, doing heroin and stealing a car."

Though stealing a car was an actual thing Thisbe might have done. Only not really, right? More like borrowing.

"And was that the part she didn't want your parents to know?"

"Well," Ted said, "yeah. She didn't want them to know."

Getting drunk was the part that would have gotten Thisbe in trouble. The most trouble. Grounded, at the very least. But it was not the part that had bothered Thisbe the most, Ted knew. "Something happened with Clay."

"What happened?"

"She said he humiliated her."

"How?"

"I don't know. She wouldn't say."

"You're sure?"

"Yes. But then later I heard that it was something he said."

"He didn't do something to her?"

"No."

The woman did not believe her. Definitely not. She probably thought that Ted knew something more, like maybe Clay had given Thisbe roofies or something. Stuff like that happened to girls at parties, supposedly, though not any girls Ted knew. It was why their mother went along with Hugh's overly strict rules.

Officer Lord said, "Oooooh-kay. Have you had anything to eat?"

"Yeah."

"Do you want to come downstairs now?"

"No."

The light shining between the curtain and the window frame gleamed bright yellow. She had wanted the sun to come out so much and now she couldn't even enjoy it.

42

GRETCHEN

Weedie called while Gretchen was watering an upside-down tomato plant. "A girl jumped off the bridge," Weedie said.

Water dripped out of the plant and ran over Gretchen's bare feet.

"They can't find her body," Weedie went on.

Lots of water running all over. Wasted.

"The Locke girl. The one with brown hair."

"*Thisbe?* They think it's Thisbe?"

"That's what they say."

Peek was grooming Roll's back. Seagulls dipped overhead. Tiny waves lapped the sand at Tidelands beach.

"Do you think Carl is working on the case? I thought since you used—"

"I'll call you back later," Gretchen said.

Take it out on him, not yourself. That's what she'd told Thisbe. A week ago, right about *there.* She sat down on the deck and looked south at the blank water between her boat and the bridge. Indigo-ebony-turquoise water holding saucers of light that never stopped moving.

No.

You should never look under the water when you could look at the waves instead. Underwater was the grave, the lost, the tumbled, the dropped. Hope and illusion above; truth below.

No.

Her whole childhood had been spent looking at boats like these and imagining each one as the tiny, happy floating house of a person who would never have a boring job or a boring life but would live all the time in communion with the sea. Now she had it, free and clear: Richard Whistler's sloop. Not just to use on vacation but to live aboard. A postcard view of the bridge. From which people killed themselves.

The blue-black flickering water rocked and flowed. The boat next door was empty and decrepit, its slanted windows plugged with rotten cloth. The boat next to that went out sometimes on weekends and the chrome was shiny. Beside that, where Frank whatever-his-name-was kept his depressing tub, the *Sayonara,* a slimy white mooring ball floated by itself. So Frank was out cruising or maybe had left the mudflats? Since he hated Peek and Roll and hated Gretchen and hadn't even helped her that time her dinghy got loose in a storm, this was a good thing. She hoped it was adios, *Sayonara.*

Think back. Should she have done something more for Thisbe? Yes. She should have. But what?

Gretchen had been sitting on her deck in the darkness with Peek and Roll on her shoulders. Late. Not a bad evening, one of the good times when you felt like a bohemian woman of the world, not an aging spinster. She held a book on her knees but had switched off the light so she could just stare at the water and the lights of the hotels and high-rise apartments, each glow full of disappointment or happiness, she couldn't tell which. She found she could *assume* happiness, could imagine some girl getting dressed for, say, an art opening or a birthday party in that tiny window way up at the top of the tower, and that was when she heard splashing. A glint slid forward in the water, became human. "Are you okay?" she called out to it.

No answer.

"Where are you going?"

No answer.

"It's not safe in the dark. A boat could hit you." Gretchen unclipped the flashlight from the wall and scanned the waves with it. "Where are you going?"

Still ignoring her.

"You know the tide's against you."

No answer.

"Are you staying aboard one of these boats?"

Mute.

"I'm going to call the harbor patrol," Gretchen said, an empty threat, really, because it would take them forever to get here. "It's not safe!" she said again.

Finally she decided she had to do something. She had to put the birds in their cages and dig out the Jim-Buoy ring before she could climb down into the dinghy and row in what she hoped was the right direction.

So annoying and shocking when the swimming girl turned out to be Thisbe, especially when Thisbe treated Gretchen like a stranger! "What the hell are you doing? Didn't you see it was *me*?" Gretchen said. She threw the buoy thing at Thisbe and it landed close to her arms. Thisbe grabbed it and hung on, gulping and spitting.

"You could have answered me," Gretchen said. "You could have said, *I am swimming in the bay like an idiot. Leave me alone.*"

Gulps and spits, but no laughs. Then Thisbe started doing that hiccup thing that came from crying, and then she was crying hard. Gretchen pulled her closer to the dinghy and nearly fell in trying to help her climb aboard. She rowed them back to the *Broker* with Thisbe like a glum seal huddled in the front, not a light load by any means, plus the tide was against them the whole way. No explanation, no *Thank you, Gretchen!* Even when Thisbe was wrapped in a nice blanket on the deck of the *Broker,* she didn't say thank you. She said, "I thought it would be easier if I just disappeared."

This was hard to take from a seventeen-year-old girl. It looked like self-pity, not despair, and it was not attractive.

"It would *not* be easier if you disappeared, you idiot," Gretchen said. "You're too young to be so unhappy."

No answer again.

"You have so much to live for! It's all ahead of you!" Gretchen tried them out one after the other, as if they were Tylenol and Motrin. "Things change!"

"Grown-ups always say that," Thisbe said. Scornful expression, scornful voice. Black sky, black bay, slivers of light rippling around the boat.

"Because it's true."

"Things *don't* change," Thisbe said. "Things just are what they are. And I'm like this. I'll always be like this."

"Like what?"

No response.

"You're seventeen, for Christ's sake," Gretchen said.

"So?"

"Did that obnoxious boy drop you?"

"Who?"

"That guy who brought you to Clayton's."

Thisbe didn't even have to nod. Gretchen knew.

"Oh, God. You should take it out on him, not yourself."

She tried to think of a Life Lesson she could impart. After four years with Harry in Hawaii, Harry had said to Gretchen, "I want you to move out," and Gretchen told Harry she'd rather drown and Harry said he was leaving for the trade show the next day no matter what, which he did, and she didn't drown herself right then because, well, it was so dark out, and even though Gretchen wanted to disappear, she was afraid of sharks and tides and jellyfish. Every day for two weeks she thought she'd do it, just drown herself, but she stayed in her chair at Pua's house, dreaming of painless obliteration, and then the call came from California. Her mom was sick. Stage four. Gretchen left Hawaii and came home to take care of her and the crazy birds.

"Things change and you feel better," Gretchen said. "Not right away, maybe, but later."

Thisbe stared with what looked like hatred at the black water in the bay.

Gretchen felt impatience. She wanted to tell Thisbe what other people had to do when you so-called disappeared. You didn't vanish like sea foam in the bright air. You left yourself for others to find. You floated in pieces. You became a pair of hands someone had to reach out and grab, put in a yellow bag, take to the surface. All in a day's work. *Here are the hands.*

Lots of people went back to work after finding things like severed hands. It was their job. They went back to work the day after they had cleaned up train accidents and murders and bits of victims stuck to the grilles of hurtling cars. Not Gretchen, though. She quit diving and went to work as a waitress.

She looked at Thisbe in the blanket, a beautiful, bitter mermaid of a girl. She thought of saying how she had found the girl's hands in the water and put them in a bag because someone who'd wanted to disappear had not made sure she was over water before she jumped off the bridge.

She couldn't say it, though. It was too grim. "You are *not* the problem" was all she said to Thisbe. "He's a black hole. Take it out on him, not yourself. That's what I'd do."

Thisbe had not asked Gretchen how to go about this. Thisbe had not even seemed to be listening. Gretchen should have told her the terrible story instead, she thought now, looking down into water she was afraid to touch.

43

THISBE

They know she's gone, so they'll be looking, right? They'll publish her picture and the taxi driver from Eritrea will see it. He'll call the police and say, *I saw her. She didn't jump. I took her down.*

She considers this in the bathroom. Instead of stabbing him, she could just scream. Shout her name and situation. *I'm trapped in here!* If they're near a boat of any kind, someone could hear her. How far could they have sailed by now?

Listen. She needs to listen. No motor. The whipping cloth of a sail. Is that a sail? The flapping is like a sail. She hears Frank's boots as he shuffles around. Creaking hull as the boat rolls side to side. The click of the jars full of sand dollars. The repetitive chime of metal on metal, a high ring as if someone were playing the triangle. It's not the feel of a boat speeding forward, when you could hear the water flowing and splashing and falling away, the gush of two streams as she sailed the blue sabot around the mark in last place. "DFL," she had heard Hugh say one time. He probably said it about her, because that's where she usually placed. *Dead Fucking Last.*

She doesn't hear the gushing sound of water going around the hull. And the man isn't steering. He would be steering if they were in the ocean, heading someplace like Pismo.

She leans on the bathroom door. An accidental bump of her sore arm makes her cry out. The borrowed pants slide. She's upright and she isn't falling, but she's dizzy, and the boat, burbling and groaning, is like a living thing. What if she just falls over while she's holding the knife to stab him? She's Jonah and Frank's boat is the whale. Is the whale swimming? No. More like it's waiting. Waiting like the nurse shark in the tank at Birch Aquarium, gray and still.

Thisbe takes a breath of stinky bathroom air. She prepares to scream, to run out, to grab the knife. She thinks the words she plans to scream: *Hey! Help me! I'm kidnapped in here!*

This boat is how many feet? Smaller than Hugh's and Clay's boats. Fifteen feet of cabin, tiny bathroom, tiny galley, maybe a twenty-six-foot boat, the kind at the yacht club. The boat set sail from Coronado, right? Because he took her from under the bridge? But maybe not. When this kind of thing happened to other girls, they were put in cars first. The car took you somewhere. She has no memory of a car but she has no memory at all between the underside of the bridge, where she was running in the dark, and the boat. In between, there was . . . what?

Maybe if she went on being Julia, if she pretended *very, very well,* the crazy man would leave the duct tape off her arms and legs and then when he was on deck she could move the jars around and look out one of the portholes and figure out where they are?

He's crazy but she's not. Sane beats crazy like rock beats scissors. The boy in the red truck had thought she was nutso, she'd seen it in his face, and something in her wanted him not to think that. She'd gotten sane again. She'd thought about jumping but she didn't jump. She opened the passenger door to the Honda and sat herself back down in the car and leaned over the gears and the driver's seat and she pulled the driver's door closed so the door would not be torn off by a passing truck and the wind would stop coming in and she could think. A crazy person would not have done that. Headlights filled the car with whiteness like spotlights on a stage. The headlights went slowly around and the car was yellow. A yellow taxi that pulled over in front of her. *Eritrea,* it said on the trunk. A black man, it looked like, turned his head and used two fingers to say, *Come here.*

Come here, two fingers said, *come here to the taxi and I will take you from this situation, this pickle, this car that isn't yours and never has been.*

She got out. She walked forward. The wind blew. The stars were not mica shards floating in outer space but white dwarfs that could burn up matter.

She opened the back door and got in.

The backseat of the taxi smelled like oil and dust, and the seat drooped beneath her, the springs broken, the hollow deep. The driver was a slender black man with long arms in a white dress shirt. "Your car, it is broke down?" the driver said, accelerating, taking her away from the situation, taking her down to the island, down to the ground.

"I'm sorry," she said. "I don't have my purse. I forgot it."

Was there another car? Did the crazy man have a car, too? A car with a backseat that sank into the springs? The boat lurches and she falls sideways like a bowling pin, hits the shower wall with her scabby arm, already throbbing, and her knees buckle.

She cries out but doesn't scream because the sound is unmistakable now: the churning thrum of an outboard motor.

She opens the bathroom door and no one's there. He's gone out of the cabin and she's not taped up. Her chance! The motor cuts out and the silence is like a layer of fog. He starts it again, and she reaches for the knob of the cabin door, to let herself out. She could go on deck and jump into the water, any water, who cares where. The knob turns but when she pushes the door out, it hits something. She pushes again, harder. Harder and harder but there's a latch or something. It's locked from the outside. The roaring motor stops and she stands still. *Green light, red light.*

44

FEN

While Fen waited for his uncle in the Lockes' house, he sat in their living room wishing he could go back to the car. The coffee table was the kind with a glass top, and he stared through it, wondering if he should pull out one of the giant books and pretend to read, or if it would be weird to check out the board games. Five minutes passed. Then six. His uncle didn't reappear, and no one else came in. He could hear muted voices upstairs—a girl's, a man's, a woman's. Creaking sounds now and then, as if people were walking. He quietly opened the Monopoly box and took out two dice, one white, one red. He closed the box and put it back under the glass, then set the dice on the table so it was clear he wasn't stealing them. He'd have stuffed them in his pocket if he meant to steal them. Then he turned a picture frame on the table beside the sofa so he could see it better. One of the girls was the Ted girl he'd met at the snack bar, but younger and smaller and flat-chested, her dress pink with skinny straps. He was brushing dust from the glass with his thumb when he heard footsteps on the stairs. Ted came into the room and caught him looking at her picture. He didn't know what to say to her. Had his uncle told her parents yet? This was a freaky-bad situation.

She was still wearing her board shorts and he could see the bikini lines under a white shirt. "Hey," she said, not smiling.

He wished he hadn't grabbed the dice out of her Monopoly game, but they were in his left hand now, so—

"Did your uncle make you come over?"

He shook the dice in his hand a little. "No." When Fen's father had died, the school secretary and the principal and all his teachers had said, "I'm sorry about your dad," but only one student besides his friend Greg had even mentioned it. Hillary Tieran had walked up to him at the cafeteria and said, "Sorry about your dad. That sucks the worst."

So Fen said, "I'm sorry about your sister. That sucks the worst." Then he wondered what she'd think about him saying that once she knew he'd been up on the bridge and had done nothing to help.

Ted stared at the floor for an uncomfortably long time. What she was looking at was a red-and-blue Persian-type rug, and in the part of the rug where she was looking, a tree grew out of another tree and flowed into another tree. Finally she said, without looking up from the tree chain, "She's not dead."

This wasn't what he'd expected at all. It wasn't what his uncle had said. Carl had said she jumped. Fen rolled the dice and they stopped on four and two.

"What are you playing?" she asked.

"Nothing." Fen knew that it was hard to let it sink in. Fen's father hadn't looked believably dead in the hospital. You had to say to yourself over and over, *He's dead.* His nose and one cheek were bruised from falling but not so bruised that you'd think he couldn't be fine. His running shoes were in a bag like he might want them when he woke up. The piece of toast he'd been eating before he left for the run was still sitting on the plate in the kitchen. It still had jam on it. The jam was shiny.

Then Ted said, "They're not going to find her in the water or wherever. She would never do that."

"Would never do what?"

"Jump."

He just stared at her. He really, really wanted her to be right.

"They say she did but they haven't found her. Because she didn't do it! She was too scared of stuff. She couldn't even jump off the high dive! She didn't like to sail because she was scared when it got windy. She's not going to jump off a giant bridge."

He should say that he'd been there and he'd seen her and she'd told him to go around her car, but that might mess with what Ted was believing, and he didn't want to be the person who made her stare right at death.

"Where'd my mom go?" Ted asked.

Fen pointed toward the kitchen and picked up the dice again, rubbing them against one another, mentally begging her not to go see if that's where her mom had gone, because that was also the way Carl had gone, and they were probably talking.

"I wish everyone would just go home," she said. "No offense."

She was leaning her elbows on her knees and turning a braided string bracelet around on her wrist like she'd never noticed it before. He was so glad she didn't leave.

"I'm going to make signs and put them up," she said. "Want to help me?"

He did and he didn't. "What kinds of signs?"

"Missing person signs."

He studied the trees in the rug. Making signs could be good, or it could be bad. If Ted was the only one who thought Thisbe wasn't dead, would Carl be angry with him? "Well," Fen said, "are you sure that's the right plan?"

"Yes. She wouldn't jump because she's a chicken, which is a good thing for once. She has to be somewhere. Somebody has to have seen her."

He didn't want to say, *Well, she didn't look chicken when I saw her.* He shrugged, like to say, *Okay.* When she went upstairs, he followed her.

45

JEROME

Ted kept texting him, and Jerome didn't know what to say.

Did you see her?

Do you know where she is?

The police say she jumped off the bridge.

No, he said. *No no no no no.* **I didn't see her. I don't know where she is.**

Fuck Clay for not answering his text. For not even saying, "Yeah, I heard" or "No, I haven't" when Jerome asked if he'd heard what happened to Thisbe. On the shelf in his room Jerome had a picture of the two of them: Jerome "Jeronimo" Betchman and Clay "Killer" Moorehead in their soccer uniforms, eleven years old. Jerome ripped the photo out of the cheap frame and tore the two of them into little pieces that he flushed down the toilet. He felt no better so he tried screaming. His mother wasn't home but the neighbors might be, so he held the pillow over the back of his head and screamed into the mattress. Maddy whined and turned in circles and poked his arm with her nose, so he petted her, but he felt no better. He got his phone out and texted Clay again, right under his own unanswered question. He typed: **She jumped off the bridge, you fucker.**

He turned off his phone and dropped it in the trash and went back to lying in his bed with the pillow smashed into his face, but the pillow couldn't stop him from remembering the way she sat drinking by herself the last time he'd seen her, the night he should have said, *If you want, I could give you a ride home.*

46

FEN

Fen watched Ted type words into a computer. The books on the mahogany shelves had all sorts of legal titles he read to himself while she typed: **MISSING**.

He couldn't help asking, "Who's that?" and pointing to a framed photo of Ted and Thisbe with two muscled-up college guys.

"Josh and Aaron. Stepbrothers. They go to Duke and Wharton. As my stepdad will tell you if you give him five seconds of your time."

She found a digital photo of her sister laughing, and said, "What about this one?"

"Nice."

Ted typed, **Last seen**, and then stopped. "I don't want to say she was last seen on the bridge."

"How else will you find witnesses?" Fen said. *Like me, for example.*

"Yeah," she said. "That's true."

He wiped his hands on his trunks and saw that he had sand

stuck to both ankles. Also his calf. He was not a complete ass, was he? He could tell her he had been on the bridge and he was a witness before his uncle or her mom came upstairs and said it for him?

She typed, **Last seen beside a white Honda on the eastbound Coronado Bridge.** "Is it eastbound or westbound?"

He definitely had sand inside his trunks, too. He felt sick and light-headed. Sandy, itchy, sick. "What?"

"They said she was coming back to the island. Is that the eastbound or westbound side? Or maybe north?"

After she wrote **westbound**, she stopped again. "I wonder what she was wearing. These things always say what she was wearing."

He would tell her, and telling would be the right thing. "Pink boots," he said. *There.* It was done. Confessed.

"Yeah," Ted said without even turning around. "My mom said she was wearing them when she left here but would she keep them on? They're so dorky."

Pause. Inhale. Exhale. *Tell her.* "That's not what I mean. I mean when *I* saw her, she was wearing pink boots. Also a black hooded sweatshirt. And shorts."

Now he was a different type of ass, based on her expression.

"What?"

"I saw a girl beside a white Honda on the bridge last night. I didn't know it was your sister until my uncle told me why we were coming to your house. I didn't know how to tell you." Fen turned the dice over in his pocket and watched Ted's fingers resting on the keyboard but not typing anything.

"What else."

"She, like, waved me on," Fen said.

"What do you mean?"

He shrugged miserably. "Like, *I've got a phone and I'm fine here.*"

"Then what happened?"

"I don't know. I thought she must have called somebody to tow her or bring a gas can. So I left."

"And she was, like, still outside the car."

He nodded.

"Was she crying or anything?"

"No."

Ted frowned. "What about, like, other cars?"

"Other people passed. Not a lot, but a few. They saw us. Saw her, I guess. They'd have to."

The dust on the venetian blinds had been smudged by a finger. A steel fan turned slowly overhead. Fen tried to think of what Thisbe could possibly have done next that would mean she was hiding somewhere and not coming home. Walk off the bridge? With nobody seeing her? If so, why would she hide all the next day?

Ted typed: **Wearing pink rain boots, black sweatshirt, and shorts.** He tried to read the back of her head, the way she was sitting, to know if she blamed and hated him as he deserved to be blamed and hated for not going up to Thisbe and asking if there was something wrong and could he help her in some way.

Ted wasn't crying. She wasn't talking. She was telling the print button to print. So he hadn't killed her hope? He felt like cold juice had just shot up through all his veins and into his brain, but he didn't know if he should be relieved. Fen rubbed the dice in his pocket and they made small sounds.

"There," Ted said. "Now maybe those other people who drove by will say something." She waited for more copies to slide out, more and more and more, and grabbed two rolls of tape from a drawer. "Let's go," she said.

He assumed they were going to show the flyers to her parents and his uncle and the police, which would be excruciating, he bet, but she pulled a blank piece of paper from the printer, and while they were standing in the hall, she closed her bedroom door and taped the paper to it. Then she wrote:

WENT WITH PHIN TO SEE IF ANYONE HAS SEEN THISBE LATELY.

"Fen," he said.

She looked blankly at him.

"Never mind," he said. He wanted to hurry. He could text his uncle, which would be so much easier than talking to him face to face.

"We need to go out this way," she said, and she took him downstairs and out a side door in the laundry room that he hoped was hidden from everyone else. "Take that one," she said quietly, pointing to a ten-speed parked under a little roof that protected three bikes. He was relieved to see the tires weren't flat. Ted gently rolled a cruiser out of the rack and opened the gate, glancing behind her to a yard that was obscured by a flowering bush. She pushed the bike to the road, climbed on, and looked back to see that Fen was following.

"Stop watching me," she said to a boy who was sitting on his lawn, throwing a beach ball at a homemade basketball hoop that was nailed to a tree.

"I'm not," the kid said sullenly, but he was, Fen was sure of it, and they went on down the road.

47

CARL

Sometimes the weather changed in an instant on summer afternoons. The fog was coming in fast now, whiting out the sky, flattening out the light in the backyard, chilling the air with drops of water that Carl could feel on his bare arms.

Carl stared at the bark of the ficus tree in the Lockes' backyard and pressed the phone to his skull as if he were still listening to Howard say there was no point in searching again so soon. He felt relieved that Fen had texted him a few minutes earlier to ask if he could go for a walk with Ted because she'd asked him to.

Sure, he told Fen. **Go ahead.**

48

FRANK

Kelp, it looks like. Blocking the water intake and overheating the engine. Frank unscrews the top of the strainer, finds a skewer to poke out the kelp, curses when the water shoots up and soaks his sleeve and pants, picks the kelp out in long stringy pieces and short slimy bits. Edite the cat paces the whole time.

"What are you looking at?" he says to Edite. She licks a paw.

Still the motor won't keep going for more than ten seconds. He has to buy a new pump impeller. Nothing else to try but that. He'll have to go ashore, find the nearest marine supply, make quick work of it, then sail or motor around the point, head north.

He has only an hour, maybe an hour and a half before dark. A cloud's rolling over the water, swallowing boats, sky, jetty, the navy jets sitting on the tarmac. He can no longer see the bridge or downtown, just the choppy little breakers that rise and fall below his bow. Nothing to do but find a marina and go ashore. Shelter Island might be the closest—that or Point Loma. He needs a bank and a marine supply right together. Maybe he has the addresses on a card in his wallet? He puts his hand into his back pocket, but he knows it's empty before he reaches in.

His pocket is a blank space.

He opens the black box by the wheel, the one where he keeps his wallet when he's working on deck and doesn't want the bulk to bother him, and inside the black box are spare keys, a flashlight, a few coins, and a can opener. No wallet. Had he worn his coat ashore last night? His coat is flung over the cushions, getting damp in the foggy air. The cushions are wet already, the skin on his face is slick. No wallet in the coat, not the first time he checks the pockets, nor the second.

Think back. He hadn't done the whole circuit Sunday night, had interrupted his plans when he saw Julia walking like a vision across Tidelands Park. He had not gone to Albertsons. Had not gone to the ATM. Had only sorted through the first three trash cans, the ones by the playground. No time to do the other things. If he hadn't taken the wallet out of his back pocket to pay or collect money, how could he have left it anywhere? It might have fallen out of his pocket when he was maneuvering things. When he was sorting the cans. Could it have fallen out in the acacias, where he zipped up the sail bag?

No cash, no pump impeller. If someone had found the wallet by the trash cans, they would have taken his cash, sixty dollars at least, then gone to the ATM, emptied his account. But he had a PIN code. A thief wouldn't know the PIN code. Maybe he just lost the cash. Bank would give him a new card and he'd be okay. It would take a little longer, that's all. The women behind the counter in their jewels and heels would look him over; the men in their gray suits would see his shoes and judge. If the wallet was gone, it would take some time.

He could just go on to Pismo. Hope for wind the whole way. Make do.

Or there could be days and days of stillness. Fog or heat. No fresh water, not enough food. Wind pushing him out, a storm.

A wave slaps the boat as he checks his pockets again. He can see less and less of Cabrillo as a layer of clouds rolls over the point and thins.

It would be much safer to find the wallet and buy the pump impeller. Within the haze, the old lighthouse suddenly appears, trim as a sugar cube. Then the fleece thickens and the whole hill is blotted out.

Barely enough wind at present to turn around and sail back. May take hours. Once he gets back to his mooring, he can anchor the boat and row ashore and go to the trash cans and find the wallet if the wallet is there to find. It will take forever, forever, forever. Get the cash and buy the impeller. One more day was all it was, not forever. A day and a night.

"Frank!" Julia is calling him, her voice surprisingly faint, but he doesn't answer yet. He doesn't want her to think he can't take her home. Still a failure. Still incompetent.

"Hey!" she says, as if from far away. He looks to see if there are boats nearby, but the nearest is fifty yards, a day-tripper heading back.

Edite the cat jumps down to her cushion. She doubts him, too, from the way she stares.

He will have to bind Julia's feet and hands again. Tell her it's necessary. Tell her to pretend it's part of the game.

49

THISBE

"Frank?" she shouts.

The water flows hard and fast around the boat.

Her boots aren't here. She wasn't wearing them when she first woke up, and they aren't on the floor. If he put her in a car to bring her to this boat, did he bring the boots?

"Hey!" she shouts. Maybe she dropped the boots and he forgot about them, and right now her boots are lying near the bike path, where a jogger or a cyclist will see them. *What's this?* the jogger or cyclist will say. *A pair of pink boots? Suspicious!* They will call the police.

The boat turns hard and she falls against the table. She gets up and kneels on the cushion, pushes jars aside. The long, narrow window is covered with a ruffled cloth, stained and dusty like everything else on the boat. She forces it aside and sees drops of water on the glass, a misty world, the choppy white waves of a wide choppy sea. Then a thing comes to the window: dirty ivory fur, the face of an animal. A cat looks in at her and she looks back. The cat goes away and she sees reddish land. A cliff without a beach, mist floating, clouds gathering thickness and weight. Houses appear on the hillside: colored boxes and roofs, everything silent, as if asleep. A long white building that must be a hotel, not a soul on a single balcony, not a sign that she can read. Where, where, where, where. She can hear Frank moving on deck, can hear ropes and sails and rudder. She finds the knife in the drawer—how silly he was to leave it there—and she holds it while she watches the cat stalk back and forth outside the porthole, waiting for a sign.

50

FEN

"Whose house is this?" Fen asked.

"Clay's," Ted said.

It was weird how fast the fog was moving. He could see it floating along the street, cloudlike and cold. They were near the bay now, and Ted was shoving one of the flyers into a mailbox on a locked gate. Behind the locked gate stood a strange house with a gleaming silver wall. All over the wall were metal swirls. The fog made him cold, but he didn't say anything, just turned his bicycle around and followed Ted when she said they were going to Albertsons next.

51

THISBE

The fog changes color but that's all. It gets darker as night falls, and they're moving—why or where, it's hard to know, because certain lights look the same: a gold blob sharpens into focus and becomes BEER and then it's a gold blob again, first behind the boat, then ahead of it, as if they're going to it and away, then to it and away, the boat swinging and rocking until she's sick to her stomach and sweaty and prickling and she lies down to make the nausea stop.

It's a long time before she can stand up, but when she looks through the little porthole, things have changed. There's no gold light that says BEER, but stacks of lights. Towers of lights. Rows that are floors and stories. They glimmer green and red, white and gold, in familiar patterns. San Diego. She knows the shapes of the buildings, the big gray wedge of the *Midway,* the aircraft carrier with a number the size of a house: *41.* As the boat wheels around, she has to grab the wooden rail to keep from falling, and the bridge appears. Where have they been? It doesn't matter. They're home now. The bridge gleams like an arc of candles on a giant cake.

"Help me," she says to the cat, but the cat walks away, and the longer she holds the knife the more she worries that it's no use.

"Hey!" she says, but he doesn't answer. She says it over and over until she's hoarse. She can hear the chain, the low, steady clink of a sinking anchor, feet scuffing, feet stumbling, weight on one side, then the other, and when she tries the door, when she pounds and pounds and says, "Let me out, Frankie! Julia wants out!" he doesn't hear or doesn't care. Whatever he's doing, he goes on doing, and when at last there's no noise on deck, she hears the foghorn. Then a train. Then nothing. The sounds are faint, so does that mean her voice is fainter? From the outside, do they hear nothing, as if she were in a freezer? It reminds her of what she used to wonder when she closed the jewelry box over the dancing ballerina and the ballerina bent over in the dark. Did the ballerina feel scared in there? Scared that you would never open the box again?

"Hey!" she screams, but her voice is weak and broken and cracked. Nothing happens. And then it does. She hears the lock snap open, and she's standing with the knife in the darkness when he opens the cabin door.

"Don't touch me," she says, her voice a strange, whispery cry.

"I have to go ashore," he says. "I'm sorry, Julia. You have to wait here."

"No," she says, holding the puny knife like it's a sword and she's a fencer. She wishes it were bigger. As big as an ax.

"Don't be mad, Julia," he says.

"I'm not Julia," she says.

"Don't say that." He's coming closer. He has a mournful look. His bristly beard shines in the light that glows above the cabin door. The light shines down on him as if he were a statue in a church. She hates him.

"I want out," she says, and she hates how it sounds like she has laryngitis, like she's too sick to hurt him.

"Not here. Not now. I want to take you home. You'll remember when you see. It takes a while. The Seer warned me."

"I don't know who the Seer is but I want to go home."

The cat swishes by his feet. It comes into the cabin as if nothing is amiss, as if this is an argument the cat hears all the time. The cat jumps up on the cushion and arranges its tail in the near darkness. Ready for the show.

The man uses his hands to talk. He holds them up to show he's reasonable, but she knows he isn't. He's insane. "I should have showed you the article."

"I don't need to see any article."

"You're confused."

"No, *you*'re confused," she says, her voice annoyingly weaker when she tries to shout. She decides to walk toward him. Maybe he'll let her go past and out of the cabin if she holds the knife in a threatening manner. It's a steak knife, but it's sharp.

"Don't," he says.

She keeps walking. He doesn't step to the side, and the boat is so narrow she can't pass unless he steps into the galley. She can't bear to touch any part of him. She's near enough to stab but she doesn't. She holds the knife a little higher, and he reaches behind him and brings his hand back holding the gun.

She forgot that. She stands still. He points it right at her chest.

"Hand me the knife," he says.

She hates him.

"I don't want to use this again," he says. "It isn't a good part of my plan."

She will never forget the sorrowful face he makes, as if he's a good person. She hands him the knife and he makes her turn around. The cat watches stiffly the whole time that he wraps and tapes her wrists behind her back. She can see what the cat sees: the man has set the gun down on the floor to tape her ankles together. She could kick it backward, kick him, but then what?

He tells her to lie facedown on the cushion and she thinks she doesn't care what happens as long as he doesn't rape her. He tapes her ankles and ties the gag in her mouth.

"I'll be back as soon as I can," he says.

When he goes out, the cat follows him and she's alone again.

52

FRANK

There's no wallet by trash can number one. Not by the others, either. The trash cans stink and spill over in pools of yellow light, papers and bags pecked by birds and mashed by feet, smeary and torn. He looks and looks but there's no wallet. It isn't late enough that all the joggers have gone home so he keeps his eyes down. Girl, boy, man. He can tell by their calves and how fast they run whether they're old or young, fat or thin.

Sand scrapes under his shoes because water has made flat rivers across the sidewalk where the swimmers wash their feet. More runners passing, the swish of a bike. The clack and thrum overhead as cars rush onto the island or rush away over the bridge. Water gleams on the waves lit below the pylons, and fog wets the empty grass of the golf course. He waits until the path is empty behind and ahead of him, and he darts into the place where it says NO TRESPASSING. Walks along the path in his usual manner, as if he's an official of some kind, a gardener here from Parks and Rec, his purpose known and important. Break in the water line? Electrical failure? He can fix that sort of thing. He hears the soft rhythm of a woman's running feet, but she doesn't stop to report him, just goes on running.

There it is: the cave of dry acacias. No one can see him here. The bag of bottles and cans is waiting as he remembered. It will make a certain amount of noise to dump them out, so he doesn't want to do that. He searches quietly under and around the cans but there's so little light. The streetlight is blocked out by branches and leaves. It's hopeless. If he were to dig up his flashlight and switch it on this early in the evening, someone might glance over and see light in the place where no one is supposed to be. He shuffles and waits for his eyes to get keener, leans down and gropes with his hands under the bag, tears open the thick plastic, and lets the bottles and cans spill out. He holds his breath and kneels in a state of perfect stillness while he listens for a bike or a voice, hurrying feet. Nothing. He feels in the dirt for the wallet, but there are only jagged cans, crushed plastic bottles, pine needles, and rocks.

He's lost it, and Julia waits on the boat. All this time, all this looking and waiting, waiting for her to return, was that for nothing? What if it's like last time? With the girl in Oceano who was not really Julia, sitting on the boat, waiting for him, time passing, too much time.

This is different. This time the girl ate. This time he gave her water. And it's just one more night. He can wait until morning. Go to the bank and say who he is and how much money should be in his account. Nobody says you have to be clean-shaven and wearing a suit to have a bank card. He can prove it's his signature. He can prove he's Frank Le Stang by writing his name the way it was on the card and by telling them his mother's maiden name, Serafim. He, Frank Le Stang, has money from the sale of the Serafim house in Pismo Beach, California, all of it guarded and saved, which is why he isn't dressed in a fancy suit, wearing a fancy tie, driving a big black car. The money is saved, sitting right there in his account, and in the morning they'll see by the way he writes his name that he has plenty of money even though he's lost his wallet, which can happen to anyone. He'll get a new card. Take the Rib to buy an impeller. Setbacks are setbacks; nothing can stop him now. This time is different.

53

HUGH LOCKE

Hugh sat barefoot in the dark. He'd given Ambien to Anne and promised to take some himself but instead he roamed the house. Ted's room: quiet. The kitchen: a row of glasses by the sink, an uncut pan of enchiladas under foil in the fridge. Pillows askew on the couch, a Monopoly box sticking out of the stack under the coffee table, the neighbor's porch a globe of lighted mist. He was often awake this time of night, his mind three to eight hours ahead, but that was different. Normally, he could just work, go for a run, read the paper, send emails. His phone and Anne's had rung repeatedly after Ted's stunt: *Missing.* Thisbe's face everywhere. *Last seen on the Coronado Bridge.* Emails from neighbors and friends had started arriving in an ever-lengthening queue: **Oh my God! I'm so sorry. I'll keep an eye out. Is there anything I can do?**

Hugh sat down at his desk without turning on the light. He clicked through the new emails, all of them short, none of them informative. Anne believed Ted had a point. Why assume the police were right? She could be missing, couldn't she? Thisbe wouldn't jump. It was impossible. Therefore she must be alive somewhere.

Hugh walked up the stairs and stood at the threshold of Thisbe's room. The door was ajar, as it never was when Thisbe was home. The girls kept their doors closed as a matter of principle, something he hadn't allowed his boys to do.

Hugh pushed the door open and stepped in. Thisbe's room smelled sweet, as she had. Her laptop was closed and plugged into the wall. Another cord was wrapped neatly in a bowl. He could hear nothing except a far-off bark. Josh's and Aaron's rooms had always smelled of sweat and deodorant. Despite their higher-than-normal ability to sink basketballs through hoops and throw footballs into outstretched hands, they could not get a tissue into a trash can. But here the pillows were arranged with precision on the bed.

He stepped forward and opened the top drawer of Thisbe's desk, slowly in case there was a squeak. No squeak. The pencils rolled once and lay still.

Checking the room for the letter he'd written her wasn't wrong. The policewoman called Lord, she had said they'd found a letter from him, and did he think Thisbe was upset by it? He said of course she was upset! It was easy to make a teenaged girl upset! He hadn't meant to hurt her, but to make her see that he was serious, this was serious, life was serious. College mattered to Thisbe, so college was the carrot and the stick.

He told the policewoman and Carl Harris and the giant guy the truth: that Thisbe had been mad at him after she'd read the letter, but there was nothing out of the ordinary about that. Her emotional ups and downs were not abnormal, from what he could see, but he'd had boys the first time around, and boys were different, people said. He could tell that Anne was mad about the letter when Officer Lord brought it up. Hugh hadn't shown it to Anne first, so naturally she was mad. Anne was always saying vaguely that things would work out if you didn't make yourself into the enemy. But she hid away from problems she didn't want to face. Pretended they weren't there, meditated, closed her eyes.

Now that Hugh was alone and awake, the letter seemed like a bigger deal. What if it was a trigger, as they had seemed to imply? They hadn't handed him the letter, which he was grateful about, just said they had found it in Thisbe's room. Hugh didn't ask where or in what condition because he didn't think of it at the time, was still shocked and defensive, to tell the truth. If they'd left the letter where they'd found it, that meant the letter was not a piece of evidence they felt they had to collect. And if Hugh found the letter in some particular state, that would be illuminating. Say she had wadded it up. Say she had folded it up inside a pocket. Say she had written something back to him in the margins, as his ex-wife had done with emails he'd sent to her, which she had printed out, for some reason, and then scrawled on in pencil and left inside an envelope he found months later instead of sending a letter back to him like a normal communicating person.

Moonlight chromed the shelves. He opened the second drawer, the one big enough for files, and it squeaked. Ted was next door, so he held still and felt the carpet under his bare feet and tried to hear whether she was awake, too. Six years was enough time for Ted to accept him, you'd think. From the age of eight, she'd received nothing from him but encouragement. The sabot that had started her love of sailing, the money he had shelled out for overnight regattas and the best gear and clinics and coaches and memberships, not to mention clothes, donuts, caramel-mocha-peppermint-pumpkin lattes, were they nothing? Still she seethed.

The files were full of what looked like old homework. He didn't look through them all. He didn't open the yellow tin box where the police had found fortune cookie messages that looked homemade, the edges crooked as if cut out one by one with scissors. *Do you know where these might have come from?* they asked. No, he didn't. *The boyfriend?* Maybe, he said. Though it seemed like more work than that boy was capable of.

He poked the wastebasket with a pencil: just a few tissues and gum wrappers that sat forlornly in the bottom. The letter was not in the trash, so Thisbe hadn't thrown it away, or the police had sealed it in an evidence bag.

Anne thought Clay had definitely given Thisbe the fortune cookies. Why else would she keep them? But kids kept all kinds of junk. Witness the "Wacky Island" map still pinned to Thisbe's bulletin board, a school project from years ago, a hand-colored, made-up place she'd labeled (he winced for her) *Poetry Island*.

If Clay *had,* in fact, seduced Thisbe with sappy messages (the only one he could remember was *Pleasure awaits you by the sea,* which made him sick to his stomach) and she had slept with him, which she probably had—they all did it; it was different now—that was likely why she'd turned into a different person. She'd started going with a whole different crowd. Drinking experimentally. (He hadn't quite been able to bring himself to tell the cops she'd gotten wasted at Clay's house and then denied it when they asked her point-blank: *Were you there?* A woman he knew casually had been only too glad to tell him—prefacing her remarks with the assurance that *she* would want other parents to tell *her* if the tables were turned—that her daughter said Thisbe got so drunk at that party that she fell on the rocks underneath Clay's deck and cut her scalp and practically bled to death. "I cut my head on Nessa's gate," Thisbe insisted. "It hardly bled at all. Mrs. Creevy is a nurse and she said I didn't need stitches.")

"I've heard all about Clay from friends at the club," Hugh had warned Thisbe. "In addition to holding parties when no adult is home, he doesn't study at all. Doesn't have to. You know why?"

"You're just against him because he's rich."

"Here are two SAT words in the same sentence: I'm against him because he's a wastrel on his way to a sinecure."

Sullen face, no response.

"Do you need me to define the words?"

Still sullen, lips together. "This town is so racist."

"This has nothing to do with race," Hugh said.

"Yes, it does. You just won't say it. He's rich and his family's Mexican so you think their money's different. Other people's parents help them get jobs, too. And there are all these really nice families here who came from Mexico. Like that kid on the tennis team."

He didn't know who she was talking about. "It has nothing to do with that. That's a whole separate issue. The problem is that he deals drugs and uses them. I've heard it from more than one person."

"You *said* he was a good-for-nothing person on his way to a cushy job. Like the problem was that his dad is giving him a job in the family business, so he doesn't have to study hard at school."

"My problem is with how he acts. Not where his family's from."

She walked out the door even though she knew she was forbidden to walk away from an unfinished conversation.

Was Thisbe suicidal in recent weeks? the policewoman had asked. No, he wouldn't have said so. Acting different from her normal self? Decidedly. Was Hugh homicidal as a result? Yes. A hundred years ago, or maybe it was more like four hundred, Hugh could have shot Clay. All the village elders would have clapped him on the back. Roasted him a pig.

On Thisbe's bedside table sat a couple of girlish-looking novels, a wrinkled *New Yorker* magazine, and the big fat paperback guide he'd bought for her before they went on their first college tour together: *The Best 379 Colleges*. Sticking out of it like a bookmark was a folded paper, and he knew before he slid it out of the book that it was his letter:

Dear Thisbe,

I do not understand what is not clear to you about the rules of this house. I have always been straight with you and your mother. I told you I would pay for your dream school if you could show me your mettle and get in. You are absolutely on track to get admitted to USC or Cal or even Stanford. But ever since you started seeing Clay Moorehead, you have shown reckless disregard for us, your schoolwork, and your teachers. I don't even know who you are anymore. What happened to your judgment? You have time to turn things around. Applications are coming up. I need proof that you can follow rules and be smart or you can plan on living at home and going to school around here.

Love,
Dad

Thisbe didn't actually call him Dad, but he called himself that in hopes that Ted and Thisbe would eventually see him that way, and he'd asked Anne to do it, too, and she usually remembered to say *your father* when referring to him at home, though sometimes the way the girls looked at Anne or curled their lips when she spoke made her falter and touch the pendant on her necklace.

Perhaps it was characteristic of certain women that they wrote responses they didn't send. Cryptic ones, in Thisbe's case. At the bottom of his letter to her, in her beautiful, precise printing, she had written:

This will not work.

The rest of the page was clean and white. He read the letter again to see what she meant by *this* and then looked out the window at the bridge, slim and silent in the darkness. *This will not work,* meaning, *I won't be bullied by you*? That's what he would have thought if he'd seen it before today. Now Thisbe seemed more confusing and fragile than he could ever have imagined. He refolded the letter using the exact creases she'd made and wondered why the police hadn't taken it as evidence, but it didn't matter. He would blame himself whether they blamed him or not.

54

FRANK

He doesn't sleep. The cars diminish but never cease. There is always, after a long pause, the clattering of weight on steel, the whine of acceleration. The light stays the same, a haze beyond the branches, artificial and cold. Water drips from the leaves. Now and then he's seen a tortoiseshell cat in the urban forest, wandering where it shouldn't be, but it doesn't come into his cave. There aren't many spiders, and he isn't afraid of the ones that walk over his knees, the spindly ones that want nothing but to disappear. Tonight a possum comes waddling and sniffing. Ugly little pointy face, bright frightening eyes. It hisses before it runs.

His mother, Francisca, was the daughter of a Portuguese fisherman. A Serafim was supposed to marry the man picked out by her father, but she fell in love with Bruno Le Stang, a boy she met at the cannery, and they eloped. It was his hair that was yellow-white, his skin that was too pink for sun. Frank took after their mother, Julia after their father. They all lived upstairs in Cousin Telma's house, but their mother had an idea that she could be a movie star if she only lived in Los Angeles, and Bruno Le Stang thought so, too. They left Pismo, when Frank was eight and Julia was four, promising to fetch them both when things got going. Julia looked for Francisca Le Stang in all the movie magazines their grandmother bought until Telma said, "You're never going to find her in there, you know." In the summers, Frank and Julia and Ben Crames started playing pirates down at Harlow's Cove.

The neon sign was visible from Frank's grandmother's attic window. He asked what *Seer* meant and his grandmother answered him in Portuguese. She pointed to the white neon hand containing in its center a blue neon eye and said it was a house of evil. He should pray if he wanted divine knowledge. Never, never to go to that false prophetess. To visit the *adivinho* would be a mortal sin.

But maybe the *adivinho* knew if Julia, when she was resurrected, would still be eight years old and if she would know what had happened to her and get to live as herself again or only as an angel, and most importantly if she would blame Frank, as everyone else did. Maybe if he couldn't visit the *adivinho,* he could send a letter. He could mail the letter from a mailbox where nobody he knew would see him, because the Seer's house was right on the busiest corner in town, one hundred feet from the church, in full view, night and day, of his grandmother.

The hardest part was figuring out how the Seer could write back. The letters couldn't come to his grandmother's house. He told the Seer his trouble, though, and the Seer understood. When the first letter came to Frank with the return address of Iron Mike's American Fitness, Santa Monica, California, he was lucky to be the one who was sorting the mail. That way he could open it by himself and act unsurprised when the next one came and he had to explain that he was tired of being so puny and weak, getting beat up by older boys; that he could earn more, too, if he built himself into a man, and that's why he'd been doing so many push-ups in his room. "Iron Mike" never failed to write as long as Frank never failed to send money from what he earned fishing and clamming. It was quite a shock when Frank visited ten years later and found Iron Mike was an old woman. It didn't take away from her wisdom, though. Far from it. Are not many things an illusion? Is not the physical world a mask?

He sleeps and wakes, sleeps and wakes. It's important to come out of the urban forest before the sun rises, before the runners and bikers might see him, so in the dripping black hour before dawn he goes to the park bathroom and washes his face, so old now, so different from what he really is, no wonder Julia can't remember.

55

THISBE

Knowing that she's close to home makes her stronger. Either that or the duct tape is more clumsily attached. This time she doesn't stop pointing her toes and sliding her ankles up and down when she feels the tight panic that stops her breath. She keeps pointing and sliding, stretching and wiggling, up and down, side to side. She chews on the gag in case chewing will work. She grunts like a pig and chews the wet edges of wet cotton. The skin is raw on her right calf when she finally frees her ankles. It stings when she stands up and looks in the moonlight for something sharp. The knife she pointed at him is not on the table or the floor but there must be other knives. She can walk now and she can open drawers by standing backward and groping at the handles behind her back.

There are other knives, but she's no contortionist. One after the other she drops them. Her hands are cramped, her fingers are cramped, her head is cramped. She thinks of things that would never work—light a match and burn through the tape (match after match falls without lighting, then one flares only to burn her fingers, nothing else), rub the tape against the side of a drawer (hurts and doesn't work), rub the tape against the metal edge of the counter (hurts even more and doesn't work)—but maybe all the wriggling and chafing and scraping has made the glue dry up, because she's jumping up and down in a semi-hysterical state, chewing with sore jaws on the disgusting gag, when a hand tears free. One hand, then the other. All she has to do now is take off the gag; she can untie it and throw it down.

"Help me!" she screams. Her voice is still wrong. Crackly and faint. The only sounds are of distant machines: foghorn, train horn, train wheels on staccato tracks. A weird chirping bird noise. Or is it bats? Owls? It goes on and on, a kind of far-off shrieking. She cries till she's even more hoarse, till her voice sounds like crackled paper. Outside, the light is pewter. She can see one streetlight and the edge of the island, the square lights of hotel rooms, shadows passing now and then, water dipping and cresting, hollows of moonlight, the night. Out the other side of the boat, the bridge like a smeary crown.

Her lips sting at the corners where the gag made sharp cuts she can't help licking. The boat has never been cleaned. The dirt of it makes her scared and sick but it's like when you have to do something gross, like unclog the toilet or reach into the disposal; you just say what her mom always says, which is you can always wash yourself afterward and you'll be clean again. She finds pasta pinwheels in a box and sucks on them like cough drops. Cans of tomatoes and cat food and Mrs. Dowder's Major Chowders. Books she would make fun of if she saw them in a store: *Same Soul, Many Bodies. Reincarnation and Karma. The Path to Wisdom Through Past Lives.* She looks on the shelf where Frank put the picture of the little girl. A zippered book, fake leather starting to tear, is full of envelopes from someone named Iron Mike. Iron Mike is a cartoon muscleman showing his pecs. Lines radiate from his arms as if he's the Virgin of Guadalupe. There's a business card that says *SEER: Reuniting Souls in Transit, Pacific Coast Highway, Pismo Beach.* A picture of a large covered porch where a woman stands with her face in shadow. She might be pretty, based on her figure, the clear skin of her chin, and her slender neck. *Serafim House,* someone has printed neatly on the back.

A newspaper clipping that has been cut out and folded says:

GIRL DIES IN BEACH ACCIDENT

BROTHER NOT TO BE CHARGED

PISMO, CA: A girl, 8, was found with her hands and feet bound at Harlow's Cove around 6 p.m. Monday and could not be revived, having been buried by an apparent rockfall. The girl's brother, 12, and another boy, 11, came running after the collapse, as did Agostinho de Ferro, a Grover City fisherman, who answered the boys' calls for help. The three children had been playing a pirate game, according to the testimony of both boys, and had dug a cave into the side of the cliff, leaving the girl with her hands and feet bound while they went to "gather the ransom." Due to the age of the two boys and the instability of the cliff, the death has been ruled an accident. The city is urged to make plans to block off Harlow's Cove, which is accessed by a footpath known to locals. "It is a tragedy for all concerned," said the investigating officer.

He'll come back, won't he? Frank will come back and unlock the door and she'll be ready to lunge out and grab the gun. She lies down with the box of pasta and tries not to lick the corners of her mouth, tries to stay awake, closes the white jewelry box over the ballerina, imagines the stingray, the sea in darkness, the sand dollars 625 to a square yard, purple cilia quivering.

56

JEROME

On Tuesdays, Jerome hit with Rolf at ten o'clock, which he couldn't cancel, not without telling his dad why he didn't owe the money, and if he told his dad he canceled, what reason would he give? *The girl I liked but who didn't like me and who I never mentioned to you is dead somewhere in the bay?*

He went to the courts and played horribly, which made sense if you thought of what might happen to your game if you no longer cared about your game. He played Brian Banks after that and beat him 2 and 0, which felt better because winning always felt better than sucking even if you were a monster for caring about a game on a day like this one. Neither Rolf nor Brian knew anything about Thisbe so at least Jerome didn't have to talk about it.

When he got off the courts, though, there was a message from Camilla Waller, who wasn't even a friend, asking if he'd meet her at Panera at six o'clock. She said she had something to tell him about Thisbe.

Camilla was a CoSA girl, meaning she went to the school

of the arts part-time, and her hair was currently sherbet orange. At first he couldn't even figure out why she had his phone number, but then he remembered they'd been forced into the same Spanish group last year. OK, he typed, because he hated it when people just said *k,* and he fell asleep in his tennis clothes even though he never napped unless he had a fever, and then he took Maddy to the dog beach and threw the Kong into the water about a hundred times because the new manager of the apartments hated Maddy and always looked like she wished she could revoke permission to have dogs, so it was important to tire Maddy out.

The ocean was gray and the beach was gray and he found himself watching the low curl of the surf like it owed him something. A lady throwing tennis balls for her Lab said what at least one person always said at the dog beach: "I thought Dobermans hated the water." "Not this one," he said, and threw the Kong again. There were no dolphins. Nothing but pelicans, their bodies like swords as they pierced the water.

57

THISBE

Before she's aware of the daylight, it seeps into her dream. The dream is memory, early spring. Outside the tennis court where Jerome is playing, Thisbe stands like an animal that wants not to be seen. If she gets closer to the mesh, trying to see Jerome better, the light splits and bends to the shape of his body waiting for the ball. He's a crouching shadow, an animal that waits to pounce. The ball comes so hard she doesn't think he can possibly hit it but he does. She can't see the other court well enough to know where it lands but the far shadow of a boy hits the ball back with a popping sound, and Jerome runs for a spot he must be able to predict, because he's there, *pop,* and she creeps to the place where there's a gap between the giant pieces of green mesh that make the tennis court a cage. Jerome is so intent on protecting himself from the balls that keep coming like bullets that he won't notice her there with her face unshielded, nakedly watching him. Then he stands still. Nothing between her and the sight of him holding the bright neon ball as he stares down at the ground. He bounces the ball once, twice, a third time, and then he throws it straight up. She knows it's called a serve, everyone knows that, but the serving they did in PE was not like this. When he throws the ball, it goes straight up out of his hand and the palm of his hand goes flat like he's offering it for benediction. It seems to her that he doesn't so much throw the ball as summon it from himself, and all the straightness of his body then coils and his other arm comes down to hit the ball hard over the net to a place she can't see through the narrow chink. It is not returned. "Sooo *big,* Jeronimo!" someone says from the bleachers, followed by a cackling laugh, a clap, and a cry of "Let's go!" Jerome smiles slightly, more of a grimace, but she thinks he was amused, and she knows that voice later, knows that the voice cheering him on was Clay's.

The next time I see Jerome, she thinks, she'll tell him that she dreamed about his serve, his hand open like a water lily, the ball suspended high above him, hovering, beyond gravity.

No, she won't tell him. It would sound weird. She'll just say his serve is awesome. Really awesome. And then she's awake, a box of pasta wheels on her chest, the light gluey and grainy, the wooden shelves dull and dark, the world when she parts the curtain lost in fog.

58

TED

At breakfast, Ted's mother wanted to know what Ted knew. What had Thisbe told her?

Nothing.

What had she seen on the Internet?

Nothing.

Why had she printed up all those flyers that said MISSING?

Ted didn't lift the flyer off the table, but she didn't answer yet, either. Her mother sounded upset but not angry. She held a pale blue coffee cup. She offered to make toast, and when the toast popped up, she spread butter on it and the butter melted. Normal things. The day outside was white and still, the lawn furniture glazed with dew. The sky was featureless, the air like a struck gong.

"There must be something," her mother said. "Something you know."

"There is."

"What?"

"That she couldn't do it."

Her mother didn't take a sip of her coffee. There wasn't any steam rising from the cup so maybe her mother had been sitting there not drinking it for a long time.

"She'd be too chicken," Ted said.

Her mother shook her head and looked like she was going to cry but didn't say anything.

"Mr. Harris's nephew saw her," Ted said. "The boy who was here yesterday."

Her mother nodded.

"He saw her on the bridge and she was standing there awhile. Long enough to make him go away. So she would have had to think about jumping."

"I know. Carl told me."

"So the high dive. Remember?"

Everyone in line for the high dive had had to wait and wait for Thisbe. She was ten. Ted had been jumping off the high dive all summer and she was only seven. On and on, Thisbe stood there, until pretty much the whole pool was watching. Ted was annoyed at first, then ashamed. "Just jump!" people said. "It won't hurt!" Thisbe was probably the only person in the history of the world to climb back down.

"Do you think it's the same?" her mother asked.

Hugh came into the kitchen all dressed up, as if for work, slippery-smooth white shirt, tie knotted. Ted braced herself for what he would say about the flyers.

"So you put these up around town?" he said.

"Yeah."

"Did you tell the police you were doing that?"

Ted shook her head. It wasn't a crime. It was a factual fact that Thisbe was missing.

"We're going to talk to the police right now."

Ted waited. She was required to pay attention when Hugh was talking, and to keep her eyes basically trained on him, but he couldn't make her smile.

"Don't post any more of these while we're gone."

Ted's mother would have finished that sentence with a question. It would have been, *Don't do this, okay?* Hugh never talked like that, though.

After they left, Ted tried watching TV but the laugh track was too weird. She caught the Greenbaugh kid watching her close the curtain. She ate two pickle spears and eight Rolos but what should have made her feel better made her feel worse. She had to go somewhere, learn something. She called Clay again. Again. Again. *The voice mailbox of the person you're calling is full or has not been set up.* She texted and got the red exclamation point: undelivered.

At noon, her parents weren't home. House screaming with emptiness, so she sent a message to her mom: **Going for a bike ride. I can't just sit here.**

Keep your phone on, her mother said back. That was it.

She saw people she knew, Camilla Waller with her freaky orange hair, and Mr. Peck, who always did race committee and bought about eight dinners from her when they were doing fund-raisers at the club, but she didn't stop, even though Camilla turned her bike around midblock and Mr. Peck held out his hand from the car and clearly expected her to come back. At Clay's metal-and-stone megahouse the entry gate was locked (of course) and the windows were like mirrors for trees, for the misty sky, for knowing nothing. She pushed the buzzer but no one came. The flyer was still in the mailbox.

The bay was choppy, a muddy, ugly, freezing abyss. She wanted to drain it like a tub, part it like the Red Sea, fly over it like a pelican that knew what to kill.

If only she could find Jerome and get his help. She checked the high school courts where she'd stood with Thisbe between the green mesh of the fence and the prickly hedge.

Today the high school courts were empty. Wind rolled an empty tennis ball can into a pile of leaves. Across town, the Glorietta courts were crowded with not-Jeromes. Old guys playing some sort of mini-tennis with plastic balls. Tiny kids hitting oversize balls into the gloomy white sky. Ted found a new green ball in the hedge and held it, squeezing it, rubbing the white seam, until she noticed that a high school–ish girl in a pink spandex dress was looking at her. Ted tossed the ball over the high fence, and the girl in the pink dress said, "Thanks," with a normal smile, but then she must have figured out who Ted was because when she leaned over to say something to the girl she was playing with, she definitely said, *Thisbe's sister.* They must have seen her flyers.

Before she could stop feeling strange, Jerome stood before her, his huge tennis bag like the shell of a hermit crab on his back.

"Hey," he said.

"Hey."

"What is going *on*." More like a demand than a question, and she was suddenly afraid.

She'd stuck a flyer in between the screen and door of his apartment but she hadn't knocked. For one thing, she barely knew him, and it was weird that she even knew where he lived. She couldn't explain that she'd seen him there once, opening the door with his tennis bag on his back, and remembered which door as if marking it with an X in her mind. She wanted to explain things to him now but her mouth screwed up in a funny way. She had to un-tense all her muscles and all that came out was, "Thisbe's missing." Which of course he'd already read on the flyer.

The popping sound of tennis balls and the squeak of shoes went on. Cars passed on the street. "I thought she jumped," Jerome said.

Ted heard something raw in his voice. She didn't know what it was. Intensity, anger, relief, pain. Something of hers went out to meet that feeling and she found it hard to talk. "She wouldn't jump. The police don't know her."

"So where is she?"

She normally didn't have trouble talking to anyone, but she didn't know how to answer him. She just stood there. Finally she said, "I don't know."

"Is there going to be a search or something?" he asked.

This was a good idea. She could do that. "Yeah," Ted said. "Later on. Would you come?"

"Yeah."

It got easier to talk now. "You have a dog, right? I saw him through the window."

"Her. It's a her."

"I thought she was going to, like, break the window and kill me."

"Nah. She's a softie."

"You could bring her to help." A silly idea, something you got from watching hounds in the woods on TV. Ted blushed. She normally never blushed.

"Where is it? The search thing."

She wanted it to seem planned out. People followed when you had a plan, but she didn't know yet. She had to stall. "I'll let you know, okay?"

She noticed he was thinking all kinds of things he didn't say. She could see doubt or resistance in the way he didn't look at her, in the way he clicked a tiny flashlight on the key in his hand, which flashed red and went out again. His hair was sweaty under his cap. She was glad he didn't ask her the questions a normal person would ask, because she didn't know the answers to anything, but she was afraid of him turning away from her. "Near the bridge," she said. "We're going to search near the bridge."

He looked down at her with his pale green eyes.

"I mean, where else?"

"Right," he said, and she felt balanced again, like when you saved a boat from flipping by leaning your whole body out.

59

FEN

Fen sat with his uncle in the backyard, moving the dice from Ted's Monopoly game around in his pocket. He dreaded what his uncle was going to say about the flyers, and the cloudy day made him feel worse. If you took a picture of his uncle's dead yard right now, you'd think it was a cold day in North Dakota.

"Grilled cheese?"

"No, thanks."

"Peanut butter?"

"I'm not hungry."

They sat facing the spiked fence of the navy base, the pink Victorian gazing ball, the dead tomato vines and their withered fruit. He hoped his uncle wouldn't ask him anything about Thisbe or Ted.

"So . . . the flyers," his uncle said.

"Yeah."

"I understand the impulse."

"I'm really, really sorry."

"No, it's okay." His uncle chewed, swallowed, scratched his

knee. They sat in the rusty chairs before the pink gazing ball. The two of them in its surface were shortened and obese. Overhead, a navy jet split the sky with sound.

"Do you think Ted is wrong?" Fen asked. He brought the dice out and rubbed them in one hand.

"Probably. But it's past experience with the situation that makes me say that. People don't believe you when you're still looking for the body. It's normal to hold out hope."

"Has anyone ever been right? Like they thought someone jumped, and they didn't?"

His uncle stared at the pink globe for a while. "I can't think of a time."

Alea iacta est, Fen thought bitterly, but he didn't say it aloud. It wasn't really whether the die was cast but whether you could see what you'd rolled. "Would you always die if you jumped?" Fen asked.

"Yes," his uncle said, then paused. He shook his head. "No. But the effects are always horrific."

Fen remembered lying facedown on the surface of the pool at the Isle of Capri. He breathed through the snorkel and studied the plaster through thick layers of chlorine; the slope, three feet to eight feet; the drain at the very bottom. The plaster was chipped and fragile in places, full of holes like popped blisters that hadn't healed. His head was underwater, and yet he breathed. "What should I do?" he asked his uncle. "I mean, with Ted?"

"You don't have to do anything to change her mind. It'll change if circumstances change."

He decided to ask the question that bothered him the second most. "Will they blame me?"

"No. They shouldn't, anyway. If they do, it's not because you did anything, but because people need someone to blame."

This didn't help at all. He blamed the people who could have stopped to call an ambulance for his father, and he blamed himself now.

"What should I have done?" he asked. That was the top question, the sharpest needle he used to poke himself.

"What you did."

His uncle clearly meant it, but Fen was unsatisfied.

"I've got to work this afternoon," Carl said.

"Okay."

"What are you going to do to keep busy?"

"I don't know. Watch TV."

"You brought your skateboard, right? You should go out. Here's money for the skate park. Or something to eat later."

"Thanks," Fen said.

After his uncle went inside to put on his uniform, Fen rolled the dice around in a cupped hand. He decided to throw them out into the garden. Just throw the stupid things away. Why had he come here? He would have been just as bad off in Brazil with his mother. He didn't know people in Brazil, either, but at least they would have all been foreigners saying stuff in Portuguese. He threw the dice hard at the grass, the way you would if you were skipping stones in water. They skipped, kind of, then were stuck somewhere in the tangled plants that had been vegetables once. He could hardly make himself stand up afterward.

60

FRANK

He's been waiting outside for half an hour because he thought the bank opened at 8:30, and then when they finally let him in, the nice teller isn't there. Frank only came into the bank once a month, on the day before his mooring fee was due, to buy a money order, and he timed that for the late afternoon, right before the bank closed. She was a Spanish girl, a lot friendlier than the other people who worked behind the counter, flashing her white teeth and asking if the fish were biting, if he wanted to open a savings account, if he needed anything else. She remembered, every time, that he used to be a commercial fisherman and that he lived on the water, which she seemed to regard as brave and interesting. El Capitán, she called him.

The only teller behind the counter is the skinny kid who drives a BMW, a tall guy with hair pushed up like mown grass, sipping coffee out of a tall paper cup. Black-framed glasses that look like part of a costume, and hands soft as a girl's.

The security guard is watching Frank from his stool beside the door.

"Good morning," Frank says to the guy with his hair pushed up. Jay, his name is, according to the sign on the counter.

"Good morning! What can I do for you, sir?"

"I've lost my wallet. My bank card. I need a new one."

"I'm sorry to hear that. Would it have been stolen?"

"Maybe. It could have been. I lost it in the park."

"Then we should check and make sure there's been no illicit activity. Let me—one sec. I'm just gonna ask the manager what all the steps are, okay? I'm new." The manager is a heavyset woman in an orange skirt and a long gold necklace. She gives Frank a glance and says some things he can't hear. A coffeepot ticks in the corner. He hasn't had breakfast or coffee.

Skinny boy comes back. "I'm Jay Thorne, by the way."

Frank nods. He can read.

"What we need to do is check activity on your account. Can you print and then sign your name here?"

Frank signs carefully, slowly, so as to make an exact replica of the last way he signed his name in a bank, which would have been five years ago, when his cousin Telma said it was time to sell their grandmother's house and retire, all of them.

The boy's shirt is so tight around his waist and chest that he looks like a Christmas package. When Frank hands him the card, Jay studies a screen Frank can't see while Jay pushes each of the knuckles on his right hand, then each of the knuckles on his left. Whatever's on the screen takes Jay a long while to read, and it doesn't change his expression. "Okay. Just one more sec. I see a Frank Le Stang here. Can you just confirm your address?"

"General delivery, Coronado."

"What?"

"General delivery, post office, Coronado. I move around. I live on my boat."

"But I need the address on the account."

"Maybe it's my cousin's address?"

"I don't know. The one you put down as permanent."

"Let's see. It's my cousin's. She mails me things that need to be mailed. Telma Cardozo, 314 Stimson Avenue, Pismo Beach."

As soon as he says it, the number sounds wrong. "Maybe it's 413. It's 413, I think."

"That's right," Jay says. "So that's where we should mail the new card?"

"Mail it? Can't you just give it to me?"

"No, sir. I don't think so. I'll check again if you want."

"I'm right here. I'd like to just take it with me. It's my money, isn't it?"

"I'll check with the manager. One sec."

The woman is reading something at a desk behind the counter, but she looks up as if she had expected this. They're tiresome interruptions to her, the boy with the toy glasses and Frank with his lost wallet. After a low conversation, Jay Thorne and the manager approach the counter with an air of defensive diplomacy. They expect him to be unhappy with whatever they're about to say, but they're going to pretend they're giving him excellent service, that they have his best interest at heart.

"Mr. Le Stang?" the woman says. "I'm Carol Ambrose, the manager. I'm so sorry for the inconvenience. We have to mail the cards as a security measure. We're required to verify your identity by the Patriot Act."

"But you just verified my identity."

"You could get cash today with a counter check. But to issue a new card, that takes two weeks."

"I don't understand. Where's the Spanish girl?"

"What Spanish girl?"

"The one with dark hair. Works in the afternoons."

"Elena?"

"That's her. She knows me. I come in every month. I always wait until her line is open."

"Elena is on maternity leave."

"She could tell you who I am."

"Even if Elena could come in, and she can't, that wouldn't be enough for the Patriot Act."

"This is not right."

"I know. It's frustrating. There's nothing I can do about it, however. Did you report the wallet stolen to the police department?"

"No. I dropped it, I think. I don't know that it's stolen."

"If you dropped it outside, you should assume it was stolen. Where did you say you dropped it? The beach?"

"The bay. Tidelands." Saying this makes his flesh warm. He's blushing. They'll think he's done wrong when it's just that he's aware people don't look kindly on canners, though they all say recycling is tip-top. Okay to sort your own trash but not to sort others'. Thoughts of Julia pass through his head so he looks down.

"Well, it could have been stolen just as quickly at Tidelands. I'm sorry for your trouble, Mr. Le Stang. Do you want to write the counter check now?"

He has to get money for the impeller and for whatever might go wrong along the way. Two weeks. "It's my money," he says. "All of it. I never should have given it to you people."

Others have come into the bank now, a middle-aged woman and an old man in a suit, and they give him disapproving looks. The guard is standing now instead of sitting near the door.

"I understand your frustration, but the card will come, and

meanwhile you can write a counter check and withdraw up to your limit, which is two hundred dollars."

"What if I need more than that?"

"Did you also lose credit cards?"

"I don't have any of those. It's a racket."

"I admire your stance. A lot of people don't have that kind of self-control."

"Maybe I should just take all my money out of here and put it in another bank. That's what I ought to do."

"You wouldn't be able to withdraw it all today."

"You people are robbers, you know that?"

The middle-aged woman and the natty man flinch. They exchange glances and little smiles. He knows what those glances mean. *Crazy old coot.*

"I have a lot of money in this bank," he says to the woman in line.

"I'm sure," she says, but she isn't. The security guard takes a step forward, but the manager holds up her hand to the guard as if to say, *Stay.*

"You should report the wallet as stolen," the manager says to Frank. "You know where the police station is? Just down the street a block? Not even a whole block."

"I just need what's mine. The card to get the money that's mine. All of it. I'm going to take it all out of here."

"You can do that through the proper channels if you want, but you'll need to wait for the clearance anyway."

"This is robbery," he says, and he walks out the door.

61

FEN

Six. Funny how he didn't even want a six this time.

He stared at the dots for a few seconds, picked up his skateboard, and opened the gate. *Okay. I'm leaving the house.*

In the yard across the street, two girls sat behind a folding table that held a pitcher of lemonade. They saw him standing on the step, so he had to wave. He started riding away, but they were looking at him, waiting for him, looking all disappointed because they had no customers. It was a long way to the skate park and he wanted to get there before, like, July.

But he had gotten a six. *Alea iacta est.* Gotta go with it.

He handed over a dollar to drink a small Dixie Cup of highly sweetened, possibly germy lemonade. "Mmm," he said. Beside the pitcher of lemonade and the jar that said *Pay Hear* was a paper plate holding the three smallest carrots he'd ever seen. Like peeled crayons, except that at the ends they became long threads.

"Did you grow those?"

"Yeah."

"How much?"

"Ten cents," the one with hair like a dandelion said.

"Each," her older sister added.

He set a dime down and ate one whole. "Yum," he said, though it was like eating old thread. The littler girl smiled her face off but the older one just nodded, like selling produce was a serious business.

There was a certain feeling, an antigravity state, that he liked to reach when he was riding his board a long way, when the rolling of the wheels and the slight bump and jiggle of the pavement began to flow through his legs and arms and the vibration of rolling onward became more normal than standing still. He felt that way after leaving the little girls. The air was cool on his skin like a layer of ice over metal, and it cleaned him, brightening the late afternoon oranges and greens, the rolling road underfoot, the whole earth moving away from him as he traveled.

The air thickened and chilled as he neared the water. Cyclists passed him often on either side of the bike path as he rolled toward the bridge: neon-bright racers in clumps, a kid on a tiny bike, staring all around and wobbling, his helmet like an eight ball, followed by a jogger who looked, for a jarring second, like Fen's dad. It wasn't him, though. Just some other man.

Before him, on water the color of lead, two tall sails coasted in silence, and he stopped to watch. The sun was finally coming out and things were starting to have a shimmer. As a kid he would have run ahead to see the rest of the bay and count all the boats with a tight happiness in his stomach that was like pain, it was so intense.

He didn't feel that happiness now and he didn't run, didn't even care if there were more boats, but he still felt a kind of rightness and calm. A chain-link fence separated the bike path from the rocks that led down to the water and the huge numbered pylons. The two sailboats slid in silence under the bridge, disappearing for a second behind the concrete legs, and he remembered, with a jolt, that Thisbe might or might not be in that water. He shouldn't have come over here at all. Stupid idea. He stepped back on the board and started rolling again. There was a line waiting to pay at the skate park, and he joined it, kept his eyes on the skaters going up and down the little concrete hills of the course, the helmeted heads and confident bodies, letting his mind go dumb in the clatter of wood and steel.

62

FRANK

His cousin Telma had shown him how to use her computer because he might want to use the free ones at the library. "You could shop for things or look up what other people are doing on their boats."

"Why would I care?"

"You can look up government agencies."

"Why would I do that?"

"Remember when your Social Security didn't come? Things like that. Or you could send me a message," Telma said.

"A message about what?"

She shrugged. "*Merry Christmas. Happy New Year. Hey, Telma, I'm coming for a visit!* Anything, Frank. And you can look up news or mooring prices or weather."

This was the cousin who had thought, when he'd tried to explain about Shiva and the reuniting of lost souls, that he'd become a Jew. "Sitting shiva?" she said. "You're sitting shiva for Julia now?"

She'd stuck by him more than the others, though. They

all got tired of hearing him talk about Julia, all of them. He'd heard Telma's daughter say, when she didn't think he was still in the house, that it was creepy how Uncle Frank said that if Julia came back, he would be the exact right age to be her grandfather, and he could raise her the way their dad and mom should have raised them both, and Telma said it was just a symptom of the poor man's grief. He knew even Telma hoped he wouldn't accept when she invited him to Thanksgiving or Christmas dinners. He was seated farther and farther from the brides at weddings.

He walks his bike past the police station. No bikes are allowed on the sidewalk, so you have to get off and walk. One block, that's all it is. A long block.

Once he's safely past the station and the giant banyan tree with its strange roots hanging down like hair, he sees that a small crowd is waiting on the walk in front of the library doors. Yet another impediment: the library isn't open yet. A few people, some of them as old as Frank, stand around by the door with bags in their hands. A young woman in tight clothes is rolling a stroller up and down the front walk while her child, sticky and blond, eats crackers. Frank can smell them: cheese crackers. It galls him again that he couldn't get the card. He needs something to eat now and that's how it'll be for ten days. Less and less money to buy things and more and more times that he's hungry. Will they even send the card now that he walked out of the bank? He's not going back. No way. He'll have to ask Telma to watch for the new one. She'll ask where the other card went and if he tells her he lost his wallet, she'll say he's too old to live on a boat anymore, he should live somewhere in town.

The cracker smell hangs in the air and the door stays shut and the people shuffle their bags from hand to hand, trying not to look at him, not saying good morning or anything at all to him, though they speak to each other, say, *How old is the child? Aren't those crackers good? Do you like to read with your mama? I bet you do!*

He parks his bike in a rack like all the signs say to do, and sits on a stone bench. Water drips from the rubber trees and gleams in the folds of pink and red roses. A crow eats the orange cracker crumbs the little boy in the stroller dropped on the sidewalk. All is green and lush and simple and cold. At last, a woman inside the library comes to unlock the door.

It's not easy to remember what Telma said to do. He can't remember how to send her a message, but he doesn't want to ask the librarian, who wears glasses attached to a little chain and looks very busy as she types types types. He'll go to the bathroom and wash his face again. The books on the library shelves wait in their plastic sleeves. His shoes make a shushing sound on the low carpet. People settle themselves into armchairs, begin to read. They don't look up. It's 10:15 a.m. and Julia has been alone on the boat for twelve hours. That isn't as long as the last time. That was two or three days. And this time he's given the girl food and water. Soup. A very nice tomato soup.

When he returns to the room full of computers, he still doesn't know what to do. The screen has so many pictures on it, tiny pictures labeled with words that don't make sense. Why is there a Safari?

He turns to the person next to him, a young man in black motorcycle boots and a jean jacket, but he's wearing headphones and watching some kind of film. Time ticks past. He has only one hour, according to the cardboard sign, and he's already used twenty minutes.

He has to ask. He walks to the librarian's desk and waits for her to help someone who wants a book she says is not on the shelf. The librarian's look when she returns to the desk is cold. She might be repulsed. He says, "I want to know how to get a bank card in one day."

She doesn't smile or say she can help. She acts as if he's come to the wrong building. "Did you try at one of the nearby banks?"

"I have my money in one of them. I need to get it out."

"Did you ask them?"

"Yes. I need to use that computer there to learn my rights."

She doesn't want to help him, he can tell. He was fine-featured and handsome once, five foot nine, a good shortstop for the Pismo Diggers, strong as anyone. He used to be able to sing, was a tenor in high school, though his voice isn't the same now. After the librarian tells him what to type into a box she made appear, somehow, on the screen, she goes quickly away, and he reads what's there but it isn't the right thing, it leads nowhere, and he doesn't know how to turn the page or make a new box appear.

He should go back to the boat, but he doesn't have the impeller yet. To get the impeller, he has to go to H & H, where he went last time he needed parts, but that was on Rosecrans, and he'd need to take a cab over the bridge or motor over there on the Ribcraft and tie up at the landing and walk. The Rib and the walk to H & H would take too long, and for all of these things, he needs money, which he can't get.

What might Julia be thinking now? Disappointed. It's just like last time.

You never change.

When his time on the computer is up, he goes to sit in one

of the carrels way in the corner, where no one will look at him with disgust, and after some time has passed he can have another turn and ask a different person how to find his rights and get a new card. The room is absolutely still except for the whiskery sound of turning pages. He sets a large book on his lap—pictures of England, it appears to be—and he opens it to the first page, but he feels so tired now, tired all over, and he lets his eyes close so he can get a minute's sleep.

63

JEROME

Camilla was already sitting at a table by the window when Jerome got to Panera at 6:10.

"Sorry," he said.

"It's okay. Want to order something?"

The line to pay for food was gargantuan. "Nah," he said.

"You can have half my sandwich, if you want."

He wasn't that hungry.

"I feel so terrible," Camilla said. "I couldn't sleep last night."

He didn't say, *Join the club.* He didn't want to say anything, but she looked so uncomfortable, rolling her bangles around her wrist, that he muttered, "I didn't know you guys were friends."

"We weren't." Her food came: a grilled sandwich with cheese spilling out from the cut edge.

Why do you care, then? is what he thought, but why did *he* care so much, given that he hadn't really gone out with Thisbe?

"Do you want half?" Camilla said.

He said no. She had a very nice smile, which he'd forgotten about, and pretty hands. The year before, when they'd done the

Spanish project, her hair had been coal black and she'd worn goth clothes and scowled all the time. Now she was wearing a tight ballet top under a military vest that was open so he could see lots of cleavage. He wondered if that was what made him think she was nice, but he hoped he wasn't that much of an animal.

"Did you get one of these?" she asked. She unfolded a paper that revealed itself to be a flyer. Thisbe smiled out of it.

"Yeah."

"So do you think it might have been, like, the party?" she asked.

He shrugged. "What do you mean, the party?"

"I mean why she'd go to the bridge? My mom says she probably jumped if she went up there."

He didn't want to have this conversation or these thoughts. "Her sister doesn't think she jumped."

"Yeah?" She seemed to think this was sad, not happy.

"Yeah," he said.

"You're best friends with Clay, right?"

How to answer this slowed him down even more. There was the truth, and he didn't know exactly what that was, and then there was what you should say to people who would repeat it to other people. "Used to be."

"You were there that night, right?"

He didn't see how he could lie about it.

"I thought I saw you. I don't normally hang out with those people, but I went because Nessa—you remember her, right?—heard Jason Elwood was going to go." She took a small bite of her sandwich, chewed, and swallowed. "You sure?" she said, pushing her plate toward him. "I'm never going to be able to finish it."

He took half of the sandwich and put it on a napkin, and while she talked, he ate.

She said the first weird thing had been Thisbe showing up at the party alone. She walked in solo and poured herself a drink, light on the margarita mix, heavy on the Don Julio, and stationed herself for a while in one of those mega-white chairs out on the deck, sipping way too fast, like someone with a goal.

Jerome had seen Thisbe, too. He stayed inside the kitchen so he wouldn't have to talk to her, but when people weren't in his way, he got glimpses of her downing the whole cup, getting really wasted like she said only idiots did. Clay was out there, too, off to the side, laughing with a whole group of people, and it looked like Thisbe was waiting to talk to him. Thisbe just stared and stared at Clay until Jerome felt sick. The two people who were sitting closest to Thisbe, Mandy Shue and Jake Grossman, talked only to each other, all snuggly-cozy, arms and legs intertwined, completely ignoring her, and then they left, so she was alone. Clay walked right past her to go into the house and Thisbe said, "Aren't you even going to talk to me?"

Clay just ignored her while everyone watched.

"I would definitely have gone home if I were her," Camilla said. "I mean, you know? Clay dissing her like that. I went to see where Nessa was, and, whaddaya know, she was sitting down on the rocks with Jason Elwood, so Nessa's night was going superwell. Thisbe's chair was empty when I came back and I thought, *Thank God. That's over.* I felt kind of guilty that I didn't figure out a way to talk to her but at least she wasn't embarrassing herself anymore. Honestly, she never talked to me once we started high school and I was in the normal classes and she was in AP all the time. Not that I care."

Jerome didn't say that he'd been sitting on the counter in the Mooreheads' kitchen when Thisbe made her drunken way to the door. She hadn't noticed him, as far as he could tell, so he hadn't gone after her to see if she had a car or a bike or was on foot. She wasn't there to see Jerome. That was obvious.

"So Nessa asked me to go with her to the bathroom, but we somehow wound up in the parents' giant bedroom," Camilla said, and Jerome could picture the wrong turn in the hall. The house was confusing and the walls in the upper hallway were dark green so it felt kind of foresty. At the far end of the hall, behind a closed (but not locked) door, was a giant bedroom where there was the most magnificent bed, so tricked out with embroidered cotton that Camilla said she had touched the edge of it to see if the thread count was a million or two million, and beside that room was a closet with a dozen glossy white cupboards, a room Jerome had been inside only once, when he was young enough to play hide-and-seek, and he had hidden in one of the white cupboards where Clay's mother's shirts hung in perfumed darkness.

Nessa wanted to get back to the rocks because she was afraid Jason would leave, so they left the master suite before Camilla could do anything stupid, like try on some of the epic shoes. When they got down to the bay, the tide was up a little more and Jason and four or five other people were standing around Thisbe. She was facedown—they said she'd slipped—and when Nessa used the light on her phone to check and see if Thisbe was awake or unconscious or what, blood was like red paint all over her forehead.

"It totally freaked me out. It was like a horror movie, I swear. Like, here's the ax-murdered person. So I'm like, 'Go get Clay. We have to call an ambulance.' And they're all like, 'If we call an ambulance, we're screwed,' and Nessa's like, 'What if she's in some sort of coma and she dies, asshole?'

"Viviana goes, 'I'm out of here,' which is just typical of her, and she ran off with two other people I didn't know, and I guess they told Clay what happened on their way out. I'm patting her on the face, going, 'Thisbe? Thisbe?' and Jason's like, 'Jesus. Can't she even drink right?'

"Then Nessa holds a tissue to Thisbe's head and it gets soaked, and I'm about to barf because I do not do well with blood, and we're trying to decide how to pick her up safely, you know, and more people come down to gawk at her, like, a whole bunch, and they're all saying what they think Clay ought to do, because Clay's suddenly standing there, and that's when somebody on the patio goes, 'The cops are here.' People above us start, like, running into glass doors, swearing, and Clay just stares at Thisbe from the edge of the rocks—he doesn't even go up close, like he would be contaminated—and he goes, 'Get her the fuck off my property.' "

The glass over the smeary painting of a light-blue-and-yellow piece of toast had splatters of something on it, and the crumbs all over the table made Jerome's skin feel dirty. He saw Thisbe again as she had looked that day walking across the quad in her white skirt.

"Wait a minute. Clay said that?"

"Exact quote."

"Then what?" he asked.

"I didn't want to move her just because Clay told us to get rid of her, right? But, what, we're going to leave her there? So Nessa asks Jason to help us, and I go get Nessa's car while they carry her, and they get her into the car without the cops seeing us because I parked behind one of those big construction bin thingies, and of course Thisbe barfed as soon as they stuck her in the backseat, facedown, like Nessa said we had to because her mom's a nurse and her mom's always freaked out about people choking on their vomit. It's practically the only thing her mom says when we go out the door on Friday nights: 'Don't choke on your own vomit, girls!' "

This would have been funny at another time, he imagined.

"Then Nessa's like, 'My purse! The cops will find my purse!' and Jason's like, 'We have to get out of here now.'

"We drove to Nessa's to see if her mother thought we needed to take Thisbe to the hospital, and Mrs. Creevy was mad as hell and said, 'Yes, absolutely, you need a doctor,' and Thisbe said, 'No, no, no, no, please don't make me, please don't, my stepdad will be so angry, please no,' and Mrs. Creevy said, 'She should at least go to urgent care because Thisbe might not have thrown up all the alcohol yet, and if she still had a lot of it in her stomach, it would keep getting into her bloodstream and, like, toxify her, and in addition to that, she probably should get a couple of stitches,' and Thisbe said, 'Please no, he'll be so mad and my mom will get in trouble,' and Mrs. Creevy was like, 'Why would your mom get in trouble?' and Thisbe said, 'That's just the way it is. I'll never do it again. I'm not drunk anymore. See? I'm not. I'm talking just fine.'

"She was sobbing but she was pretty sober, it seemed to me, and Nessa said, 'Maybe she can prove she's sober by helping clean the barf off my car!' Then Mrs. Creevy looked at all of us and said, 'I am never doing this for you again. Remember that, all of you,' and she called Thisbe's mom and asked if Thisbe could spend the night with Nessa because we were watching a movie and having such a good time. Thisbe's mom said yes."

"Wow."

"Yeah, I know. I said to Thisbe that everybody knows Clay's kind of a jerk and he treats girls like they're disposable or something, so she shouldn't care what he said about her, but she just said that made it even worse. I don't know."

Jerome looked out the window at a family walking by with their two little kids on leashes.

Camilla sounded like she was about to cry when she said, "I didn't know she would kill herself over it."

Jerome felt like he hadn't slept in a month. His stomach hurt. He didn't want to tell Camilla what he had said to Clay before he left the party, when Clay saw him crossing the lawn to the front gate and said, "Hey, bro, where're you going? We're just getting started."

"Home," Jerome said.

"Why? Are you mad about Thisbe still? I'm not seeing her anymore. Somebody said she went downstairs with some guy from Point Loma, though."

"I'm done, Clay."

"What do you mean, done?"

"With this. With being here."

"You mean with me?"

"Yeah. That, too."

"Because of Thisbe? I didn't know that you wanted to go out with her. You told me you didn't care."

"And then you asked who I would pick, remember?"

"Yeah," Clay said. "I remember." The party was loud, but not so loud that somebody couldn't overhear. Jerome was worried about running into Thisbe again, especially if she was cheesing with some cheesing Point Loma guy.

"I'm out of here," Jerome said.

"See you tomorrow, right? I'm going to drive over to Barnes for your match."

"Don't bother."

Clay didn't move while Jerome walked over to where he'd locked his bike, and Clay might have still been standing there behind the gate when Jerome rode by, but Jerome didn't turn his head.

"Why do you think this says that Thisbe is missing?" Camilla was asking him, holding up the flyer again.

"What?"

"I mean, other people said she jumped."

"Ted made it. She's the one who told me they were searching."

Jerome broke a potato chip in half and then crushed both halves with a fingertip. He rubbed the crumbs off but the oil stayed. He remembered when he had first started playing tournaments against kids who wanted to win as much as he did, or whose parents wanted them to win so much that the kids were scared witless, how hard it had been to referee themselves. No umpire, no ref, no parent could call the balls in and out. Just you and your enemy deciding what was fair. There was this one boy with white-blond hair and ears that stuck out on either side of his cap, just a pusher, but in those days, when Jerome was still playing in the under-tens, pushers beat Jerome all the time. They just kept lobbing the ball back over and over and over until Jerome couldn't stand it anymore and he smashed the ball hard, trying to end it all, but it usually went into the net or way over the baseline, which made his dad go, "Ah!" really loudly and cover his head with both hands. But that one kid, Benson

Hart, was a pusher and a poker. If Jerome called a ball out, he'd say, "Are you sure?" "Yes," Jerome would say, but the more times Benson asked, "Are you sure?" (and he asked every single time Jerome called an out ball out), the more unsure Jerome got, until finally Jerome was returning serves even when they were a foot out and his dad was practically wearing both hands on his cranium and his face was purple. Jerome lost to Benson Hart 4–6, 6–4, 0–6 in the finals and cried on the court.

Jerome rubbed the oil from the potato chip off his fingers. "I don't know," he said. "It looks one way from where you're standing, and totally different from the other side."

Camilla looked kind of confused, and he hadn't said anything about lines or learning to call balls in or out, so why wouldn't she be?

He said, "What they say in tennis is, *One percent on the line is one hundred percent in*. Meaning, if you think it might possibly be just a tiny bit in, you have to call it like that."

"That's cool, I guess," Camilla said, still confused.

"If there's still a chance that she's not dead, I mean, then you have to call it like that."

"Let me know if you hear anything," Camilla said, and he said he would. It was seven o'clock now and maybe Ted would have a plan. He would text her, and then he could do something with this awful feeling he had.

64

FRANK

"You can't sleep here, sir," a voice is saying.

He stares. It's not the same librarian, but she has a name tag on. The book is open to the same page and the man who was reading in the carrel way ahead of him is gone. A lady who's scanning the shelves across from him pretends she isn't listening but she's watching to see if the librarian will make him leave. Perhaps it was she who told the librarian an old man was sleeping in the chair instead of reading.

He closes the book and sets it on the desk before him. Then he stands up. The librarian crosses her hands nervously and waits to see if he'll go.

"I'm going," he says.

She doesn't say anything, just waits for him to walk in the direction of the exit, down the shiny hall. The light outside is different: it's late afternoon. Somehow he's been asleep for hours and hours. Can that be? It's as if he were drugged.

There's nothing to do about the impeller or his money now. He must go back to the boat and do without the motor, do without the card. He needs to hurry. So much time has passed. If he doesn't hurry, when he opens the hatch to the cabin, it will be like the other time, in Oceano. The girl's body so still. What did Shiva think when Frank sailed out from Oceano after dark, when he pushed the body off the deck, when the boat sailed away from it, when the ocean failed to swallow, then opened, then she was gone? So far away. Or when he and Ben Crames decided to have an ice cream while Julia was tied up in the pirate cave because there wasn't enough money to buy three. He and Ben would buy one scoop each and then go back to find Julia and never tell her about the cones.

So much time gone now.

65

CLAY

First Clay found the rolled-up flyer. Tossed onto the deck of his boat, evidently, where he stepped on it. One more proof that people thought this was his fault, but also good news. Maybe Thisbe was missing instead of dead.

He needed to check the stash. Maybe Thisbe had taken all thirteen bags. They could be hidden all over the island like land mines if her last act before disappearing had been to ride around dropping his stash in places the police could connect to him. Should he go by the house? He wasn't supposed to disturb the tenants but this was an emergency.

Once he'd unlocked the cabin door and opened the cupboard, he found the bags lined up, thank God. He flicked through them to count them, just to be sure, and a blue card slipped to the floor, one of those playing cards Thisbe had brought the night she surprised him and he should have told her to go back home. The letter *J* on one side of the card, a blue-and-white striped flag on the other. What that one meant he couldn't remember, though he remembered stuff about being on fire and going down in flames. *Pilot me* and stuff. The thing was, he really did like her. She was not much like the girls that he normally went out with. The *facilones*. She was the opposite. More like a *difficult-oh-nay*.

He needed a plan, though, so he made one, and then he started going through it, step by step.

Wait until dark. *Check*.

Drop by Mark's and snag one of his mom's Tupperware things. *Check*.

Transfer all baggies into Tupperware. *Check*.

Borrow the half shovel from the junior toolshed. *Check*.

Skateboard to golf course, where he received a message from Isabel Knapp, who said she could meet him wherever. **11th green**, he said. **30 minutes**.

Cross seventh green to Stingray Point. *Check*.

Stash shovel on sand beyond the green. *Check*.

He had plenty of time, so he took care to count his paces on the golf course from the seventeenth tee to the weird rubbery plants that grew at the edge of the grass, where the golf course stopped and Stingray beach began. *Check*.

Bury Tupperware really deep. *Check*.

Heave half shovel into bay. *Check*.

Cross golf course to eleventh green without being seen. *Check*.

And there was Isabel, sitting on the bunker beside the twelfth fairway, listening to her iPod, water bottle in hand. When his movement caught her eye, she pulled out her earphones.

"Clay?" she called through the damp evening air, and he felt the usual flicker of anticipation when things were fresh and new with someone, when only the good parts were happening, so it was no trouble at all to sound cheerful when he called out, "Check!"

66

GRETCHEN

Mandy called from Clayton's at seven o'clock to say they were slammed. Could Gretchen come in? Gretchen had been on the island all day, seeing the lawyer about her mother's estate; getting her teeth cleaned; buying bird food, milk, a new can opener; going from place to place like a zombie in the wintry air. She didn't want to go back to town again. Change into her uniform, row to shore, unlock her bike, ride to work, smile at people.

"Please?" Mandy said. "I think every enlisted man on the island is here."

"Is that supposed to entice me?"

It did, sort of. They were good tippers. While she was thinking it over, she noticed the *Sayonara* was back. The white cat was pacing around on its deck when Gretchen rowed to the *Broker,* but she didn't see Frank's dinghy. In town, apparently.

"Lady Loch," Peek crooned. With all the treats she'd been giving them, Peek and Roll had sort of learned their new chant.

"I know," she said. "Dinner."

Feed the birds, get dressed. There was a small stain by the hem of her uniform. Ketchup or salsa. She should wash the stupid dress after every shift but laundry was the royalest of royal pains on a boat. Her only other uniform was balled up in the laundry bag, so she worked the stain with a drop of water from the galley sink and a fingernail that needed all kinds of reclamation that she didn't have time for.

"Lady Loch," Peek crooned again.

Roll climbed nervously up the bars of his cage because he knew this was the way Gretchen looked when she was leaving.

"It's okay," she said. "Let's get you some water." Water being the other royalest of royal pains because she had to haul it from town in the dinghy, over the mudflats, which was crazy-hard work at low tide, so Gretchen tried to drink very little on board the boat. It was unhealthy. She needed to pee now but could maybe wait till she got to work. Or use the park bathroom. Which was gross.

Gretchen twisted her frizzed hair into the requisite ponytail, leaned close to the mirror, in which she could hardly see now that she needed glasses (which you couldn't wear when applying eye makeup, so how was that supposed to work?), and drew lines on the rim of each eye that she would have to remember to check once she got somewhere with better light.

"You look like an actress," Thisbe had said once, a long time ago, when Thisbe was little and lived next door.

"Ha ha. That's what I am," Gretchen had said.

"Peekaboo," Peek said.

"Roll again," Roll said, and the two of them kept repeating their old words mournfully as Gretchen stuck the water cups into their cages and climbed down into the dinghy and rowed past the wretched *Sayonara*. She hoped she wouldn't run into Frank when she was locking her dinghy to the stay cable.

The sun had finally broken through, and the green slime of the mudflats lay like turf before her. Only trash marred the beautiful sheen of it: plastic bags, water bottles, broken lids, the eroded corner of a Styrofoam cooler. When Gretchen had time, she picked up as much trash as she could hold in two hands and threw it away so she wouldn't have to look at the mess the next time the bay drained itself.

A shiny pink thing lay half-buried in the mud, rubber or plastic like the edge of a tube, but as she approached, the tube resolved itself into a boot. God, people were lazy and careless. How hard was it to keep track of your boots? If she tried to pick that thing up, it would get mud on her dress, so she'd get it next time. She dragged her dinghy to the stay cable, flipped the boat over on the dry grass, and turned the combination lock. The light glazing the flats was so bright that it burned stripes into her corneas. From a distance, the abandoned boot looked like driftwood, a natural lump in the finely rippled skin of the beach.

She was far away, looking left for an opening in the traffic to cross Third Street, when Roll Again pushed open the door of his cage.

67

FEN

The skate park was the right thing, actually. He got into a groove after a while, forgot everything. It was better than snorkeling because you had to pay attention or you'd wreck yourself.

But when he stood by the bay again, it came back. The bridge, Thisbe, his failure, Ted. The tide had gone out and the sun had come out and the water was a freakishly pretty shade of blue. It enticed you. It said everything was fine, perfect, living, and good. He walked out on the sand where he was pretty sure he'd written his name with a stick that time with his mom, the whole thing, not just *Fen*. It had seemed like a big beach then, but it wasn't. It was kind of gross, too, how the sand bled into mud, and the rippled mud was covered in what looked like green fur. People were disgustingly lazy, that was clear. Plastic bags and stuff. A cup here, a can there. Pathetic. The more he looked, the more trash he could see, including what looked like somebody's boot.

Fen stopped walking. He could see the boot's color, and it was pink. It could be a coincidence. The wrong size. From a distance, it looked small. If he went out there and it was maybe the right size, he should call his uncle. Or Ted. No, his uncle. Because maybe it was evidence that she was dead. This led to the much more terrible fear that it wasn't just a boot but a body. Nausea bloomed. He couldn't see anything like that, though, nowhere, not in the water, not on the green fur pelt, and he needed to man up. He took his shoes off so he wouldn't slime them and he left his skateboard balanced on the shoes so sand wouldn't get in the trucks, and he walked out a little farther until he was standing right over the empty boot. It was pink. It was not a child's. He would call his uncle now.

68

GRAYCIE

A very skinny man was sitting on her aunt's sofa. Africa-skinny. Fortyish or more, wearing a white dress shirt that was too large in the neck. New member of the Hand of the Living God, no doubt, via the Hand of the Living Estelle. Graycie had no problem with charity but it would have been more relaxing to just sit at Estelle's table by herself and eat dinner rolls and feed Genna mashed lima bean soup until it was time to get ready for her shift.

"This is Awate," Estelle said, holding Genna on her hip. "Awate, this is my niece that works for the California Highway Patrol. Tell him what happened on the bridge, Graycie. Tell Awate so he can pray for that girl's family!"

Graycie didn't want to tell him anything. She should never have told her mother about the incident, but on the phone her mother had said she'd seen a flyer for a girl who went missing on the bridge, and Graycie had just blurted it out: "We called that in. It happened on my shift." Naturally, after Graycie told her mother, her mother told Estelle.

Graycie tried not to look at Awate. Maybe he wouldn't show an interest and they could move on to other topics.

"I drive the taxi," Awate said. "I am all eyes."

Whatever that meant.

Estelle called from the kitchen, "Tell him, Graycie! He drives that bridge all the time. He knows how high it is."

"Would you like something to drink, Mr. Awate?" Graycie asked.

He pointed to a full glass and an empty plate.

"That steep hill has parched me out," Graycie said. "I'll be right back."

Graycie took time to cut a lemon wedge and squeeze it into her glass of iced tea, throw in some sugar, sneak a roll from the basket draped with a red napkin, admire the hummingbird feeder (*Mm-hmm! Look at that, baby!*) that Estelle was showing Genna on the back patio, but Mr. Awate was all eyes, as he said, when Graycie returned to the dark living room.

"You are saying," he prompted. "The highways."

She didn't go all into it, just said it was a bridge incident, car parked up there, harbor patrol called to search the water, nobody found anything. A girl's ID in the car. "We would have seen more if the cameras had all been working," she said.

Awate had very good posture on the couch. A formal way of sitting, with both of his elegant knees together instead of slouched out, his hands with their long, slender fingers resting on his knees, statuelike, but he now brought his fingers together and blinked.

"You are saying a she," he said.

"A what?"

"A she."

"Uh-huh. They found a driver's license in the car. That's how they knew."

"You are saying a white car?"

"It looked white on the camera. It's not that clear, the colors, leastways."

"Long-hair girl?" He drew a line below his collarbone, and she shrugged.

"I think," she said.

"But cameras, they are showing?"

"Well, they have 'em, but they weren't all working."

"This, it happens Sunday?"

"Yeah. Sunday night, Monday morning."

"I am picking up this girl."

"Pardon?"

"I am picking up this girl on the night."

"You picked up a girl on the bridge?"

"I do."

"And did what?"

"She say, *I am not having money. Leave me here.* So I am."

Aunt Estelle was standing in the doorway between the living room and the kitchen when he said this, and Genna was opening and closing her small hand, the light from the street muted by the drapes that shielded Aunt Estelle's red velvet sofa from the rotting of the sun.

"You're positive," Graycie said. If the man wasn't crazy and what he said was true, it was very, very good news.

He looked startled and offended. "No," the man said. "I am *not* having AIDS."

Was he dense? Like, really, really dense? It took her a second to see how he'd gotten from the word *positive* to *AIDS*. Graycie said, "All I mean is, you for sure picked up a girl Sunday night on the Coronado Bridge."

The man nodded, so she got his phone number, writing it down on a notepad with a not-very-sharp pencil. She needed to call it in for sure.

"I need to go," she said to Aunt Estelle.

"Not before you eat," Estelle said. "Not before this little one has her lima beans, right, sugar? Not before you and Mr. Awate and this little angel have eaten my famous succotash."

69

FEN

Fen stood by the half-buried boot and felt ice-cold. "Should I tell Ted?" he asked his uncle on the phone.

Carl said, "No."

"Does it mean she's dead?"

His uncle didn't answer.

Fen didn't want to talk anymore.

"I'll send someone out there to get it," Carl said. "Are you okay?"

He said he was, but he didn't feel okay.

"Wait there until I come or somebody else comes. I think it will be a woman named Elaine Lord. She's very nice. Just wait nearby, okay?"

He said he would, but he didn't want to. He walked back to where his shoes were and stared at his skateboard.

"It's important that you stay because if the tide comes back in, the boot might get covered back up and washed away," Carl said.

"Okay," he said. That was different than waiting for someone to babysit him, so he did it. He took his skateboard and his shoes to a bench and waited for his feet to dry, the boot stuck in his mind the way it stuck in the mud, half in, half out.

70

R. P. SKELLY

The number Skelly called for Awate Mebrahtu went to a voice mailbox that had not been set up yet.

"Nothing?" Elaine asked.

"Nothing."

He called Graycie back to see if he'd written the number down wrong.

Graycie had the same numbers.

"Can you ask him again?"

"He went home."

"Home where?"

Graycie was silent.

"You didn't get his address?"

Hold on while she asked her aunt Estelle.

Aunt Estelle wasn't sure, but she would call the pastor and ask if he knew.

The pastor, it turned out, was not home.

71

THISBE

For a long time she was obsessed with shells. Broken, chipped, jagged, smooth. All the broken bits mattered. Then she got choosy and brought home only sand dollars that had survived everything.

"They're just skeletons," her cousin Neil had said when he came to visit. "You're picking up bones! It's gross."

"They are not!" she said, because she actually thought they were seeds, like pinecones or maple keys or acorns. She went on looking for telltale circles in the wet sand where a wave had just come and left a long puddle, sucking things back into itself. Nine out of ten sand dollars were crushed in some way. All the joggers, walkers, and Navy SEALs running in boots, the lifeguards' Subarus, stupid Neil dragging his stupid boogie board, Ted playing smash ball with their mother—they shattered them underfoot without even looking. She developed a magic sense that told her when she was going to reach down and find the saucer whole. It gave her a shiver, the premonition.

Her mom would bring tissues and wrap the dollars like they

were teeth that had fallen out at school. *Don't hold them too hard,* she would say. *I won't,* Thisbe would say.

Sometimes they were little like dimes, and those were her favorites.

"Lady Locke," a bird is screaming. Her name. It's screaming her name.

Through the grimy porthole, the ocean is gold and promising, but she can't get there.

"I'm in here!" she says to the bird, but her voice is like a hiss now, so she kicks at the door.

The next time she hears the sound, it's farther away, and she sees a gull swoop over the water. Just a gull, like all the others.

72

FRANK

The flyer isn't unexpected. It all took too long. If he hadn't dropped the wallet, if the impeller hadn't broken, if he hadn't been such a screwup from the beginning.

The flyer on the pole by the library says: MISSING: THISBE LOCKE. LAST SEEN BESIDE A WHITE HONDA ON THE WESTBOUND CORONADO BRIDGE.

Not *under,* but *on*.

There's another one by Spreckels Park.

He needs to hurry, hurry, hurry. He rides toward his camp in the acacias, and he sees three more flyers before he gets there, Julia's face looking out at him from poles and trees, smiling and young, still trusting him, though she shouldn't have, she shouldn't have. He fell asleep and stayed away too long. He will lose her again.

73

THISBE

It's the dirtiest, oldest, funkiest set of signal flags she's ever seen. The kind all connected for running to the top of the mast and down again, flapping on holidays in the summer sun. It almost makes her laugh. It makes her want to say, *HUGH! YOU WERE SO RIGHT!*

Other people know the distress signals, more than just her and Ted and her stepdad know them, right? People learned them, didn't they? *I am on fire and have dangerous cargo.* This is a code, people!

She feels the metal edge of the porthole again but still can't find the handle to unlock it. Either it's not the kind of porthole that opens, or it's grimed shut. If she smashed it, someone could hear her better. She could hear if the bird is still calling her Lady Locke.

A can opener doesn't work. Too small. Likewise the cutting board, which slips out of her hands when it thunks the glass. But she can get enough velocity with a three-legged chair. The glass cracks and she swings the chair again with all her strength. It crackles and some glass falls out. She uses the can opener to push the pebbled glass out onto the deck, and she touches air. Cold air like fresh watermelon. Sounds are louder now: the clear ring of metal against the mast as the boat rocks. She sets the whole slippery pile of flags on the shelf and pushes one out the gap of the broken porthole. There's a deep wrinkle in the nylon that makes the flag fold in half and flip up all crooked, and this fills her with despair.

She remembers how she said to Hugh, "What's the point of a distress signal that tells people to *stay far away* from you?"

Something moves on the deck—is it Frank?—and she retracts her hand. It's the cat, though, just the cat. It draws closer and sniffs. It paws at the flapping signal flag, plays with the curl of it in the window. She tells the cat with her mind to go away and fall into the sea. It pauses, pats the bent tongue of the flag, sits like a figurine, licks a paw, stares at the universe.

In time, the cat pulls itself forward, stretches out like a rug and falls asleep. Above the cabin the wind makes a tinging, pinging sound like a child playing the triangle in a school play. She can't shout, so she goes to the galley and gets a can of Mrs. Dowder's Major Chowders and throws it over and over again at the locked door.

The next sound she hears is the scream of the cat. A green bird swoops toward the deck, wings spread out over the cat's head, and then rises at the last second to miss the cat's swipe. The cat crouches and stalks out of sight. Now the tinging, pinging sound is punctuated by the rusty hectoring of the bird.

74

FINDS

"So, like, I thought we would look around here," Ted says to Jerome.

Jerome waits with the dog called Maddy, the one he calls a softie, though the dog is sharp-eared and Nazi-ish. The three of them are blocking the bike path and Ted has to scoot over while Jerome is showing her what a softie Maddy is by stroking and patting the dog's head. It being a summer evening, plenty of runners are chugging themselves along, and bikers in neon shirts are going *zip zip zip*. Ted picked the bike path to begin the search because she thought, *Okay, if you didn't jump, where would you go? You would walk. Would you walk to the city or the island? The city is gnarly. Gangs and all. Homeless. If you were a lone girl, you'd walk to the island, and if you were Thisbe freaking out, you might go to the troll house.*

This is what she has to tell Jerome now while making it seem intelligent. Which is hard because he seemed to think there would be a whole lot of people doing the search, and the police would be in charge.

"The troll house?" he asks.

She points. He stares at the weird little shingled shack on the side of the fence where you're not supposed to go. Built for the bridge workers, maybe, back when there used to be a toll. There's a tall, tall chimney thing all covered with shingles, and the house/shack is covered with shingles, all homeylike, and there's one window and one door. "Thisbe had a whole story about it. When we were younger."

Jerome doesn't speak. He's probably thinking she's nuts.

"It was just stories she made up about trolls who live under the bridge."

Jerome says, "Won't people wonder what we're doing over there?"

He has a point. They both face the chain-link fence that divides the paved trail from a long gutter and a hillside with trees and bushes and dead leaves and stuff. The foresty part leads to the troll house.

"Oh, well," Jerome says, and even though he seems worried about breaking the law, he starts walking to the place where you can go around the little chain-link fence if you totally ignore the NO TRESPASSING sign. Ted's glad Maddy is one of those scary Nazi dogs, even if she's a softie at heart, because if they go into that underbrush or perchance yank open the troll door, whatever might be living there will have to face the dog first.

Superlarge amount of brush around. Huge, thickety mounds that are more like overgrown bushes than trees. Her heart is thudding like when a horror movie is getting bad and she has to turn the sound off.

No music to turn off here, though: just *crackle crackle snap snap*. She walks directly behind Jerome's large, comforting back. The dog's tail nub and pointy ear tips float in the golden air. The extendo-leash creaks as Maddy gets farther ahead, goes sniffing up the bank.

Should she call out? Should she say, *Thisbe?* like she's calling for a lost pet?

Maddy sniffs herself into a thicket-place that's like a cave of dead vines and branchy stuff and might be where a homeless man makes his poos. You can't see Maddy anymore, just the leash line. If Maddy weren't a Nazi dog, Ted would be afraid for her.

The thicket-place explodes with barking, followed by the strangled voice of a man shouting, "NO!" Scared look on Jerome's face as he jerks on the extendo-leash to reel Maddy back like a fish from the thicket-place and whoever's in there. Passersby on the bike path are definitely staring. They definitely are. Best to act like you belong in the no-trespassing zone.

A man pops out of the brush, holding his wrist, where there are definite bite holes, bright red and bruisy blue. "I'm so sorry," Jerome says, his face blotching red. "She doesn't normally bite, I swear. She never has."

"I'm fine."

The man has a blue spot on his lip. White hair in a circle around an elfy bald head. Dirty clothes, so maybe homeless. A gazillion dark brown wrinkles from a gazillion hours in the sun. But what's he doing here?

"Do you want to go to the hospital?" Jerome is asking him.

People on the path slow down as they see what's happening. They don't stop completely but they almost stop. They listen and stare.

The man says no, he has a first aid kit. He talks like he's in a hurry to go.

Ted waits to see if he goes back into the thicket. Does he live in there? Do homeless guys have Band-Aids?

"It's on my boat," the man says.

So he's a rich guy? "Oh," Jerome says.

"I'm fine," the man says again, though red blood is dripping from one of the bite holes. He wipes it on his not-clean pants.

"You guys okay?" a runner on the other side of the fence is asking, a middle-aged guy like Hugh, bald and sporty, his shirt dark from a good sweat. "You need anything?"

"No," the wrinkled elf-man says. "I'm fine, sir. It's fine."

Instead of going back into the thicket, the elf-man turns toward the bay, and along the gutter that Ted and Jerome followed, he begins to walk really fast with his dog-bite arm not bent in any special protective way, just hanging down almost normal, and it's kind of like how Ted pretends sometimes when she's sailing that she isn't hurt when she is—and it's weird—it really is—how he isn't mad at them for the dog bite.

75

SKELLY

After Elaine left to go get the boot Carl's nephew had found, the front desk called Skelly to say a cabdriver wanted to talk to him about a girl he'd picked up on the bridge. African guy, he said he was.

The very same.

Awate Mebrahtu has no receipts to prove he picked someone up right after he supposedly saw the girl. No subsequent fare until one a.m., he says, at McP's. He has a name that no one is going to spell right, ever, and which will mark him as a foreigner. Skelly is amazed that the guy has come into the office at all, that he is sitting in Skelly's presence to talk about a missing white girl.

In what seemed a previous life, on this man's home continent, R. P. Skelly had been Elder Skelly, aged nineteen. Elder Skelly had been the Jesus Man inside homes, on streets, and in cafés, where all the skin was walnut brown like Awate's and Skelly was a pale giant from America.

"You saw this girl?" Skelly asks. "Where did you find her, exactly?"

"On this bridge."

"Like, the middle or the end or what?"

"Middle."

"Was she wearing boots? Pink ones?"

He nods. So the boots were right, anyway.

"And where did you take her?"

"It is the football field."

Skelly holds out a map. "Here?" he asks, pointing to the high school stadium.

The man studies the illustrated map of the island, the red roof of the Hotel Del, the blue grid of streets, the green circles and yellow squares. He turns it clockwise a quarter turn. He points to a green blob shaped like a kidney bean, the outer edge of Tidelands Park.

That kind of football. "Then what?"

"Do I sit and have a smoke."

"You do or you did?"

Nodding.

"So right there"—Skelly points to Glorietta, the street that curved away from the bridge and around the green blob—"you stopped?"

"No." Awate touches the map again: a circle near the blue edge of the cartoon bay.

"You were sitting here, like, on a bench?"

"No bench. The front skirt of taxi."

"Inside or outside."

"Outside."

"The hood. Then what?"

"The girl is walking."

Skelly nods.

"Along this path," Awate says. "Under this bridge."

"Then what?"

"Nothing."

"Did you see where she went?"

"Under this bridge."

"Did you see anyone else?"

"Yes. The Boat Man." Not *boat*mun. He says it like two words, not one.

"Who's the Boat Man?"

"He live in the water. I see him two times also before. Coming shore, going out." Awate holds up both elegant hands and mimes rowing.

"Was the Boat Man rowing when you saw him?"

"No, he is walking. He is walking the same path."

"What's his boat look like?"

Awate shrugs and shakes his head.

"What about the guy?"

"Guy?"

"The Boat Man."

"He is a white."

"Big? Tall? Short? Beard? Bald?" Skelly points to his own thinning hair.

"He is old."

"Then what?"

"I finish my smoke, I drive."

"Did you see the man talk to her or anything?"

"No."

Skelly writes that down. The earth was full of holes that opened up and swallowed things. The hole was there and you could find it, or the hole closed over, smooth as water.

"Thank you, Mr. Mebrahtu," Skelly says, unable to feel much hope. A Boat Man by definition had a boat. Boats sailed away. South to Mexico, north to anywhere, surrounded by the erasing, swallowing sea.

"There is one thing," Awate says.

"What's that?"

"It is not on her feet then, the boots."

"When?"

"She is walking, she is holding boots. Like this." He holds his hands out to the sides as if in each one he has a boot.

"So she's barefoot."

"No. She is socks."

"That's weird."

Awate stares at him like he doesn't know the word or everything is equally weird.

"It's good, though." So the boot Carl's kid had found didn't mean a body hitting the water from the bridge, clothes ripping off, boots torn away and floating—which didn't make sense, anyway—all the way to shore.

He walks Awate to the door and shakes his hand, and for a second Skelly remembers the Nigerian sky, foreign and yet benign because in that time and place Skelly had been absolutely sure of goodness watched over by a fatherly God. Then the glass door of the police station closes and he can see nothing but his own reflection.

76

JEROME

"That was psycho," Ted says.

Jerome nods. He's still feeling rubbery. He thought that old homeless guy would want to sue him for sure, but first they'd have to go to the hospital and the man would get tested for rabies and need stitches and who knew what else that would cost a fortune. Jerome's mom would freak. Then maybe Maddy would have to be put down even though she wasn't vicious at all. It was Jerome's fault. Totally his fault. He lets the extendo-leash reel out a little and Maddy picks up a stick and stops mournfully in front of him. "I know," he says, and she looks sadder.

"What do you think he was doing in there?" Ted asks.

"Something weird," Jerome says. He should go back in the bushy cave-place and look around, he thinks, but it might be a toilet, just a disgusting place with tissue left all around. "Hold the leash," he says.

He makes himself stick his head in and sees a sleeping bag unrolled. Jars and cans, various types. A bag of what looks like trash. Just a camp for some homeless guy. At the far edge of the circle, where the branches touch down, he sees a white piece of paper. Small like a card. Probably nothing, but maybe not. He steps over the sleeping bag and picks up a business card that says *SEER: Reuniting Souls in Transit.* That's a weird one. He decides he has to pick up the sleeping bag and look underneath, though he's pretty sure the sleeping bag is going to smell, and he doesn't want to touch it. Maddy is sniffing and whining. He can't see well in the shade but he picks up the sleeping bag and drags it out of the bushes. He bends over and looks at the mashed grass and dirt underneath. There is something wrinkled and crushed: a piece of newspaper. Edges torn, not cut. He picks it up and thrashes out of the branches, Maddy pulling hard at the leash and poking his thigh to be petted, and then he sees. A part of the local paper, the *Eagle,* its colors and type font familiar. What has been torn out is a photo of a girl, and the girl is Thisbe. LOCAL GIRL SUBMITS SCHOOL PROJECT TO OCEAN FOUNDATION, it says. Thisbe grins in the photograph and holds up a clear glass jar. Something floats in the jar, but he doesn't know what it is.

Maddy breathes her hot tuna-can breath and Ted comes up to see, her face worried.

"It was under the sleeping bag," he tells her. "I think we should tell the police."

77

FRANK

Frank sees it as he pulls the dinghy across the mud. The boot is uncovered. It will be uncovered every day at low tide. Lying there for anyone to see.

He should pick it up. Who would question digging trash out of the mudflats? But he has a sense of misgiving. He gets into the dinghy and begins to row, and when he turns to look at the beach, a boy is standing there with his skateboard, looking out at the bay. The boy looks directly at Frank, as if he's watching him to see where he goes.

Frank's wrist throbs, and he still doesn't have the impeller. The wind is light. What if Julia is dead? The dog was a sign of something. Something bad.

He stops rowing to press on the bite mark.

What if the boy is still watching?

He is.

He should go back and get the boot. He could pull it out of the mud like a tooth.

He's passing the mint-green sloop with the fake owl on its

stern and the light is fading, the water rising, *"All the water will rise and cover us,"* that's what the Seer said. It's not just the boy with the skateboard watching him. Under the bridge he sees two people not moving, just waiting there close together, and beside them is the hulking shape of the same dog.

78

THISBE

The ivory cat hears her hitting the door with the heavy can. The sound is nothing, does nothing, brings nothing. Perhaps the parrot? But what can a parrot do! She kicks the door. She screams the raspy, hopeless scream.

The cat is the only thing listening, and perhaps the parrot is no longer teasing it, because the cat resumes patting the flipped-up flag that is telling people the wrong message: *stay far away from me, I might explode.*

79

TED

Jerome holds the news article so Ted can see the photo of Thisbe. He hands her the business card that says *SEER: Reuniting Souls in Transit.* The dog looks at them with brown eyes and brown face smoothed and shaped by little black hairs. She has a noble bearing.

Ted dials and then tells everything fast to the guy who answers at the police department: the nervous man, the newspaper picture of Thisbe in his camp, the path that says NO TRESPASSING. Ted doesn't care now who sees them on the wrong side of the fence. She wants to see where the weird man went. "Can you tell Elaine?" she asks the police person. "And the giant man?" He says he will, but she isn't sure it will happen fast enough. Nothing happens fast enough.

"Wait," Jerome says when they're almost out of the bridge's shadow, and he pulls her back before she can run.

The man Maddy bit is a shadow. The sun's down now but everything is still half-yellow, half-black. Ridges in the green mud look like furrows seen from an airplane. Bits of trash spoil the effect here and there. The man is out of his boat, standing on the mud, his hair a black halo.

"What's he doing?" Jerome whispers, as if the man might hear them. He's about fifty yards away. He holds his arm like it hurts.

A voice yells, "No! Don't pick that up!" The voice comes from a boy on the sidewalk, some skater, but the man looks in the wrong direction, under the bridge. Ted feels the man see her and Jerome. The man stands perfectly still, like that might make his physical self and Ted's physical self evaporate. The man stares for one more second, maybe two, then rolls the wheels up on the boat and climbs in. The water rises around the boat. The sky in its yellow-orange glowing is like a half-dead fire.

Should they stop him?

She wants to stop him.

"Wait," Jerome says. "Watch him."

Watch him row? Watch him leave? Jerome holds his hand on her arm or she'd run, and she's not sure what to do. When the man can't be seen because of the darkness and other boats, Jerome's grip on her arm loosens and they walk with Maddy until they reach the beached dinghies and the skater who told the guy to stop. "Ted?" he says. It's Fen, and he looks really freaked out.

"Why did you tell him no?" Ted says.

He doesn't answer her.

"That was great," she says, but he doesn't look glad to hear it.

"We need to go after him," she says. She still doesn't hear any sirens or see any twirly lights. Everything is taking way, way too long.

She finds a boat that isn't locked. Not a nice one but it will do. "Help me," she says to Fen and Jerome.

Jerome says they should wait for the police and Fen just stands with his hands in his pockets. Far off, the sound of sirens.

She shoves the boat to the mud and is glad to see the tide has come in so much. She won't have far to go before she reaches the water. Hands are helping her and the dog is barking. "What are you doing?" Fen asks.

"You come with me," she says to Fen. "But can you stay, Jerome? To tell the police what happened?"

What a slow boat this is. If she had her paddleboard, she'd be better off. She has to row harder or the man will disappear. That's her sense of it: he is going.

The sirens are louder. They might be coming this way.

80

THISBE

When she hears footsteps on the deck, she curls up to hide.

If you close your eyes, others can still see you, Thisbe. Her mother said that to her gently, so long ago, she doesn't remember why, only that she was under the coffee table and it was the middle of a school day. Something had happened at school, something mean.

She doesn't close her eyes. She watches the hatch, but it doesn't open. She hears thuds and the rake of metal, maybe the sound of a chain.

I am the devil of reality,

Seen for a moment standing in the door.

The sound is the anchor coming up, the links of the chain coiling. He's trying to take her away, and there's nothing she can do.

81

FRANK

There's no time to open the hatch. He's waited far, far too long, and there are people watching him. He can feel their eyes like the eyes of Shiva. The engine waits in the cold. Worthless.

Though sometimes when you let it cool, the engine recovered.

He gives the cord a yank. It starts right up like nothing was wrong, like he didn't need the impeller after all.

82

THISBE

The boat is moving. They're going again, going away. She raises both fists and goes to the broken window. "I'm Julia!" she says. She pushes the can of chowder out the window and hears it thud and roll. "Julia wants out," she tries to scream, but the motor is louder than her ruined voice can ever be.

83

FEN

Ted won't let Fen row. He feels that, as the guy, he should row, but she refuses to trade places with him. "Where are we going?" he asks her.

"We have to find him."

Carl had told him not to mention the boot, but maybe he should. She said Jerome's dog bit a guy who was living in the bushes by the bridge. A homeless guy who was acting weird and had a news clipping about Thisbe in his camp.

"The police are coming," he says.

"I know," she says. "I called them."

"So did I."

"Really?"

They pass the first row of tethered sailboats, and she turns the dinghy to row them down a sort of water street in the dark. The boats they pass are empty and cold, which he didn't expect. He'd always thought, when he looked down from the bridge, that they would all have families living on them, that everything would be happening there as in a campground, where you made small dinners on a tiny grill and maybe watched old-fashioned TV with your old-fashioned mutt and lay down in a hammock and were very happy. But the boats have a permanent sense of loneliness about them and a cold, mucous-thick smell of brine. Moonlight licks at the metal edges and masts. It scallops the water they cut through like silk. Ted has her back to where they're going and that strikes him, suddenly, as bad planning in the design of rowboats. Again he says she should let him row and she says they'll tip over and he remembers, with shame, how badly he sailed.

At the far end of the water street, a silhouette begins to move, and a wake begins to flow outward, licked by the same moonlight, lifting each moored sailboat and each slime-edged mooring ball. Ted turns to see the dark mass, which is boat-shaped, and she says to Fen, "That could be him!" She rows harder and keeps turning her head.

"This is too freaking slow!" she says.

She stops where a string of white Christmas lights has been draped over what he thinks is the cabin-house of a newish boat. *Broker,* says the name on the side, but he misreads it first as *Broken*. Plants of some kind are growing in pots and their shape in the dark is like Spanish moss. Ted lunges and grabs hold of the ladder on the boat's side and Fen feels that he's stuck in the getaway car of a person who's just committed a minor crime and may be about to commit major ones.

"Can you still see that boat?" she asks.

He hears *boot* at first. He starts to shake his head, but she says, "Is it still going?" and points, and he sees the light on the boat that's chugging away from them. "Yeah."

Ted climbs the ladder and says, "We have to follow him."

"Whose boat is this?" he asks.

She doesn't answer him, just calls, "Gretchen? Are you home?"

No one answers, and when Ted opens the unlocked door to the cabin, birdcages are the first thing they see and smell. In one cage, a white parrot screeches. The other cage is empty and the door is ajar.

"Where's Rogaine?" Ted asks the bird. "Or are *you* Rogaine? Where is Pick Your Boob?"

That Ted has lost her mind occurs to Fen.

"Rogaine?" he asks her.

"They have weird names" is all she says, and then she tells him to call the police again and say the man who was living in the bushes beside the Coronado Bridge is getting away. "I *think,*" she adds.

Honestly, this isn't the clearest message he's ever been asked to give. She says she can't do the calling because she has to get them under way—sailor talk, he's pretty sure, for making a boat move.

Once she's up on deck somewhere and he's alone with the parrot, which starts screeching at him, he calls his uncle instead, because that seems more direct. His uncle will understand that Ted is grieving about her sister and doing crazy stuff. "Quiet," Fen says to the very agitated, very loud bird. "Shhh."

"Pickle stew!" the bird shrieks over and over. Or maybe it's *picker view!*

His uncle doesn't pick up.

Holding one finger very hard against his left ear and standing outside the cabin door, which enables him to watch Ted unhitch the boat from its floating, slimy mooring, Fen explains the situation on his uncle's voice mail, which isn't easy, the situation being so odd, and after he hangs up he questions the wisdom of ending the message with "I think we're trying to chase somebody," but he's pretty sure his uncle will pick up the message right away and call him back.

84

CARL

At the harbor patrol office, Carl sits at a desk, hoping Elaine is on her way to find Fen. He'll go himself as soon as Howard arrives. The boat ride will take twenty minutes. Can't go fast in the dark.

"News," Chrissy says, sticking her head in. "The girl may not have jumped."

"Why?" Carl asks.

"Some taxi driver says he brought her down."

"When did this get reported?"

"Just now."

A great blue heron stands on the pier beside the patrol boat, where Carl goes to wait. Night after night, the heron flies to the same spot and takes up his post. Officer Joe, they've taken to calling him around the office, but Carl always thinks of God when he sees the giant bird with its pop-eyed expression. It watches Carl board the boat, and it watches, feathers stiff, neck unfurled, as Carl starts the motor, and only when Howard has jumped aboard and they've started moving does the moonlit bird extend its great wings and rise up for a few minutes, disappearing with whatever thoughts it thinks, and Carl feels the consciousness of the bird like the consciousness of all the creatures swimming or floating in the black bay, instinctual and mute, wise about things they can never say.

85

FRANK

It was late August. Julia was eight and he was twelve. They were playing pirates, so they tied Julia's hands and her feet, then put a bandanna in her mouth, not to hurt her but because she said it had to be real. It wasn't tied very tight. He, Julia, and Ben Crames had already dug the cave. It took all the summer days that had already passed to dig it: day after day, the three of them working. Never was anything more fun than that. Never was the sunlight more beautiful, never was the water fresher when you ran into it with sand-covered hands and knees. For hours at a time they were lost in it, the idea that they were not themselves but other, grown-up people. Julia would be in the cave, tied up, and Ben would be the pirate and Frank would save her with the ransom that was sand dollars. They had the dollars all saved up in buckets. Julia was in charge of that because she was so good at finding them.

But then they had the idea of getting ice cream. Ben said he had enough for two. Not three. "It won't take long," he said. "Just a second."

How terrible to see the cave was gone. He thought for a moment they had run too far or not far enough. But up on the cliff was the palm tree by the pink house. There was the same fisherman on the beach with his bucket and pole, and he was staring at the rocks. He said he hoped nobody was under there.

Julia wasn't standing on the beach. She wasn't saying, "Look, I got free!"

"His sister's in there!" Ben said, and the fisherman started running. Then they were all pulling at the boulders and rocks, the fisherman, Ben, and Frankie, an absurdly small number of people for a giant pile.

After the funeral, when his grandmother had to take charge of Frank, the Seer taught him how the dance of destruction is the dance of creation, the rhythm of the dance is the rhythm of a world perpetually forming, dissolving, and re-forming. Serpents coil about Shiva's limbs and from his right hand flows the promise of release.

When the letters from the Seer ceased, Frank knew that she was not dead, just as Julia was not dead, only gone to another life-form. That other time he thought he'd found Julia, he was wrong, because as soon as she said, "I forgive you!" he felt cold. He'd been mistaken. Julia wouldn't forgive him.

He can hear her nearby. He won't fail her now; he'll let her see the lights of the city, the light of the stars, the beautiful water, where Shiva is inextricably woven into all that the eye can see.

86

THISBE

The hatch opens. The air is cold and salty and delicious like that moment when you plug your nose and jump off a boat. The man is still there, but he stands still and lets her pass.

"I lost my wallet," the man says. "It took all day. I couldn't help it. But the motor started. It's working."

"Get away from me," she says. She holds the knife and she feels like she could bring it down on him, *slash slash*. The way she holds it makes him back up, so she's doing it the right way. He lets her come up out of the smelly darkness and stand on the deck in the strobelike air. Never has anything felt better than the salty cold. She keeps the knife aloft.

"You don't remember," he says.

"I remember," she says, her lips still cracked and stinging at the edges, her mind dizzy from hunger and fright, so that the parrot sitting on the rail of the boat seems a possible figment of her imagination, a figment that keeps saying *crow man*. Where the cat has gone, she isn't sure.

"I remember," Thisbe says, knife up. "And I don't forgive you."

"I know," he says. "It's really you, isn't it?"

"Stop the boat," she says.

It never ceases to amaze her, looking back. The unexpected obedience. The turning of the boat when she said to stop it. The power seemed to flow out of the knife that she was only pretending to know how to use. He jumped into the water and then two boats came up. One had her sister on it, and the other was the harbor patrol. The creepy man was still down there in the water, and he was waving a gun. He kept saying, "Don't come any closer or I'll shoot," shouting it over and over again until a policeman shot him, shot him dead.

87

TWO WEEKS LATER

On the day the *Sayonara* is to be towed to a police storage yard, a dockworker removes thirty-two jars from the cabin. His daughter is always hunting for sand dollars, so he sets two of the biggest jars aside to take home, then imagines her asking where they came from, and what kind of story is that to tell a five-year-old? He stands on the deck at midday and opens the lid of the first jar and watches the sand dollars and their beds of fine, dry sand fall into green water at the edge of the beautiful, summer-bright bay, aware that what he's doing would be viewed as inefficient if his supervisor were to pass by. It would be faster to throw all the jars, unopened, into the trash bin, but he can't quite do it, so he unscrews lid after lid and dumps. The sand dollars float briefly, then begin to sink, staring up at him like open eyes until they reach the deeper water and wait for the tide to lift them like ghosts.

Elsewhere: Telma Cardozo is eating clam chowder and a piece of rye bread when the call comes about her cousin. She'd always expected to hear of Frank's death from the police or the coroner, a heart attack while he was alone on his boat somewhere, or him drowned, the boat found drifting, and she'd expected to think, *Well, he's finally at rest*. She wasn't prepared for a kidnapping. A girl who said he called her Julia. Resisting arrest, getting himself shot.

"No," she says, "we do not have the money for that," though they do. She simply can't ask her husband for money to bring the body of a man who could do such a thing all the way from San Diego.

"Who was that?" her husband asks, eyes on the television.

"Frank died," she tells him.

"Well, he's finally at peace," he says, and she doesn't correct him.

Elsewhere: A boy stands with a girl on a tennis court. Summer, not yet dark. No one is around, so the court feels like an enormous empty chalkboard. The sky is lilac.

"I'm not athletic," she says. "I warn you."

"It's okay if you don't get it right the first million times."

"That's all?"

"Well, that's how long it took me."

"So we'll be here awhile."

"Whatever it takes," he says. A million seems like a small number of times to do something with Jerome.

"Like this," he says. He throws the tennis ball straight up and then he hits it with stinging precision into the opposing court. It looks possible, like all graceful things. She takes a ball and nods, holds it, then starts to fling it upward.

"Bounce first," he says.

Bouncing and catching it with her left hand is bad enough. "I can't even do this part!" she says, laughing, but she knows he doesn't need her to do it well. She bounces it again, badly, then throws it too low and far away from her body, and the clumsy way she reaches for it makes her laugh. "That was terrible," she says, and he says it truly was, a thing he doesn't care about in this exact moment.

Elsewhere: A boy stands on the dock beside a sailboat that a girl is preparing to make him sail. "Here's your bailer," she says.

"I thought that was to pee in."

The ludicrous thoughts of nonsailors.

"What do you say to pump people up in this situation?" he asks.

"Win or don't come in," she says, and then laughs.

"Perfect," he says, and in a peculiar way, for that moment, everything is.

Elsewhere: Clay Moorehead walks through the *jardin* at ten minutes to five. The trees have been trimmed with machetes into these giant cube-type things that are very surreal and remind him every second that he's in Mexico, not at home. As does the smell of burning corn.

He's mailing, like, ten things for his mom because he has to work for her now, and forget about going back to Coronado High, because, *What*? she says, *everybody is going to forgive you just like that? No. They're all going to think you are a criminal!*

Clay is not a criminal. He's a fighter, man. And Jerome won't answer his emails or his chats, so Clay picks out a postcard in the mailbox place that shows a superhot woman in a supersmall dress, comic-book sexy but that's what makes it cool. On the part that says *Escribe tu mensaje aquí,* he writes:

JERONIMOOOOO!

What's up? I miss you bro! I'm really sorry. I mean seriously. I didn't mean to make Thisbe feel that bad and I'm really glad she's okay. Don't cut me off bro, okay?

Your besto amigo, Claymo.

He sticks one of his mom's American stamps on it and the lady takes it and puts it with all the other mail someone is flying up to Texas to make sure it gets there quick, and when he walks back through the garden of giant cube trees, a zillion black birds are flying into them and disappearing but you could still hear their crazy screams.

Elsewhere: The boy digging in the sand near the golf course at Stingray Point submits to the sunscreen being rubbed into his shoulders for approximately five seconds before he resumes excavation with the small, rusty shovel his father nearly cut his foot on when he waded into Glorietta Bay. The sharp blade is excellent for moats and canals, so the boy goes deeper than he's ever gone before, so deep that he's kneeling down and leaning his head way down into a hole when he hits the hard top of something that looks like a plastic bowl full of cash, or maybe just old salad, but he yells as loud as he can to his mother, lying facedown on a towel, and his father, lying faceup on a towel, taking yet another boring nap: "I found it! I found the treasure!"

Elsewhere: The groundskeeper at Woodlawn Cemetery of Las Vegas, Nevada, sweeps the dice into his hand. They've not been moved for a long time and are dusty, cracked, and faded, the sort of grave decoration that makes people feel their loved ones are neglected and lonely, not tended and duly recalled. He means to throw the dice in the trash with all the torn and faded artificial flowers he has collected that day, but to throw out dice seems unlucky, so he puts them in his desk drawer one at a time, sixes up, for luck.

Elsewhere: Awate Mebrahtu's taxi contains one passenger, a blond woman on her way to Coronado Island. Awate can see all the way to Mexico from the peak of the bridge, and the air coming in through the vents is seventy-two degrees Fahrenheit, a good thirty degrees cooler than Assab this time of year. Awate stays in the inside lane as part of his plan to avoid, always, the lane where a person might pull over and climb out. The woman says she's on her way to see her teenaged son, who's been living here since his father died. Because many people tell Awate many things about their lives, whether he understands them or not, he nods and says he's very sorry for the lost, but it's a good island, very happy for the weather time.

ACKNOWLEDGMENTS

I'm deeply indebted to the San Diego Medical Examiner and the police officers on and off Coronado Island who spoke to me in detail, but anonymously, about law-enforcement procedures and the corporeal and emotional effects of bridge suicides. The compassion and resilience of those who work on and under the bridge continues to inspire and humble me.

Many thanks are due to the junior sailing program of the Coronado Yacht Club for its inclusive and transformative programs.

To my friend Janet Reich Elsbach, editors Nancy Hinkel and Erin Clarke, husband Tom McNeal, and agent Doug Stewart, who instantly read drafts of this manuscript every time I sent up a signal flag, thank you.

Big thanks to Peter Bulkley for doing a nautical edit and delivering the manuscript to me by bicycle, to Doug and Maggie Skidmore for owning and sharing a Hobie Getaway, to Sam McNeal for reading the whole thing and not disowning me, and to Cara Ryan Irigoyen for stopping to pick up the unbroken sand dollars. Lastly, I think the world would be a more coherent place if my copy editors, Steph Engel and Diana Varvara, were in charge of it.